THE RED BOOK

Gillian Newham

BespokeChristianPublishing.com

Bespoke Christian Publishing

UK

Bespoke Christian Publishing is part of the Christian Book Consultancy. More information can be found at christianbookconsultancy.com.

First published with the help of Bespoke Christian Publishing in 2020

bespokechristianpublishing.com

Designed & typeset by Pete Barnsley (CreativeHoot.com)
Cover photo: Jonny McKenna, unsplash

ISBN: 979-8-668379-19-4

Dedicated to Doreen Sharp

In memory of Amaraa
10th October 1971 – 11th October 2019
A beautiful lady who lived to glorify Christ

"Were the years I spent travelling through Mongolia,
sharing the gospel of Christ, wasted?"

James Gilmour,
missionary to Mongolia 1870–91

Family Tree

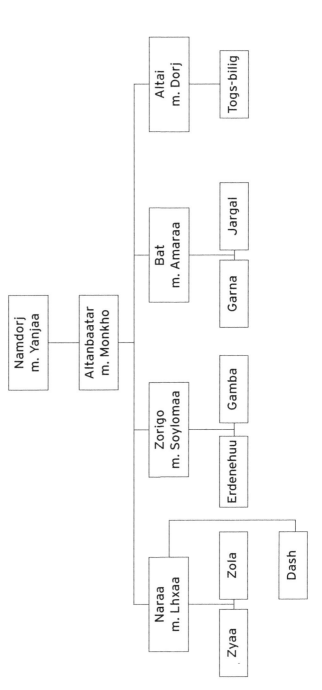

Prologue

"You're a fool, Edward Paterson."

Like a drum beating in my head, Jack's words have banged around my head all day. Perhaps he's right. Certainly, the recent Tienstin massacres this spring make it a dangerous time to travel, but I can wait no longer. I must go.

Jack and other friends have done their best to dissuade me from this journey. Last night at supper, they regaled me with tales of brigands ambushing unsuspecting travellers; of cat-burglars who prowl near wayside inns, slitting the throats of innocent victims; of peasants who, enslaved to the opium warlords, have themselves become marauders. I know they spoke the truth, but these things do not make my heart race. Rather, reports of missionaries slaughtered in the massacres do. Not because I am afraid of death, but because the emphatic decision of the field leadership here in Peking to move south fills me with panic.

What if I were to leave Peking with them and was never able to return, never able to travel north?

My colleagues' work is amongst the millions in China, but my sights are set farther north. I am bound for Mongolia. For years, no—more than that—I've felt consumed with a pain that touches every bone of my body. I must take the good news of the gospel to the untamed wildness of the Mongolian peoples.

But my superiors deemed me ill-equipped. In preparation, they required that I study the Chinese language and Chinese customs, which I did. However, after two years, they asked me to wait and further test my calling to the Mongolians. If it was genuine, they said someone else would come forward to join me.

No one has come forward and that was five long years ago. They've been hard years of waiting, during which the burden for the salvation of these people has grown heavier and the ache to tell them about the true living God, deeper.

Monday, 13th May 1872

This morning, after a restless weekend, I told my superiors and friends that I would not be travelling south with them. Perhaps it was the tone of my voice or the set of my jaw that convinced them, but eventually they stopped arguing. And, despite misgivings, they graciously released me with their blessing and I am elated.

Friday, 17th May 1872

I'd always envisioned my departure from Peking in grand terms, but it was a simple affair with commissioning prayers from the field director, who repeated the phrase that we were "fools for Christ's sake," which solicited loud "Amens" from those gathered around me.

After hearty handshakes and goodbyes, I climbed onto my wooden cart and rode through the quiet Peking hutongs towards the road that headed north. Preparations had taken longer than I'd imagined. I struggled to find a suitable camel and wooden cart, and packing my belongings, gospel books and pamphlets securely took an additional day. But finally, armed with an ancient map and my compass in my jacket pocket, I'm on my way, and I realise for the first time that apart from God and this thick-coated camel, I am alone.

Saturday, 25th May 1872

As I travel through northern Chinese villages, the days have been warm with the coming summer, and I'm thankful I chose to wear my lightweight linen suit and bring my pith hat along for protection against the midday sun.

In each village through which I passed, a group of children trailed behind me and their elfin faces beamed as they winked and leapt onto the cart. Once on board, they held out their hands and, with dark, pleading eyes, begged for a mao or two. I gave them a brightly coloured gospel tract instead, which seemed to delight them and sent them bounding home.

Countless peasants leading ox carts loaded with early vegetables passed me, while peddlers with their wares spread on the roadside touted their business. Each one fixed me with a stare: it must be strange to see a foreigner with a camel. I waved, and they returned my greetings. Villagers in navy trousers and jackets cultivated every piece of land like busy bees. Every few miles women crouching behind braziers sold stewed black tea and steaming snowy dumplings. The sweet smell of onions, garlic, and pork drew me to their stands, and I often stopped to fill up on their tasty dumplings. I told each vendor about the true God and left them with a simple tract, which they received with politeness, as I silently prayed that the words contained in those pages might bring salvation to their lives.

These days have been slow and relaxed as the steady pace of my camel takes me closer to the Mongolian border. All appears peaceful, and the threat of uprisings and violence seems like a nightmare from another world.

Each night, I have allowed myself the luxury of sleeping in a courtyard home. The cost is a little more than the wayside inns, but they attract fewer drunks. The singing and brawling of merry men tripping home late into the night and the intoxicating scent of opium still filter through the paper-thin screens of my room. Yet despite the drunks, I've still secured good rest on the thin mattresses.

Sunday, 26th May 1872

I was tempted to rest today, especially as it's the Lord's Day, but the innkeeper told me that I was a mere five kilometres from the majestic mountain pass that leads to the border town of Hal-luck or "The Gate." Therefore, I chose to press on and into Mongolia.

Entering the gorge by way of a narrow pebbly path that wound steadily upwards into the coolness, I felt suddenly chilled. Mountains so steep as to be almost vertical hemmed my camel and I in. And unbelievably, hidden in the shadows, clinging to the rocks by nothing but blind faith, families lived in tiny shacks. Voices and the steady tap of hammer on stone were a cacophony of sound in that giant amphitheatre.

My camel and I kept travelling until the path broadened and sunlight finally shed its warmth on our way and led us out of the pass. By late afternoon, I arrived in the bustling town of Hal-luck, which had once been the location of the gate between China and Mongolia. I saw no evidence of a gate, although by then I was searching the crowds for my first glimpse of the Mongols.

And then, I saw them. Clothed in their traditional coat-like deels, they were shorter, more deeply tanned, and rougher-looking than the Chinese. Their noses were thinner, their cheekbones higher, and their dark brown eyes reminded me of almonds. Their faces, I think, are more angular than those of the Chinese.

Most walked between the market stalls in sombre-coloured deels that reached below their shins, beneath which their turned-up boots poked out. Their deels, held close to their bodies by large silk sashes bound tightly below their waists, appeared to be fastened at the shoulder with three ornate buttons. The buttons secured the right flap over the left, forming a pouch-like pocket into which they merrily stuffed their purchases.

Fascinated, I continued staring until they began staring back. Their stern faces surveyed me with distaste, reminding me that they were the descendants of fierce warriors. I walked to the edge of the market. Unable to remove my eyes from them, I watched them haggle loudly with market sellers over the price of brick tea and other foreign delicacies until suddenly their leathery faces broke into easy laughter.

Tears pricked the back of my eyes. Those lost men knew nothing of the saving power of Jesus Christ.

After buying fresh supplies, I loaded up my camel, who has grown accustomed to me, and we travelled on beyond Hal-luck. With the light fading, I decided to stop at a ger, and thus I spent my first night in the Mongolian desert.

A group of five gers, white-covered round tents that are the dwellings of the Mongolian herders, stood close to the track along which we were travelling. I stopped, and an elderly couple graciously welcomed me into their home. Inside, the windowless tent was dark, although warm from the fire burning in the central hearth. A crude chimney stood above the fire, carrying some of the smoke out while the rest remained inside.

My host seated me at the head of the ger, and the wife, a woman of indeterminable age, fed me meaty dumplings while her husband handed me his snuff bottle. I realised this was a polite form of greeting. He also encouraged me to drink some clear alcohol. I sipped the bitter liquid, horrified that, after each sip, he kept adding a little more liquid to my bowl.

As I write by the mellow candlelight, my hosts regard me with curiosity. We have no words besides a simple hello to communicate with one another, and yet I am strangely at peace in this new country.

Monday, 27th *May* 1872

I woke with a sore head. A fog hung in the ger, catching in my throat and causing me to cough which sent my host into a panic. His wife handed me a bowl of salty milk tea and a plate of meat and I tried to swallow my cough.

Taking the old map from my bag, I plotted a course to Sain-shand, a southern desert town several miles north of my present location. My host sat beside me, following my finger but shaking his head as I indicated my destination. I have no idea what he was trying to say, and for the first time, there was a flutter of nerves in my stomach.

Thursday, 30th May 1872

I left my new friends' ger just after nine o'clock in the morning three days ago. They hugged me generously and pressed a cloth bag filled with dried meat and curds into my hand. In return, I handed them some simple Chinese gospel tracts, which they received with both hands and then touched to their foreheads.

I'd calculated the journey to Sain-shand should take fewer than twenty-four hours, but I must have taken a wrong turn, because I never reached the town. For two of the three days I was travelling, I saw no other man. I can't recall how many times I took my compass from my pocket and, rubbing its face, glared at the needle. But every time it told me I was heading in the right direction. Yet there was nothing before or behind me except a bleached ocean of rippling sand. Neither did any animal break the eerie desert silence, other than the footfall of my camel and the creak of the cart as we moved northwards.

My back and shoulders ached and the bruises on my arms and legs were beginning to show. I've never known such fatigue before, and I longed to stop my cart and sleep, but I would not allow myself that luxury. I forced myself to keep going; forced my camel to keep moving. Of course, there were moments when I was rocked to sleep by the motion of the camel and cart, and moments when my slim Peking bunk begged me to come back and lie on its full length. But they were mad delusions, and I would not stop or turn back. I even started counting the number of turns the less-than-round wheels made as they bumped through the sand, jarring the very teeth in my mouth.

When a gentle breeze encircled the two of us, I became convinced that I must be near a town or a ger. Shielding my eyes against the glare of the sun, I scanned the horizon for a glimpse of something. But there was nothing.

And then, on the edge of the wind, came a faint, low whistle. It grew louder, closer, and then, like some ancient spirit entombing me, it hit. Choking and blinding me and forcibly knocking me from my perch, the whirlwind gathered me in its power until, twisting through the air, I was tossed to the ground. My arms and my legs, my head, my chest— every inch of me was pelted with a thousand glass-like shards, and then—darkness.

My fountain pen is wet with the sweat of my hand. My heart slows as I remember the moment that I realised I was still alive. I lay covered with a heavy blanket of sand, aware that a shadow was moving in the stillness. Gasping for air, I threw off the heavy, scratchy blanket and stood up. I tried to wipe the sand from my encrusted lips; my vest, my trousers, and even my socks all sandpapered my skin. I groped towards the shadow, which turned out to be my cart, and held onto its frame for the longest time. Once I felt steadier, I scrabbled beneath its sand-covered canvas to search out my canteen of water. The precious liquid cascaded freely down my throat and over my face, although within a moment I had started coughing and spluttering as I desperately tried to rid my throat of half of the Gobi Desert.

Jack's words rang in my ears again, "You're a fool, Edward Paterson."

He was right. Ill-prepared and ill-equipped and knowing nothing of this strange land and its equally strange weather, I had hurried away from Peking alone. I could have perished in that storm. And what's more, I am ashamed to admit that my faith in God, like water on a hot day, had simply evaporated in the face of such difficulties.

My camel nuzzled his head into my chest reminding me that I needed to get going again. Apart from his newly matted coat, he appeared unaffected by our ordeal. I touched my head with the thought of straightening my hat only to find that it had gone. I could not see it, and neither could I see the track we'd been following.

Amazingly, although my fall had cracked the glass, the needle of my compass was still working and still pointing north. I ran my finger along the sharp, broken edges, remembering my mother's words.

"Son," she'd said, wiping a tear from her eye, "this compass will keep you travelling on the right road."

My head throbbed as I remounted and signalled for my camel to walk on. He plodded, and I scanned the horizon for any evidence of life. Eventually, images began dancing in my desert-beaten imagination. I wasn't sure whether they were real, but with each rub of my sand-filled eyes, the images became sharper. They were white dots. They were tents. Three gers together.

I smiled, giddy with relief as the gers became clear against the blue sky. Smoke curled effortlessly from one of the tents that crouched beside a small hill, sheltered from the worst of the wind. Someone was home.

With shaking hands, I tied my camel to the family's hitching post, pulled the heavy felt door open, and walked inside. Smoke and a sickly-sweet smell almost knocked me to the floor. Four scruffy men sat hunched on low stools around the fire and each cradled a bowl of steaming liquid in their knobbly hands. Mouths open, they stared at me, holding me in place with their flinty eyes. My tongue had stuck itself to the roof of my mouth, but I forced myself to speak one of the two Mongolian phrases I'd learned in Peking:

"Sain bain uu?—How are you?"

No one responded. I extended my hand towards the oldest man.

"Sain bain uu?" I repeated.

Grim-faced, he returned my greeting but remained unmoved.

"Bi Mongoloor yar-ax chad-gui—I can't speak Mongolian," I added.

Shrugging his shoulders, the one seated beside the oldest returned to slurping his drink. Not sure what to do next, I took the only vacant stool and placed it beside them. They looked puzzled. Unexpectedly, their faces broke into wide smiles, and they began thumping me on the back.

Wednesday, 5th June 1872

The horror has passed, yet the pride with which I undertook this journey has forcibly hit me. My superiors were correct. I was not ready and am still not ready to understand missionary work in Mongolia. I am ashamed of the cavalier attitude that propelled me to come here without a specific plan and without gaining further language skills.

This last week has been one of reflection and repentance as I realised how God graciously protected me. I could have been buried in that storm, lost to all. But He spared me, and I will seek to know Him, and those I've come to reach with the gospel message, more deeply.

I am thankful that my host, Dambasuren, a respected holy man in his early fifties, has turned out to be a kind, cheerful soul. By dints of signs and grunts, he opened his home to me, inviting me to stay with him. By further signs, I agreed, and he has undertaken to begin helping me in my acquisition of the Mongolian language.

Friday, 12th July 1872

Finding time to write in my diary has been hard. Although Damba lives alone in this sparse ger, there is no shortage of visitors. From first light to dusk, people come. Many have travelled miles by foot or on horseback. Entering the ger, each visitor waits quietly by the door until Damba beckons him forward with extended arms. The visitor approaches and, kneeling before Damba kisses his twig-like hands while Damba kisses the visitor's brow. He leads the visitor to a stool where, he speaks of his problems in hushed tones.

The Buddhist scriptures by his side, Damba carefully removes the brown velvet that protects them and turns the yellowed pages to find a suitable text for his visitor. Holding his knotty finger on the page, he begins rocking and chanting a low monotone prayer. Dark solemnity fills the ger as Damba rocks, mumbling indistinct words and phrases repeatedly for fifteen minutes or more, while the visitor shifts uncomfortably on his stool.

I wonder what and to whom he prays. Do Damba's mantras bring him closer to enlightened beings, who themselves have drawn closer to the nature of holiness? My current understanding of Tibetan Buddhism is limited.

When the praying ceases, the visitor slips Damba a few turgriks notes and normality returns. We drink tea or eat a meal together—a meal which I've already learned to prepare. It's a simple soup that Damba delights in asking me to make.

As I boil the water over the fire and throw in a handful of black tea our curious visitors watch silently, assessing my technique. I wait for the tea to thicken, ready for the addition of meal, a generous handful of salt, and a large lump of mutton fat. They nod with approval as I toss the few ingredients into the wok and then serve them steaming bowls of soup. They are fascinated by this foreigner, and they've even started calling me, "mini duu," our younger brother.

Their acceptance is due in no small part to Damba's warm embrace in calling me his yellow-haired friend. In fact, this gaunt, stooping man with his toothless smile and white beard that hangs in wisps beneath his chin has already become dear to me. His care and kindness are deeply touching. He is a man with a good heart, a person who wants to help everyone. In the few weeks we've been together, I have never seen him turn anyone away. He is always ready to offer his services, hopeful that his prayers will bring comfort to people's suffering.

He lives simply, as a holy man dependant on the gifts and care of others. His furniture is basic—a table, a bed, and five low stools. All he seems to own of value is a shabby wooden box filled with equally shabby books. Every morning, Damba opens the box and gently removes a tome. I have no idea what his books are about, but it is evident that he treasures them. His lack of material wealth bothers him little and appears to bother those who visit him even less, for young and old, rich and poor all find their way to his door. Obviously, his wisdom is of greater value than his material possessions.

And then suddenly, I'm reminded that despite his goodness, this man, my friend, knows nothing of the true comfort that transforms lives. He knows nothing of the saving, life-changing power of Christ. With genuine kindness, he seeks to help everyone, hoping that his prayers bring light and relief to people, but the comfort he gives is short-lived as people return time and time again. For they long for a comfort and freedom that will truly release them from the terrors etched on their faces.

Saturday, 27th July 1872

Lately, after our guests have eaten, I've taken to gathering my notebook and pencil and sitting close to the fire to listen to the evening conversations. Each time I hear a new word I jot it down with a note to ask Damba what it means. I'm already picking up the gist of conversations, which tend to follow a familiar pattern.

The herders speak of their struggles to care for their animals and their worries of the coming winter's cold. They want favour with the spirits and protection for their families and animals. But often there's despair and resignation in their voices, they realise they have no power to influence or change the cycle of life.

At this point, someone produces a bottle of some homemade brew, and the drinking bout begins. I always refuse the vodka-like liquid. As I watch them drink, a cloud descends on my heart. How can I speak to these men of better things? How can I tell them about God?

By the end of the evening, the vodka has dulled their pain, and they end up singing, remembering their great history, and rejoicing over their children. Few of them return home, but I am content to sleep alongside them on the hard-packed earth floor.

Occasionally, we have an evening with no visitors. On those evenings, I try to introduce the topic of Jesus and the God who created the world, but it's hopeless. My spoken Mongolian is not good enough, and Damba hardly seems interested. He offers me his slow, calm smile and in comforting tones tells me that life will always be a struggle between good and evil. Patting my arm, he explains that all men are the same and that it's impossible to change the heart of man.

I agree, no effort of man will ever truly change the heart of man, but the one and only true living God who created this world can.

Damba disagrees, always replying evenly, "No, it's impossible. All we can do is trust that our good deeds outweigh our bad and hope that the spirits will be kind to us. Your notion of a saviour," he concludes wistfully, "of someone who could rescue us from the power of darkness, is too tidy, too easy. Life is a battle to keep the spirits happy. Every day we have to fight our way through worry and fear."

By the end of the conversation, my head usually aches. My inadequate words do not touch Damba, and I do not know how to answer him. When I was in Peking, everything seemed so clear. My plan was simple: to convert the Mongolians to Christianity. But being here amongst them, that clarity has gone, and I'm left hanging, praying and hoping that God will come to my aid.

Thursday, 22nd August 1872

Autumn is already approaching, and it's time I returned to China. Colour is draining from the landscape, leaving the distant hills faded and the sand whiter. The grass is brittle, and it crunches beneath my feet. There's a coolness in the breeze, and the ger stove burns for most of the day. Daily, I've been chopping wood and gathering dried dung from the heap close to our ger.

During the weeks that followed, no, months—it's been almost four months since I arrived—I haven't strayed far from Damba's ger and have lived my life, as the Mongolians say, "within the perimeters of the wok." Mostly I've sat on my stool beside the wood-burning stove, absorbed in the comings and goings of this home as I've learned a little of the culture and language of these people. This home has been a safe and intimate refuge where I have received guidance and care. But on my next visit, I must explore the surrounding towns and villages and find out where the herders live.

My luggage is secure on the cart, and my camel harnessed. Damba has arranged for me to join a nearby group of traders travelling into China to buy winter supplies.

Saturday, 24th August 1872

I found the caravan of traders easily, and the journey so far has been straightforward. The first night we all slept under the stars with only the cries of the wolves for company.

Saying goodbye to Damba was painful. He begged me to stay through the winter.

Damba's keen eyes had searched my face. "We make a good team, the two of us," he said.

"Yes...yes, we do," I'd replied, pulling the belt of my jacket tighter around my waist. "And I shall be forever grateful for your hospitality. But I must return to Peking."

For two ha-pennies I'd have stayed, although the

frustrations I experienced over my short-comings reminded me that I must return and better prepare myself to serve these people.

"I think the spirits sent you to protect this old man," Damba said, checking the camel's bridle.

I smiled. "God sent me."

He smiled too. "Your god and our spirits—perhaps they are one and the same."

Lowering my head, I pursed my lips; I did not want to argue with him as we said our goodbyes.

Damba's bony frame enfolded me. "Daraa yldz-ie! See you later," he said, pushing me towards my cart.

"Thank you. Thank you," was all I could say.

I took my seat on my cart and turned my face resolutely towards Peking.

Thursday, 29th August 1872

I rode through Peking, watching the busy street life unfold like a play before my eyes. Life appeared to be carrying on as normal, and I detected no signs of the raids or riots that might have taken place in my absence.

The mission station house was locked up when I arrived. But, reaching in my pocket, I was amazed to find that the smooth, familiar door's key was still there.

Only Fong-Bing, a Chinese servant was living in the house. He told me that my friends travelled south shortly after I left. There was a letter on the desk in my room, postmarked from Edinburgh. I held it in my hand, feeling a little comforted for the first time since I left Damba.

I did not recognise the handwriting, but I took the letter into the garden, where Fong-Bing brought me a pot of tea. The tea was weak by comparison with the nomads' salty tea. The late afternoon sun danced on the last of the roses. Golden yellow, dusty pink, and deep blood red, the colours were startling after the faded Gobi landscape. I sat on the bench beneath the willow while her branches swept gracefully in time with the breeze.

The letter was short, written on a single sheet of pale blue paper.

"*Dear Mr Paterson,*" it began.

"*It is with great sadness that we are writing to inform you that Mrs Beatrice Swan, lately of 21, Leith Way, Edinburgh, E2 died on the thirtieth May...*"

I got no further. Suddenly I was a young engineering student in Glasgow again, and as a recent convert to Christianity, I was trying to work out what I should do with my life. Mrs Swan, who was rumoured to be a burly woman with a no-nonsense attitude to life and faith, had been booked to speak at one of the college's Christian meetings. Apart from that, we knew that she and her husband, who recently died, had spent many years as missionaries amongst the Buriat Mongols of southern Siberia.

We students were expecting a dry and dusty missionary report, as befitted a lady of her years. However, as soon as she stepped on to the stage, we realised our assumptions were wrong. Her face was full of light and laughter, and there was a mischievous air about her. Waving her arms enthusiastically, she was animated and engaging as she regaled us with lively tales of the Buriat Mongols.

Drawn into her stories, I pictured her and her family living and travelling with the nomads as they relocated their gers to their summer or winter places. Their acceptance into the nomads' lives gave them the right to talk about their beloved God. A few came to faith and we rejoiced, but knowing that many did not, I felt sorrowful.

Concluding, Mrs Swan had told us that there was no Christian witness amongst the Mongols of Outer Mongolia.

"Will anyone go?" she had asked, pointing her finger towards the gathered congregation.

Her finger seemed to rest on me, burrowing its way into my mind until I responded, "I will."

Friday, 7th March 1873

My friends and colleagues finally returned to Peking at the end of February. I have spent the winter studying the Chinese language further. Sadly, I have found no person willing to tutor me in the Mongolian language. However, with the aid of some basic medical encyclopaedias and the help of a local apothecary, I have made a rudimentary study of medicine so that I might return to the desert with common-sense cures for the plethora of simple ailments that afflict so many.

Tuesday, 3rd June 1873

I pushed my camel as far as I thought she could go each day and we made the journey here in less than a week. After spending the winter at a farm on the edge of Peking, my camel was happy to return to the desert.

As Damba, and the two herders beside whom he lived, loomed on the horizon, I found myself whispering silly tunes. Getting closer, I saw Damba standing outside as if he was waiting for me. My face broke into a grin that I could not remove, and before I reached the hitching post, he was by my side. Descending from the cart, I threw myself into his open arms.

"Welcome, younger brother," he whispered in my ear, enfolding me in his familiar bony frame. His hair, soft and wispy against my cheek, smelt of wood-smoke and mutton. "I knew you would arrive today," he said, releasing me and wiping his nose on the long sleeve of his deel. "I just knew you'd come."

"How?" I asked, astonished.

"I sensed it, and then early this morning," he said, clearing his throat, "there were two magpies at the hitching post. That was confirmation."

"Confirmation of what?"

"That a special visitor was coming from afar."

Tethering the camel to the hitching post, Damba escorted me into his ger. The warmth of the fire enveloped me. A rotund woman in a deel and headscarf bent over the stove, stirring a pot of soup that made my stomach groan with hunger.

"Sain bain uu?" I said, greeting her. She smiled but continued attending to her soup. I recognised her but couldn't remember her name. A tray of meaty dumplings sat on a trivet ready for steaming. Two men dressed in thick deels, felt hats and turned-up boots sat playing cards at the low table.

"Our visitor has arrived," Damba announced.

The men looked up and, gruffly acknowledged my presence before returning to their cards.

Damba gathered the blue silk cloth that lay on his bed and held his arms open before me. I extended mine beneath his, allowing him to formally kiss me on both cheeks and offer me an extremely late but traditional New Year greeting: "Amar bain uu?"

"Amar bain uu?" I replied. "Did you have a good winter? Are your animals healthy?" A flood of questions fell from my lips. "Is your body well?"

He threw his head back and snorted. "Glad to see that after a winter with the Chinese you haven't forgotten your Mongolian."

We drank the soup and ate the meaty dumplings that Damba kept pressing upon me until my stomach, like the stone-filled belly of a roasting marmot, was ready to burst.

The card-players left, and the ger was quiet. For a moment, I stepped outside to view the skyscape. It was alive with layer upon layer of sparkling jewels. I stood, letting the velvet darkness wrap me in its cloak. *This is an amazing land, God, and I am happy to be back amongst the Mongols.*

Tuesday, 10th June 1873

The first week has slipped easily by. Damba is frailer, his hands more twisted and gnarled, and his legs more deeply bowed. He has a young man living with him called Lhagva. Damba calls him "my son" or "my disciple." Lhagva, who can be no more than eighteen, says Damba is the father he's never known. The boy follows Damba faithfully, sitting beside him as he prays for people and reads scripture.

Knowing Lhagva lives with Damba, gives me the nudge I need to begin exploring this vast land.

A couple of days ago, I asked Damba where I could buy a horse. He was a little surprised by my request, and I had to remind him of my desire to visit other gers, villages and towns. Damba shrugged his shoulders, saying that all the people I ever wanted to meet came to his ger.

"Yes, you're right." I nodded slowly, not wanting to offend him. Rubbing my clammy hands together, I explained that I wanted to talk to people about the living God, the Creator of the blue sky, and that I also wanted to be able to offer them cures for their physical illnesses.

Damba's eyes became beady. "They will want your cures but they won't want your god," he said.

"He's not..." My voice faltered. "He's not just the God of the white man. He is the only true God..."

Ignoring me, Damba pulled on his boots and headed to the door, shouting for me to follow. I wondered where we were going. Seeing my confusion, he raised his eyebrows. "Do you want a horse or not?"

I grabbed my boots and followed.

"Can you ride?" he asked.

"A...a little," I replied.

He smiled. I didn't need to say anything more for him to know that I was a novice.

"It can't be that difficult. You told me that the children here ride almost before they can walk."

"But we Mongolians are born with the love of horses in our blood. You foreigners have to learn."

I bit my lip and followed him.

"Lhagva," Damba shouted. The boy came running to his master's side, carrying on his back a basket full of dried dung that he'd been collecting to fuel the stove.

"Our Edward wants a horse. Go and catch Blackie," Damba said. "Let's see if you can ride one of our small beasts," he added, giving me a sly grin.

Lhagva returned swiftly and saddled the horse, which looked like a pony to me. I knew enough to understand that calling Mongols' horses ponies would be offensive. The wooden saddle Lhagva secured onto the horse's back looked ridiculously small, and for some reason, as he was preparing the horse, people began arriving. I still don't know how they knew that the foreigner was going to try riding one of their horses.

By the time, the horse was ready, seven or eight neighbours had gathered around the hitching post.

"Sain bats-gan-uu," I said boldly, straightening my back, and walking deliberately past them to my charge. Mounting the horse, I sat on the wooden saddle and thought, *So far, so good.* One of the bystanders handed me the reins. I could see the oil smooth and shiny in his black hair. He looked me in the face and winked. He and rest of the audience stepped back. The horse seemed content with me on his back, and I let my body relax. *I'd done it.*

However, before I moved another muscle, the horse began whinnying and bucking. Panic-stricken, I gripped the reins tightly while that mini powerhouse lowered his head, arched his back, and threw his back legs out behind him. I was sent somersaulting through the air, seemingly in slow motion. With a mighty thud, I hit the earth and found my mouth filled again with the gritty sand of the Gobi Desert.

For a moment, the crowd was quiet, but once the onlookers realised that apart from my pride, I was unhurt, someone yelled, "He can't ride!" A gentle ripple of laughter broke, which turned into a roar. Gripping their sides, the Mongolians tottered like wooden skittles. "He can't ride. He can't ride," they chorused.

Even the horse turned his head in my direction and, curled back his lips to expose his yellowing teeth, as if laughing at my foolishness,

"He's just trying to show you who is boss," Damba said, holding the reins out to me. "You've got to get back on."

The crowd stepped forward. My face was hot. I didn't want to get back on that horse.

One of the herders held the bridle and the horse's head firmly. I returned to the saddle, and the horse whinnied.

"Sit tight," shouted Damba. "Grip the reins firmly and keep his head high."

I held on as tightly as I could but the small beast was violently trying to rid himself of me.

"Don't allow him to lower his head," Damba barked.

I kept holding on, and after what seemed an age the horse slowed his movements until I finally relaxed my grip. I let out a long sigh and patted his neck.

"Okay," said one of the other herders. "Now we can teach you how to ride."

"Relax in the saddle."

"Sit tall and straight."

"Hold the reins loosely."

"Hold the reins tightly."

"You can't ride like that."

Everyone had something to say. Putting my hands to my head, I laughed.

"Okay, that's enough advice, let our Edward practice," Damba said.

And with that I let the horse take his first steps.

Monday, 26th August 1878

My journal entries are more sporadic, as weariness often dogs my travels. I love the Mongolians, but staying with families in their ger, affords me no privacy at all, and long conversations into the early hours of the morning, leave me exhausted.

But I am thankful for their company, grateful for their care, especially today. Nearing this family's tent, my horse

Blackie, for no reason I could see, bucked me off his back. I landed heavily and awkwardly, and my hosts, finding me in a heap, rushed to my aid. They bathed my wounds, fussed over my needs and let me lie quietly on one of their beds. Despite my bruised body, I appreciate the quietness.

The first, and only other time Blackie tossed me from his back was more than five years ago. Since then, I have covered hundreds of miles safely on his back. Although wherever I go that story always goes on ahead of me. I wonder whether this one will be the same.

It is true, from a Mongolian's perspective, I am not the most skilled rider, but Damba no longer shouts, "Mounting askew, walking wobbly," every time I arrive at his hitching post, which is a proverb herders say to novice riders. Apparently, the way a man mounts his horse reveals whether he is a skilled rider or not, and of course, the horse always recognises a skilled rider.

Monday, 26th August 1891

I do not know how much longer I shall be able to travel north every year. The last few winters, I have returned to Peking suffering from dysentery and, latterly, cholera. Each time Fong-Bing has nursed me back to health with his preparation of sweet flag roots and other herbal medicines.

I am better, but I have lost much of my stamina. This year, I had my cart packed and was ready to start my journey by 30th May. The transition from the bustle of Peking and the busy

Chinese people to the slow pace of the Mongolian desert and its nomads has become something of a ritual.

As usual, I arrived to find Damba more withered and shrunken than he was when I left the previous year. And yet, his kind heart never changes. He always welcomes me into his home, protesting bitterly when I saddle Blackie to start my round of visiting gers, villages and towns across the plains.

Riding with the blue sky above and the sand beneath always strengthens my soul, making me feel like God is absorbing me into His vast temple of creation. And every now and then, despite being over twenty, Blackie still has the strength to race a little.

Families continue to welcome me, begging me to stay with them. I cannot stay with everyone, although I do try to stay with different families each year. But it rarely works as the children of families who know me well unload my bags and let Blackie roam free before I have a chance to tell them that I plan to move on.

Everyone knows that I carry a medical bag, and shortly after my arrival, the bag is handed to me while the gathering crowd presses me to provide cures for their ills.

The children, knowing my sealed cloth bag contains Bible storybooks with coloured pictures, love to unpick the stitching and find a new story. I could easily give the books away, but I am aware that the Mongolians place more value on something they've bought. I sell each one for a few turgriks or a little food for my onward journey. However, before anyone consents to buy any book, they insist on hearing the text first.

"No fool would buy a book containing a story he hadn't heard before or didn't like," they reason.

I am happy with this arrangement, as it presents me with ready opportunities to talk further.

They love listening to Bible stories and like nothing better than sitting around the fire by the mellow candlelight to discuss religion. Yet when I challenge them to think about receiving the gospel for themselves, they close their ears and eyes and speak more resolutely of yellow Buddhism and the ways of the shamans.

Their traditions and superstitions define them. They welcome me as a friend and invite me into their homes and lives but few are interested in becoming disciples of Jesus. And in the cases of those who have embraced Christ's message of salvation, fear keeps them bound to the unseen spirit world, and they quickly fall away.

Damba was right. They want my cures for their bodies but, in the depths of their beings, they are unmoved by the message of true healing—the message of salvation for their souls from the Great Physician.

Today I gave Damba a precious gift, the newly published Mongolian Bible. It is a beautiful tome, bright red with gold lettering. I told him that it contains the words of eternal life. He touched the book to his forehead, receiving it with the reverence due a holy book. His eyes were moist as he placed it on his god shelf next to his copies of the Buddhist scriptures.

Now Damba sits beside the fire, his head bowed in prayer as I write. We share a special friendship, the two of us, and yet the division between us remains as great today as it was on the first day I arrived, almost twenty years ago. Faith divides us, and Damba is no closer to knowing Christ. Broken, I cannot bear the thought of this frail, old man going to a lost eternity.

I've devoted my life to loving these sons of the desert but all my labours seem to have born no fruit. Throughout these twenty years, I've seen no groups of Christians established or church built. Maybe I have been a fool.

In my own weakness, I begin to realise that perhaps God's primary goal in bringing me here was to change me. Loving the Mongolians has certainly done that. Their polite acceptance of my gifts, help and even my initial message encouraged me. But their blank incomprehension of the gospel flummoxed me. I came expecting them to respond with ease. But they have not. Their incomprehension finally taught me to slow down, to take time to listen and learn, and above all, to pray.

"Lord! Please do not let Your Word return to You void,"

Part 1

Arhangai Province, Central Mongolia

June 1985

Chapter 1

"Yanjaa, my love," Namdorj whispered, kneeling beside his wife and rocking her in his arms.

"Is Emee sleeping?" Bat asked.

He'd heard his grandmother re-enter the ger, but she hadn't handed him his bowl of tea. Bat rubbed his brow. It was strange. Winter or summer, it didn't matter, her routine never changed. Lighting the fire and preparing the tea were her first jobs. While the tea brewed, she always stepped outside to ensure that all the animals were safe before returning to wake Bat. Except this morning.

His grandfather's shoulders convulsed, and Bat noticed the tears in the old man's eyes.

"She's sleeping her last sleep, Batbold."

Bat swallowed rapid breaths and held his hand to his mouth. No one in the family ever used his full name.

His grandmother, a doll of a woman with her white hair and walnut complexion, looked like she would wake at any moment. Surely his grandfather was wrong. Bat shook his head in disbelief.

"No, Bat, she's gone."

Impossible! What was *this*, ripping her presence from his life? For sixteen years—no, almost seventeen—she'd always been there for him, always showered him with love and constant care. This could not be happening. Gone, never to return? It could not be.

"Go and get your father."

Bat stood up. Pushing his heavy limbs into action. He pulled his clothes on, left their ger, and whistled to get his horse's attention. She trotted out from the herd, which was grazing close by. Bat saddled her and headed towards his parents' ger six kilometres away.

His father, Altanbaatar, tall and wiry, was already outside mending the wheel of one of his oxcarts when Bat arrived.

Before his father could utter a word, Bat spoke.

"Emee's dead."

His father's expression changed from delight to shock.

"It's true," Bat said.

"Zorigo," his father shouted, summoning Bat's older brother from his ger.

Zorigo opened his door. "What is it?" he asked, surprised at the abrupt early summons.

"Emee's passed over," Altanbaatar said.

Zorigo took a step back and let out a low breath. "I'll get the oxcart hitched," he said.

"I'll tell your mother and saddle the horses."

A chill ran through Bat's body that kept him pinned to his saddle and gripping the front of his deel. Were he to loosen his hold or dismount his horse, he felt sure he'd crumple.

His mother, Monkho, left her ger and heaved her dumpy body onto the waiting oxcart's small wooden seat. With her brown eyes set and her lips as straight as a pencil, she urged the ox forward, and Bat, his father, and Zorigo followed. Not one of them spoke. The ride to his grandparents' ger seemed endless, although the last thing Bat wanted to do was face the horror of seeing his grandmother's lifeless body again.

His mother parked the oxcart while the men tethered the horses to his grandparents' hitching post. Sobbing, his grandfather still held his wife in his arms. Bat's mother approached him and, putting her arm around his shoulder, spoke indistinguishable words into his grandfather's ear. The old man stroked his wife's silver hair away from her forehead and kissed her lightly. Bat gulped and watched his parents carry his grandmother into the nearby ger that they used for winter storage.

"Zorigo, Bat! Get the felt," said their father.

They carried the roll into the gloomy ger, placing it beside their grandmother as their parents undressed her. Bat wanted to shout, to scream, or just to run away.

"She came into the world naked and innocent," his mother said. "And she'll leave the same way."

When they removed her undergarments and threw them to the goats hovering by the open door, Bat had to force the bitter liquid back to his stomach. He straightened, feeling the muscles in his shoulders pull as the grotesque scene unfolded and his family members wrapped the roll of felt around his grandmother's tiny frame.

Bat stumbled out behind Zorigo and his mother. His grandfather, the last to leave, secured the door with the square lock and led them back to the ger where the hazy heat of the wood-burning stove left Bat feeling faint.

"We must eat," his mother said, sitting on the stool his grandmother had so recently occupied. Beads of sweat formed on her brow as she chopped onions and meat.

Sickness or hysterics, Bat wasn't sure which, rose in his stomach. He ran from the ger, pulled his saddle from his bay mare, and jumped on her back. Seizing the reins, he struck her backside hard. She reared, thrust her ears forward, and began running across the open steppe.

Faster and faster Bat pushed her. His legs clung to the horse's rough sides while his tousled hair flew like a flag in the wind.

Tears spilled down his cheeks. If only we could fly, he thought. Then surely, he'd escape this choking pain. Together they would soar into the blueness, and, like an eagle climbing above the world, he would outrun the torture that wound its icy fingers around his heart. He would reach the sun. Warrior-like, with all his strength, he would push the fiery ball back until history rewound the events of the day and everything in his world was as it had always been— carefree and innocent.

How long they'd been galloping, he had no idea, but his horse was slowing. Despite an overwhelming desire to keep running, Bat knew they had to go home. Gently pulling the left rein back, he squeezed the horse's middle, and she turned, snorting softly.

They'd be waiting for him, he thought, their solemn faces mirroring the heavy weight that had fastened itself to his own soul. A single stroke, that's all it had taken: a single stroke and his eyes were open to this alien world of grief.

In the low meadow there were flowers everywhere, buttercups and dandelions, vetch, and tiny irises. On the edge of the horizon he could see the two white dots of his grandparents' gers. The track narrowed and bent towards the hills. Bat kept going straight-ahead, passing the animals that were still at pasture close to the river until he reached his home.

His grandfather sat on the thin bench outside their ger. "Uvoo—Grandfather," Bat called.

"You've been driving that horse too fast," his grandfather replied.

"I was trying to outrun the wind."

"And here's me thinking you were trying to fly," the old man said with the faintest of smiles.

Bat had often dreamt of feeling his horse stretch out beneath him as they soared above the earth. He tied the horse to the hitching post and dismounted.

"Your father and Zorigo have gone home, but your mother is tidying up."

Bat raised his eyebrows and smiled. His mother always insisted that a home be orderly, with everything kept in its rightful place.

He entered the ger to find his mother sitting with her head in her hands. Bat shifted awkwardly, wondering whether he should quietly retreat. Finally, he decided against it. Drawing a stool close, he sat and placed his hand on her back. Her shoulders tensed, she took hold of his deel and buried her head in his chest. Bat's cheeks burned hot. A few minutes later, blinking lashes heavy with tears, she pulled away.

"A man's way is a long road," she said, recovering her breath. "And I have been slow to learn life's lessons."

"Um," said Bat, suddenly confused.

"I'm saying that I'm glad you grew up with your grandparents."

Bat raised his eyebrows. What was she talking about?

"Yes, I know. You wonder what this is all about."

Bat moved his stool a little farther away. He didn't want her to continue, but he also realised that she wasn't going to stop.

"You see—we persuaded your grandparents to leave their home and family in Uvs and move to the plains of Arhangai with us. Sensing it was the place the spirits had chosen for our new home, your grandfather readily agreed, and your grandmother followed." His mother smoothed her long black hair. "However, no sooner had we settled here than your grandmother wanted to turn around and go home. 'I can't live without children in my ger,' she whinged like a bleating lamb.

"If she had a child in *her* ger, then she could stay. Of course, many grandparents bring up their grandchildren but I'd always vowed to bring up my own children. Angry words passed between us, igniting a fire that flared with every mention of her childless ger or her real home.

"And then you were born," she said, patting his hand. "After the birth, I was very sick and unable to care for you. Your soft-hearted father, eager to see that your needs were met and to please his mother, coaxed me to let your grandmother take you home." She winked. "I wasn't happy, and your father knew it. But I let you go, promising myself that it was just a temporary arrangement and that you'd return to me once I was well. But seeing the joy you brought your grandmother—I knew I could not take you back." She wiped her hand across her tear-stained face. "And today I can say that I'm glad she brought you up because your presence gave her something to live for."

Bat smiled. He knew nothing of this. To him, living with his grandparents had been normal.

She pulled his hand to her face and kissed it. Then she stood, tucked the stool beneath the low table, and straightened her belt. "We'll see you early in the morning," she said leaving the ger as if everything were all right again.

Bat covered his eyes with the palm of his hands. The pain burned in his soul.

"That horse of yours is thirsty." His grandfather's slight figure stood silhouetted in the doorway.

Bat followed his grandfather outside. The old man, holding his hip, swayed from side to side as he made his way back to his bench. Turning his attention to his panting horse, Bat walked to the well. His heart was heavy, but the warm air cheered him a little. He filled the empty bucket and took it to his horse.

Thud!

The bucket hit the ground sending a tide of water splashing onto the dry sand. With a loud snort, the bay buried her head in the bucket. Sucking and gulping with undignified splutters, she took large draughts.

"Move over."

Despite himself, Bat couldn't help but laugh as he pushed the horse's head to one side so that he could scoop handfuls of the water into his own mouth.

He looked at his grandfather, who suddenly appeared old and lost. The old man held his beads. He twisted each one gently between his thumb and index finger as the beads steadily moved through his hand. It was a ritual his grandfather had observed all of Bat's life.

"Do they help?" Bat asked.

"Do what help?"

"The beads."

Namdorj's eyes narrowed. "I'm not sure."

"Why use them then?"

"Because..." He stopped and gazed at the smooth, blackened beads before adding, "Each bead concentrates prayers that, hopefully, will bring us favour with Tsenger, the god of the blue sky, and the *others*."

His grandfather didn't need to explain who the *others* were. Bat knew. Everyone knew. The others, the spirits. Lurking in the mountains, amongst the trees, in the holy fire and sacred springs, they lived *everywhere*. The hairs on the back of Bat's neck stood tall. There was no way of knowing where they were and whether they were watching. People said they saw everything and would pay you back double for any wrong you did.

"Why did you leave the lamasery?" Bat asked, eager to change the subject.

The old man straightened as best he could, and his tired eyes stared beyond Bat.

"Well, that's an interesting question."

Was Bat wrong? He'd always been curious but never had the courage to ask. However, today seemed a day for honesty, as his mother's strange revelation showed. "Eej-ee—mother—said you left because you met Emee and were beguiled by her beauty," he blundered on hurriedly.

Namdorj dragged the sleeve of his deel across his face, which was moist with tears. Bat busied himself searching for a wedge of wood. The sun, sliding closer to the horizon, brought soft shadows creeping across the steppe.

"Well, your grandmother was a rare beauty. And I am certainly going to miss her. But she's not the reason I left the lamasery."

Bat skimmed the wedge of wood across his mare's flank, until a pool of sweat formed beneath her.

"I felt trapped," his grandfather said.

"Trapped?"

His beads fell onto the bench. "Perhaps I was just a hot-headed youngster, impatient with the endless ceremonies and mantras, but I remember feeling like a wrestler pinned to the ground by a powerful opponent I couldn't beat. In the end, I just had to escape."

"So, you ran away?" Bat asked in surprise.

"Yes! I ran away. Haven't you heard the old women gossiping about the truth? How they found out I've no idea, but the news followed me from Uvs to Arhangai, slipping from someone's tongue and taking up residence in people's heads with no effort from me at all."

Bat rubbed the horse's flank one last time. "Then why you keep using the beads?"

"Because," his grandfather said, casting an eye skywards, "beyond the ceremonies and mantras, I'm convinced that there is some sort of supreme being."

Bat followed his eyes. "What? Where?"

"Medgui—I don't know, Bat." He stroked his chin. "But there's a belief in me, a sense I can't explain, telling me that there is something bigger than me, bigger, even, than this world."

"Is it Tsenger?"

He picked up his beads. "Perhaps. Certainly, there's a presence that brings order and rhythm to the world, patterns to the seasons, beauty to the wilderness and majesty to the mountains and the rivers. When I see that beauty, thankfulness rises in me."

"Is it the spirit of the mountains and the rivers?"

"I don't think so. It's more the marvel of the creation that directs me beyond to hope."

Bat rubbed the back of his neck.

"Just look at that tree. It's perfectly formed and fitted

for this place. Look at your horse," he said, pointing to the animal swishing her tail to keep the flies away. "She was created for a purpose, created for us to enjoy."

"I've never thought about it like that."

"Of course not, but I've spent my life tramping these hills, reading the seasons and caring for our animals. I've watched lambs survive the coldest of winters and seen lost calves miraculously find their mothers in the worst of blizzards. True, plenty have perished but again and again, I've observed a kind of tenacity that drives the animals to fight for life." He touched the beads to his forehead.

"Aren't they just the lucky ones?"

"Perhaps they are. But it set me thinking. Was the hunger for life placed in them by a creator?"

"It must be Tsenger," said Bat, untying his horse so that she was free to graze.

"It could be," his grandfather answered. "We certainly believed in Tsenger before we believed in the lamas and maybe even in the shamans." The old man pursed his lips. "Perhaps Tsenger is the father of heaven who created all."

His grandfather's face, lined and leathery from the harsh climate, wore a bewildered expression. Bat bit his lip. He'd learned so much from this man, including how to tend the animals and how to read the daily life of the steppe. His grandfather was also a spiritual man, who respected this land, but his questioning made Bat's stomach tense.

Bat thought the sun was slow to rise the next morning. Bat and his grandfather were up and dressed while the world was still black and white and the animals dozed. Drinking bowls of milk tea, they sat on low stools beside the metal stove. They listened, fixed in colourless silence. And slowly, coming closer and closer, came the creak of the oxcart. Minutes later, his father opened the door to allow his mother, Zorigo, and his brother-in-law, Lhxaa, to enter.

Their shuffling entrance pulled Bat back from the edge of some dark abyss. Heads bowed, Zorigo and Lhxaa, offered no greetings but simply sat on one of the beds. Bat and his grandfather remained seated while his mother collected four bowls from the cupboard beside the door and filled them from the flask of tea that his grandfather had made earlier.

"Bat, I need your help." His father's sharp words jolted Bat to follow him to the small ger where his grandmother's body lay. Watching his father struggle to undo the old square lock, Bat let his foot grind a patch of grass bald. As the door to the darkened ger opened, a smell like rotting apples hit Bat, causing him to turn away. His father turned him back to face the ger.

Entombed in felt, his grandmother lay where they'd placed her yesterday. His father loosened the felt to reveal her face, and he took a new blue cloth from his deel pocket. Handing it to Bat, he instructed him to cover her face.

Bat stepped closer. His grandmother looked peaceful, perhaps younger in death than in life. His lips trembled as he lifted her cold head, wrapped the cloth, secured it with a loose knot on one side before replacing the felt. Lhxaa and Zorigo, who must have been lurking in the shadows, stepped forward to gather the roll of felt and carry it to the waiting oxcart onto which a long board had been secured. They laid her on the board. Lhxaa sat at her feet, Zorigo at her head, holding her steady as they walked to the burial ground.

Altanbaatar guided the ox while Bat and his grandfather walked alongside. His mother, as was customary, remained in the ger, since everyone knew women were more vulnerable to the evil spirits that frequented funerals.

They moved slowly, his grandfather leaning on Bat's arm as they made their way to the foot of the sacred mountain.

"I'm glad we're breaking with tradition," said Bat's father.

"Me too. I couldn't bear the thought of my beloved being tossed carelessly from the cart and abandoned," said his grandfather.

"But will we anger the spirits?" asked Bat.

"I don't think so. Surely the place we choose to lay the body is as valid as the place it lands after being hurled from a fast-moving cart," said his father.

"Exactly!" answered his grandfather. "Tsenger, the blue-sky god, can easily direct us to a designated burial spot." His grandfather touched his eye. "Sometimes, we just have to stand against our traditions."

The dirt track took them to the foot of the mountain, and by the time they reached the grassy knoll where they'd chosen to lay the body, the sun was already bringing colour to the day. Zorigo and Lhxaa unloaded the body, unrolled the felt, and placed his grandmother on the grass, facing the sky.

"That's how she entered the world," his grandfather said simply.

"She belongs to the wolves now. May they carry her to the gods," said his father.

"Yes, we'll see whether the goodness in her was enough to gain her entrance into heaven," added Zorigo.

Three days later, in the stillness of the evening, Bat and his grandfather walked to the burial site. All traces of the tiny naked woman were gone from the hillside.

"The wolves, eagles and vultures have feasted on her flesh and bones," his grandfather said quietly.

Bat clenched his fists as images of those birds tearing her corpse apart flashed through his mind. Gone. She was gone forever.

"They have taken her," his grandfather said.

"So, her virtues were enough to grant her soul entrance to Tsenger?" asked Bat.

"They were."

Chapter 2

"Pup-pup-pup-pup-pup-pup." Bat heard the familiar sound of his father's motorbike approaching. Beneath its battered exterior, the Russian bike had a throaty roar and Altanbaatar rarely let the motor run above a low purr as he crossed the steppe.

Listening to the bike, Bat slowly washed his brown face with a damp cloth and gave his rugged neck and arms a perfunctory wipe. It was more than two weeks since his grandmother's death and his parents were still visiting him and his grandfather every day. Didn't they know that Bat and his grandfather could care for themselves?

The night of his grandmother's funeral, after the rest of the family had reluctantly returned to their own gers, he and his grandfather had sat by the fire, talking far into the night. This was their valley, their home, and they'd decided that they were not going to leave. In a few days, Bat would be seventeen and fully a man. He didn't need to go to school anymore.

"With your knowledge and my strength, we can make it here," he'd told the old man.

His grandfather's eyes had shone.

"We can care for the animals and keep our home going," Bat added.

His grandfather agreed, and Bat had slept peacefully that night, confident that all would be well.

But his parents' constant visits and their sideways glances to one another bothered him. Bat pulled his shirt over his head, tucked it into his trousers and came to sit beside his grandfather who was patting the fire down and letting the wok of tea brew on the blackened stove.

Their ger door opened. Monkho pulled her short ample figure inside.

"Sairhan amaas uu—Did you have a good rest?" his mother asked.

"Sairhan. Sairhan," Namdorj and Bat replied automatically.

Moments later, Altanbaatar followed. Closing the door behind him, Bat's father straightened and cracked a grin. Despite his peppery grey hair, he was still lean and strong, and Bat was proud to say that he stood head and shoulders above everyone else that they knew.

"Sairhan amaas uu?" Altanbaatar said.

"Sairhan. Sairhan," Bat and Namdorj repeated.

"Sky's clear. It's going to be another fine day," said Altanbaatar.

Bat glanced at his grandfather with widening eyes. Why had his parents, come so early? His grandfather shrugged his shoulders while his mother drew a stool close to the fire and poked the embers Namdorj had just patted down.

"Fine days are good for the animals," she said, removing the wok from the stove, and skilfully pouring the tea into the nearby flask. The three watched her move to the cupboard, pick up four bowls, and wipe each with a rag before filling them with tea. Beckoning them to drink she said, "I've got something to tell you."

They sat on low stools around the table. Monkho tried to catch Bat's father's eye, but he was busy cooling his scalding tea. She cleared her throat. "We'll move your ger tomorrow."

"What?" Namdorj said, scrambling to his feet so that his stool tumbled across the floor.

"We'll move your ger tomorrow. Put it beside ours," she said, deliberately smoothing the ragged oilcloth that covered their table.

"And what if I don't want to move?" Namdorj asked.

Bat's mouth was dry. His mother's words hammered his soul. Bat gripped the sides of his stool. Move! They'd never move. His grandfather stood tight-lipped in sullen silence, the veins in his neck twitching nervously. Monkho continued fiddling with the oilcloth while Bat's father kept his head low.

"Aav-aa—Father, you have to move. You know you can't manage on your own," Monkho said.

"He won't be on his own," Bat answered, fixing his mother with his bravest face. "I'll be here."

"No. Son you won't be here. You'll be at school," Altanbaatar said.

Bat quelled rising panic. Surely, he reassured himself, once his parents knew their plans, then everything would be all right.

"I'm leaving school."

His father slammed his empty bowl, on the table spilling the dregs onto the cloth. He stood up tall and straight. "You are not leaving school," he said, his face taut. "You have your education to complete. You have opportunities before you."

Bat's hands trembled; his father's words brought a stench to his nostrils that reminded him of rotting meat. "I'm not interested in school."

"You say that now," Altanbaatar said slowly. "But in the future when all the opportunities are gone, you will feel differently."

"No! I want to be a herder. I want to stay here with Grandfather. I can care for the animals, wash clothes, keep the ger warm, prepare food. We can…"

"This is not a discussion. You are our son," his father said moving closer and jabbing his finger in front of Bat's face. "Our responsibility. You will do what we say. You *will* finish your education."

Bat's cheeks burned red as he quietly shifted his stool away from his father's fiery eyes.

"You'd better do as he says," his grandfather said with a shake of his head.

His grandfather's words cut like an axe into his soul. Weren't they partners? Hadn't they made an agreement?

And yet his grandfather had deserted him. He wanted to answer back, but the words stuck in his throat, strangled and voiceless. They couldn't tell him what to do.

"Aav-aa, we'll come and move your ger tomorrow," Monkho said with an air of normality that shocked Bat. He would not move; his grandparents had always allowed him to follow his own way, and his parents were not going to change that.

The old man sat heavily on his stool with his elbows balanced on his knees as he stared at nothing. "Za-aa—okay," he said.

"That's settled then." His mother slapped her thighs. Standing to leave, she added, "Even large rivers follow the path of the ground."

Another of her foolish proverbs, Bat thought.

"Everyone knows that large rivers cannot go where they want," she said, retying her headscarf. "They must follow the contour of the land, and so we too must follow life's rules."

Altanbaatar moved towards Bat, but Bat stiffened. He didn't want his father's reassurance. Instead he lowered his head and focused on the packed earth beneath his feet.

Bat heard the roar of his father's motorbike. His parents were going back to their own ger. Bat leapt to his feet, flung the ger door open and raced to his horse tethered at the hitching post.

"Bat! Bat...Wait!" his grandfather called.

But Bat wasn't waiting for anyone. Unhitching the horse, he jumped on her back and slapped her side hard. The mare reared and bolted for the mountains with an ear-piercing neigh. Her hooves pounded the ground.

"They can't tell me what to do. They can't take this place from me," Bat chanted, pulling the reins back as horse and rider slowed to zigzag their way up the scree slope. Halfway up the mountain, they reached a ledge where Bat drew his mare to a halt. They were both breathing hard. Bat rubbed his chest. His anger spent, he shielded his eyes against the cloudless blue and watched a black kite soar, rising buoyant on the thermals. With his finger, he traced the bird's flight.

"Amazing," he whispered as the bird climbed and then effortlessly descended. Lowering its legs, the kite swooped to snatch some small, living victim from the doorway of its hillside home. "Now that's hunting," Bat said, patting the mare's neck and dismounting.

The valley stretched out below him. One step forward, he thought, and he too would be flying with the birds. He smiled wistfully. Clusters of white gers dotted the steppe all the way to the horizon. His parents', brother's and sister's three gers lay tucked in the next valley.

Above them rose the craggy mountain he'd climbed a hundred times with his younger sister, Altai, who always insisted on calling him by his childhood name, Ulanaa, or Red One. He wished she wouldn't use that name, as his red face had faded a long time ago. On summer days, the two of them would walk the ragged ridge, find a ledge they called their throne, and sit, imagining themselves king and queen of all they surveyed. Bat's stomach ached; those were blissful days.

Horses and yaks, sheep and goats roamed, mingling freely as they feasted on the lush greenness. A single row of stubby, deformed trees bent over the bank of the long river, trees that Bat had climbed and, yes, fallen out of. The river glided quietly past, snaking its way across the valley floor. The mountains, like the outspread fingers of a giant's hand, skirted the valley, enclosing either side and keeping it a haven.

"I don't want to leave," he groaned. His horse made no reply. "I want to be free."

Bat knew that he was as wise and grown as any man and yet his father seemed to treat him like a boy who needed caring for. He let out a long sigh and finally accepted the awful truth: he must follow his grandfather. Mounting his horse, he turned westwards to their valley one last time.

Ahead of him, a few yaks sauntered home. Catching the sound of hooves in their ears, the yaks quickened their pace to outrun their pursuer. The sheep and goats were already close to the ger.

Namdorj sat in his usual spot, beads in his hand. Bat wished his grandfather were stronger and could have stood up to his mother. But Bat knew he couldn't. His grandfather's heart was too soft. As he dismounted, a smile crossed his face—no doubt that shabby bench of two chunky log legs, a plank, and two long nails would travel with them and his grandfather would continue sitting outside.

"You'll kill that horse."

"Never!" Bat replied. "She loves speed."

Namdorj stood and held his arms out, trying to regain his balance. "You're a wild boy, that's for sure."

"Take my arm," Bat said, walking to the old man's side.

"These legs are shaky. Your mother tells me I need to eat more carrots and onions."

"What does she know?"

"Come on," Namdorj said, holding Bat's arm and staggering towards the wooden corral where they kept the young sheep and goats. "Let's get the animals settled."

Bat opened the gate and ushered the animals towards the pen. They crowded in bleating, although one renegade darted back towards the steppe. With acrobatic movements Bat sprang forward, fell to his knees, and grabbed the sheep's hind legs.

"Oh, for the nimbleness of youth," exclaimed Namdorj.

"Yes," Bat replied, rubbing the dirt from his knees to inspect the tear in his trousers. "Hear the wolves last night?"

"I heard them rallying for the hunt. Prince amongst animals is the wolf—handsome and magnificent and yet deadly. I've known a pack to destroy an entire herd in one night."

Bat imagined the pack meeting in the depths of the forest to discuss their battle strategy. Wolves were intelligent animals, more intelligent than men, some said. Crafty and ruthless, hungry males trailed their prey, learning their habits and spying out the stragglers of herds. In the daylight, the wolves laid low, sleeping and resting in preparation for their night raids. When the call came, they responded, moving with stealth in the darkness, ambushing and massacring the fit and vulnerable alike.

"Make sure the horses and yaks are fed and close by," his grandfather said.

Bat nodded. They didn't want any attacks on this, their last night. Bat gathered hay and scattered a little on the ground; the animals munched and followed him closer to the ger.

His grandfather watched. It was getting late. "Let's eat," he said. "Your mother brought us a tray of buuz."

The old man leant on the younger as they stepped inside. Namdorj sat on the low stool beside the fire and began shaving thin strips from a log.

"You should listen to your father," he said, placing the shavings in the stove, and striking a match. The fire crackled into life. Bat held the wok in his hands and felt his heart pounding beneath his shirt.

"You should listen to your father," Namdorj repeated.

Bat removed the lid from the stove and, placing the wok over the fire, poured water into a metal pan. "Why?" he asked, returning their water scooper to the top of the water barrel.

"Your father knows how important education is."

"But he never went to college."

"Precisely."

"He's a herder. You don't need an education to herd animals."

"You are right, and your father knows that. He loves the countryside but it wasn't always that way."

"Why?"

"He didn't want to be a herder."

Bat blinked in disbelief.

"He wanted to be a teacher."

"A teacher?" Bat dropped the tray of meaty dumplings on top of the boiling water and replaced the wok lid.

"Yes, a teacher," Namdorj said, pulling his silver pipe from his boot and filling it. He lit it and inhaled a mouthful of smoke. "When he was a boy, your father did his lessons well. He was also kind and patient and helped others who struggled to learn."

Bat drew his stool closer, remembering the times he'd gone to his parents' ger to ask his father to help him with some point of grammar, or a maths formula that Bat couldn't fathom. His father had been patient and always managed to explain in ways that made things clear.

"His teacher told him he should study further, even go away to college. She promised he'd get a scholarship and that he could become a teacher." Namdorj kept smoking. "He came through that door bouncing and bubbling with chatter. I remember it well. He'd found his vocation, he told us. He was going to go to college in Ulaanbaatar or beyond—Moscow, Sofia, or even Eastern Germany—some exotic place in the world we knew nothing about."

Namdorj placed his thumb over the pipe's opening and inhaled.

"But your grandmother," he said quietly, "she would hear none of it. She cursed his teacher for filling his young, impressionable head with such fanciful ideas. She told him he was a herder from a herder's family and that nothing was going to change that. She told him there would be no further study and that he'd leave school at the end of that term."

"What did you say?"

Namdorj dropped his head. "I said nothing. She was adamant, and I never challenged her. Your father pleaded with her, but it made no difference, her mind was made up."

"He left school at the end of the term?"

"Yes. He left. He never mentioned it again, but he was quieter after that, more reserved."

Bat's stomach growled. He was hungry, and the buuz were emitting fragrant steam. "I think they're ready," he said, lifting the lid and carefully placing the hot tray of meaty dumpling on the table. "Ouch! Ouch! Too hot," he said, dropping four or five into their empty bowls.

Namdorj laid his pipe on the table and grasped Bat's arm.

His grandfather's expression was steely. "That's why he's so determined to see you finish your education. He wants you to have the opportunities he was denied."

Bat nodded. He didn't agree, but at least he understood why his father had been so angry. Bat stuffed buuz into his mouth. They were delicious. He couldn't deny it; his mother was a good cook. Juice dribbled down their chins and Namdorj rubbed the palm of his hand back and forth across his chin. "Fat's the best face cream ever."

Bat pulled his sleeve across his face and sniffed. "What's wrong with being a herder?"

"There's nothing wrong with being a herder. Herding is the foundation of our lives," Namdorj said, tapping his pipe on the edge of the table. "And as far as I'm concerned, it's the best. I could have wished for no more contentment in my life. Battling the elements, feeling the freedom of the open sky, and yet knowing the constraints that come from living in this wildness have sustained me. With every bone in my body and every fibre of my being, I know that I am a part of this landscape and that it is a part of me."

"Uvoo, I feel the same."

"I know, I know," he whispered. "An old poet wrote:

In the eyes of those accustomed to the steppe,
The very edge of heaven appears.
By the actions of horses used to galloping
Our homeland stretches out before us."

His grandfather held his pipe. It was one of his most precious possessions, purchased from a trader for five cow hides long before Bat was born.

"Sometimes, we have to lay down our dreams."

Bat opened his mouth.

"No." Namdorj raised his hand. "It's time to listen. I've seen you running with the wind. I've seen the rage, as savage as an unbroken horse, that rises in you when someone crosses your will. Your grandmother and I were too soft. We have not taught you to follow another's words."

Bat wanted to protest, but his grandfather continued.

"That is a great weakness in a man, and you need to learn to follow other people's words. For a while, just a while, think about your education. Finish your schooling. Go to college, and after you graduate, if you still want to return to live the life of a herder, then you can. But," he said, waving his pipe in Bat's direction, "you will never be able to recapture your school-day opportunities. And if you do not learn to follow another's words, you will never become a great man."

His knobbly fingers caressed the stem of his pipe. "The knowledge you learn when you are growing up becomes like the morning sun, lighting your path and leading you to wisdom, which is amongst life's most precious virtues."

Bat listened. Was his grandfather, right? They sat quietly, letting the fire burn low, watching as sparks spat on the floor.

Later, lying on his bed, he tried to make sense of his grandfather's words. Knowledge, wisdom…he would try and find answers. He fixed his eyes on the wood-burning stove. Fragments of light escaped the ill-fitting lid, and the light comforted him.

Tomorrow they would move; his parents had decided. The light from the fire touched the furniture giving it a lustre it lacked by day. It flickered and turned, dancing in the shadows, dwindling as the fire died and the darkness closed in.

His grandfather lay on the bed at the head of the ger, and from his even breathing, Bat knew he was already asleep. In the distance he heard the long, mournful cry of a lone wolf—was that one left behind? He turned and lay on his back. Gazing through the open toono, the skylight of the ger, he saw the inky blackness, crammed with dazzling stars that sat like snowflakes on a velvet blanket. Their nearness made him feel safe, and as he had done as a child, he started counting them.

Chapter 3

"Sit on your bed," Monkho said. "You need to rest."

Picking up his pipe, Namdorj followed his daughter-in-law's directions. His family was working around him, clearing shelves and cupboards and bundling his belongings into blankets. The pipe in his hand had been his father's, although for some strange reason that Namdorj could not fathom, the family insisted that he'd traded hides for it. He had not, but perhaps they thought their version of the story more colourful.

The pipe was old, too old to keep using, but he used it anyway. Its delicate stem, once engraved with flowers and leaves, had long since become smooth and the silver mouthpiece was paper-thin. But its familiarity, like his beads, brought warmth to his soul.

Thud!

"Careful!" Namdorj shouted. "That box is precious."

"What, this?" said Zorigo, opening the flaps to remove a tattered volume. Tracing his finger through the thick dust, he added, "This can't have been opened for a century."

"It is a while since I looked at the contents," Namdorj admitted. "But that doesn't mean the books aren't valuable."

"Valuable to whom? I wouldn't give you ten turgriks for the lot."

"Valuable to me," he said, putting his hand to his heart, which seemed to be fluttering alarmingly. "You never were a book man."

"Gui, gui—No, no," said Zorigo emphatically. "I've no time for reading strange things that do me no good."

"But you could learn more about the world," said Namdorj, picking up a thick tome entitled *Ancient Civilisations*.

"I did all the learning I needed at school. I can read and write and do my numbers, and that's enough."

Sighing, Namdorj slid his pipe into the top of his leather boot. Once upon a time, he'd have argued with the boy, urged him to open his mind to the world beyond his ger, but today he was quiet. He was tired, tired with a weariness that clung to his every bone and made his flesh as heavy as a dead cow. Perhaps it was the grief touching the very fabric of his being that weakened him. He didn't know.

At least if you were here, we could share the weariness, he thought, imagining his wife could still read his thoughts. But you've gone, and the pain is beyond endurance.

His hand flew to his chest as he remembered the knifing agony, that, like some tortuous evil spirit, visited him every night, leaving him reeling and biting back the cries that threatened to break free and wake Bat, who knew nothing of Namdorj's suffering.

Bat removed the drying aaruul from the strings above the stove. The curds were still soft, as they'd only hung them a few days earlier. Carefully, Bat stacked the wedges in a cloth bag. His long hair hung loose, hiding his face and making it impossible for Namdorj to know what he was thinking.

That morning he'd woken the lad early and given him a talking-to. "You need to be a man," he'd said. "With Emee gone, life will be different. You need to be strong."

Bat had listened, his serious face attentive.

"Listen to people's words," he continued, repeating with urgency the advice he'd given the day before. "Listen to their advice. Don't be offended or wounded by every strong word that comes your way, but humbly accept instruction. This is part of being a man."

Bat bowed his head and stared at his hands.

"Do you understand?" Namdorj asked.

"I understand, Uvoo," he replied quietly.

He patted Bat's head, just like he'd done when he was a small boy. They washed themselves, ate breakfast, and removed the stove's chimney, putting it outside just as Monkho and Altanbaatar arrived.

Monkho came armed with two flasks of milk tea and a sack of chewy biscuits, which she set on the table as she announced that Zorigo and Lhxaa were following with two more oxcarts. "So, there's no time to lose," she said, giving each of them a task. "You sit on the bed and tell us what needs packing and what needs to be burned," she said to Namdorj.

Hearing her words, Namdorj smarted. None of his possessions were going to be burned.

Although Monkho was his daughter-in-law, she could easily have been his daughter.

Physically, there was no resemblance. Monkho was a rounded woman with an enormous stomach and long, plentiful black hair that hung plaited down her back, whereas members of his side of the family were thin and wiry. She wore her gold drop earrings every day, while his family believed jewellery was for special occasions. But that's where the differences ended; her character was so similar to his wife's it was uncanny.

Monkho was a good woman, and her large, lustrous eyes were loving and kind. Namdorj's grandfather had always believed that the light in a man's eyes reflected the love in his soul. But there were times when her tongue was sharper than any razor he'd ever used. He'd seen the way her thoughtless bossiness crushed her family, and he didn't like it. Even though he had loved his own wife dearly, he knew what it was to live under a woman's domination and to have his abilities undermined. It left him as inept as a drunken monk. Watching his daughter-in-law, he worried that she too would crush the life out of her family.

When Altanbaatar met her, Namdorj had warned his son, "Don't marry her; she won't respect you."

But Altanbaatar had not listened. He was young and determined to choose his own spouse. In the end, Namdorj and

Yanjaa had consented to the marriage. Six months later, Zorigo was born, and Altanbaatar became a father and a husband.

"Bat," his father called through the open door, "help me roll the ger covers back."

Bat joined his father. Namdorj was pleased to see Bat's eager response.

His ger was almost bare. Shelves and cupboards emptied; his goods sat on the beds tied in bundles with brightly coloured sashes. Lhxaa and Zorigo packed the remaining ornaments and photos into the last blanket.

"You boys made quick work of the packing, but don't forget my telescope," said Namdorj, pointing to the instrument that lay on the table.

Zorigo and Lhxaa laughed. "We won't."

The two boys were in-laws, but with their dark skin and shaved heads, they could have been brothers. Although, once he started walking, Lhxaa's limp made him easily identifiable.

"You haven't got much stuff," said Zorigo.

It was true; he and Yanjaa had lived simply.

"Let's start moving the furniture out," said Lhxaa.

"Teem—yes," Zorigo agreed.

"Let me give you boys a hand?" said Namdorj, grabbing his stick and trying to get to his feet.

"Gui, gui, you stay there."

He settled himself on the bed again. Bat and Altanbaatar were folding the thick felt and placing it on one of the oxcarts. His ger was a naked lattice skeleton. Namdorj shook his head, it felt strange to be moving so soon after their arrival. Ever since he was a boy, he'd followed the same pattern, moving with the seasons to different ground: to their autumn place, their winter place, and their spring place. Occasionally, if the winter was too long or the summer came early, they'd miss a move, but moving had been another routine of Namdorj's life.

The late morning sun lit up a sea of floating clouds, and sunbeams bathed his wizened face in warmth. He sighed. This place had been his summer home for more than twenty years.

Altanbaatar and Bat were already loosening the roof poles and removing them. One by one, they laid them on the ground. Altanbaatar went first, and then, with a nod of his head and the movement of his eye, he directed Bat to the next pole on the opposite side. Namdorj watched them working in harmony and realised a bond existed between them that he'd never noticed before. Father and son understood one another. Altanbaatar had a quiet confidence about him, a presence that Bat recognised and was following. Namdorj shut his eyes and shook his head. With spine-chilling clarity, he understood. His long-held opinions were wrong. His son Altanbaatar possessed a strength of character that he himself had never known.

Monkho was packing up his bowls and spoons. Had he misjudged her? Despite her dominating ways, she had not crushed Altanbaatar. He was still his own man, still the husband and father of his children, not just the figurehead. Namdorj was sweating.

"I read the situation all wrong," he muttered. "How could I have been so wrong?" The ground seemed to be moving. "I lamented my son for what I thought was weakness when really quietness was his strength." He gasped. "I judged his and Monkho's lives through the lens of *my* own experiences and reactions. I didn't stand up to my wife." He put his hand to his chest. "I wasn't man enough to stand firm for what I believed in." His chest felt tight. He couldn't breathe. The pain was intense. He tried soothing it away.

"Aav-aa, are you okay?" Altanbaatar asked through the lattice wall.

"I...I..."

Zorigo was at his side, putting his arm around his shoulders and laying him down. "A...a...mom..." The words wouldn't come out.

"Don't try to speak," said Zorigo. "Just be quiet."

Pain engulfed him, carrying him into the darkness. His bones were calling him home.

They were whispering; he could hear them. He forced his eyes open. Monkho sat by his side, patting his hand.

"What was all that about?" she asked.

"A touch of indigestion, I think. I ate too many of your delicious buuz last night."

She arched her eyebrows. Bat sat beside his mother, and Namdorj saw the fear in his face. "Indigestion and dizziness," he said hoarsely. "That's all, no need to worry. Help me sit up."

Zorigo and Lhxaa sat him up. The pain had passed, and he smiled with relief.

"You're good boys. But haven't you all got work to do? I thought we were meant to be moving today."

"Yes, but we need to move you out so we can take the toono down," said Bat.

"I'll take the toono down."

"U-gui," they chorused.

He raised his hand. "The toono is the central, pivotal piece of my home. The crown that holds everything else in its rightful place. You can help me, but you're not going to stop me from taking down my own toono." Namdorj's jaw was set.

"Let's do it together," said Altanbaatar.

Namdorj heard the gentleness in his son's voice. "Za, za," he replied, happy to receive their help. "It is right that the young support their elders."

"Then let's do it," said Zorigo, taking one of Namdorj's arms under his own.

"You're as light as a lamb," said Lhxaa, grasping Namdorj's other arm and helping him move to the centre of the ger.

Namdorj smiled. "I feel more like the dried-out branch of a dead tree than a young lamb."

Lhxaa gave him a crooked smile. Namdorj placed his two hands on the posts that supported the toono. With their help, he rocked the toono gently back and forth. His earthly home was being dismantled. *There would be no more fires in this hearth*, he thought as the orange toono tilted forward. Altanbaatar and Bat grasped the wooden crown and lowered it to the ground.

"It's done," said Namdorj. That's the last ger he'd ever take down, he thought.

Lhxaa and Zorigo carried him through the doorway and set him on his bedframe. The lattice walls creaked gently, bending to the rhythm of the breeze. He shifted, trying to get comfortable, but the old wiry springs pressed against his body. His furniture, a worn and dirty assortment of beds, cupboards, stools, and a table were ready for loading onto the three oxcarts.

He leant his head on the frame. The air was heavy with the scent of summer grass and beyond there was the faintest scent of mountain onions and wild garlic. The haze shimmered with the sounds of chattering grasshoppers. Two white swans glided effortlessly down the river, and Namdorj's heavy eyelids fluttered shut. His head fell forward.

A faint wind brushed the river's surface, ruffling the stillness and sending tiny white crescents forward. The river beckoned. In his mind's eye, Namdorj rose and walked unburdened to the bank. Underfoot the grass was tender and his step light. Although gnarled roots broke the surface, he had no fear of falling, for he was once again agile and fit. He lifted his gaze. The trees were close, their branches arched like a tunnel shielding him from the sun's heat. These trees were a refuge, holding him safe in their embrace. The leaves, lush and full, curled upwards towards the sky. He marvelled. "What is this place?" he asked, delighting in its peace, revelling in its glory.

The beads moved through his fingers as a voice whispered in his soul, "I am the creator. And this is my home. It is close. Come and join me."

The words soothed Namdorj's heart, washed away his pain, and filled him with joy. "I feel your presence. I am coming. Take me quietly and show my family the way."

"Are you ready, Aav-aa?" asked Altanbaatar.

Namdorj's eyes snapped open. "Yes," he replied shocked to see the face of his son so near to his own. He took a breath. Had he been dreaming? He wasn't sure although the feeling of peace remained.

Bat and Altanbaatar had concertinaed the lattice walls and removed the door. Monkho, Lhxaa, and Zorigo had almost finished packing the oxcarts, and it wasn't long before they were securing the toono on top of the last cart.

"A patch of pale grass, that's all that's left," said Namdorj.

"No need to be maundering," said Monkho taking the sack of biscuits. "Bring the flasks," she continued, waving to the red flasks on the ground. Altanbaatar picked them up.

I'm not maundering, thought Namdorj, just reflecting. All that remained of the place where his ger stood was a balding scrap of land. Compared to the vision he'd just seen; it was dry and lifeless. Namdorj heaved himself upright and tottered to the faded grass. The boys gathered large smooth stones.

"Make a good circle," said Altanbaatar. Zorigo and Lhxaa arranged the stones carefully on the ground and they all squatted outside the circle.

Monkho poured milk tea into a large bowl and took a long drink. "Fire opens out of the stones," she said, drenching the stones with tea. "Fire warms the world and illuminates the darkness."

She passed the bowl to Namdorj. "We call the fire into the hearth, and our ger becomes a home giving birth to life," he said.

Lhxaa grasped the bowl with both his hands and drank. "The horses rest at the hitching posts, the fire blazes. Father sings, and Mother spins yarn."

"Emee watched over the fire and kept it glowing red and warm. We lived peacefully and in contentment," said Zorigo.

"She stoked the fire, and life continued," said Bat. Namdorj touched his grandson's head and smiled. The boy was beginning to understand.

Monkho moved to the waiting carts. "Aaraa...Aaraa... aaraa," she hummed, pouring milk over the wheels. "Aaraa..." Her voice rose and fell:

"Through the mirage gentle as the dove,
My white ger flashes like lightning in the air.
How can one of these dots be my own palace...aaraa..."

Bat and Altanbaatar mounted the horses and gathered the cattle. Monkho ambled from ox to ox, dribbling milk across their woolly heads. "Oo...oo...oo," she sang.

Lhxaa sat Namdorj on the first cart.

"Oo...oo...oo...From afar, this tent is hidden from the world. But when I'm in it, it's the world to me."

Lhxaa and Zorigo sat on the other two oxcarts and Monkho squeezed next to Namdorj.

"The fire burns in Father's hearth." Taking the reins, Monkho drove the ox forward. The others followed.

"Chu, chu," said Altanbaatar, squeezing his horse's sides. "Bat, keep the cattle together."

Slowly they walked away. The carts, one behind the other, lumbered across the steppe. Goats, sheep and yaks followed as Altanbaatar and Bat guided them.

Monkho sang, but Namdorj heard nothing. He was listening to the sad song of the mountains. And beyond, there was a whisper in his heart, like the faintest mutterings on the gentlest of breezes. "Father! Father," he cried in response, rubbing each bead as it passed through his fingers. The mountains were mournful that he was leaving his beloved place, but in turning to bid them goodbye, he smiled. He would return to rest here again and await the coming of his creator.

Chapter 4

Conversation ceased and, thankfully, Monkho's singing did too. Even the birds were quiet. Only the rhythmic creak of the cartwheels dominated the stillness.

"With luck we'll be home before it gets too dark," said Altanbaatar.

Zorigo twisted his face and shook his head. "Not with those oxen."

As they reached the top of the hill beyond their valley, the light was already slipping. The group stopped at the ovoo and his parents walked to the sacred stones. Littered with silk cloths, the ovoo stood as an altar to the mountains or the sky, Bat wasn't quite sure which. But he knew that they marked a holy spot of worship. His parents each picked up a stone and began circling the mound: once for the past, once for the present, and once for the future.

As they walked, they prayed. His grandfather, who would normally have accompanied them, remained seated on the cart.

They moved on, watching the daylight languish into a cool, eerie dusk. They were powerless to make the stubborn oxen quicken their pace. Zorigo was right; they would not be home before dark.

Bat tried to stretch. The wooden saddle chafed against his leg. He hated riding sitting on a saddle, but he knew the easiest way to carry it was to sit on it. He looked past the sheep, but the dusk greyed the images, melting them to a blur as they moved farther into the night. Was his grandfather okay? He could see nothing. A sudden cool breeze made his skin crawl. Bat's head throbbed, and a lump the size of a boulder lodged itself in his throat. Gently, he drove the cattle forward, refusing to look back, afraid that the ache in his head would burst into a fresh torrent of tears.

"Too hard," he whispered, patting his mare's neck. But his grandfather, usually so mild-mannered, had sternly told him to be brave. And Bat was trying his best.

"Light," Zorigo shouted, pointing to three shafts of yellow that lit up the night sky.

"The lights are guiding us home," said Bat's mother.

She was right. The lights were coming from their family's gers. Sensing they were nearing the end of their journey; Bat's horse began shaking her head. She wanted to run, but Bat held the reins firmly and smiled, remembering his grandfather's often-repeated words: "The smallest light always pierces the darkness and leads us to safety."

The lights were getting brighter, and he could see the ger chimneys poking through the toono. They would soon be at his parents' home.

"That six kilometres was a long ride," said Bat's father.

"A long, slow ride," agreed Lhxaa.

The dogs barked madly. In his mind's eye, Bat saw them straining at their chains as they stretched their necks in response to the sounds of their masters' return.

"Someone's happy we're home," said Zorigo, jumping from his cart to grab his ox's bridle and lead it towards the gers.

A door banged open. "Coming now, they're coming now." Altai's voice rang out above the barking dogs.

"Aav-aa, Eej-ee," she shouted.

"Coming, we're coming," Monkho answered her daughter.

They heard her tripping and stumbling, "Ow... aaugh...ouch."

"What is she doing?" asked Zorigo, narrowing his eyes as he tried to see his youngest sister in the light of the open ger door.

"Pulling her boots on as she tries to run," said their father.

"Where have you been...why are you so late?" Half-running, half-skipping, she careered towards them. "Been worrying... made noodle soup," she continued between breaths. "It's hot and ready to eat," she yelled, finally reaching her father.

"No need to shout, we're not deaf," said Bat.

Her black hair tumbled in tresses about her face. In the darkness, Bat saw her eyes flicking from one person's face to another. Five years younger than Bat, she really was a child. In her baggy trousers and shirt beneath her deel, she stamped around in their father's old boots like she was trying to be a boy.

Their father pulled Altai up behind him. She flung her arms around his middle and sank into his back as they rode the last few yards home.

The dogs howled and snarled. "You'd think we were strangers," said Lhxaa as he reached the hitching post.

"They're just excited, and they're not used to us being out at night," replied Altanbaatar.

Soylomaa and Naraa opened their doors. "Shut up!" Naraa shouted at the dogs, whose whimpering ceased.

Behind Soylomaa her two boys, Erdene-huu and Gamba, stood in the doorway. Although there was one year between them, Erdene-huu was twelve and Gamba eleven, they look liked twins and were the best of friends.

"Erdene-huu! Gamba!" Zorigo shouted. "Help us." The two boys ran to their father. "Feed the animals and get them settled," he said, sending his boys bounding off to the fodder store.

Bat tied his horse to the hitching post and went to help his grandfather down from his seat. The old man's eyes were barely open.

"A long journey," he said, and turning his head skyward, he chanted something beneath his breath.

Bat led him to the ger door. "Lean on me, Uvoo."

"My old bones ache! I'll have a drink and lie down."

"You don't want to taste my soup? I am sure it will make you strong," said Altai, coming to her grandfather's side.

Touching her hair and cupping her face in his worn hands,

he smiled. "I'm sure your soup's delicious, my precious, but I'm too tired to eat. Save me some."

"Of course," she said, moving inside. Three pots filled with butter, and a wick that burned with smoky softness, lit the ger. Altai had placed her wok of noodle soup on an upturned wooden stool close to the squat table, and before the family was through the door, she was ladling the soup into bowls.

Bat guided his grandfather to the bed. "I'll have a little rest," Namdorj said with a sigh. "Just a little rest...just a little sleep."

In a moment, or so it seemed to Bat, his parents' ger buzzed with chatter. Bat's older sister, Naraa had come in. Married to Lhxaa, Naraa and her husband lived in the ger next to her parents. Zorigo's wife, Soylomaa, who lived in the last ger in the row of three, was handing out bowls of Altai's soup. Zorigo and Lhxaa bent to wash their hands at the tiny washstand by the door while Bat's parents were seated, and Bat's two nephews were taking turns feeding the fire with strips of wood and paper. Bat thought the noise would disturb his grandfather, but the old man lay with his eyes firmly shut.

"This is good soup," said Altanbaatar. "You have learned well, my daughter."

Altai blushed.

They ate soup and drank bowls of milk tea. As they finished Bat's mother shot their grandfather a glance. He was still sleeping. "We need to get to bed," his mother said. Erdene-huu and Gamba moaned. "That's enough," she added. "There'll be time for stories another night."

Zorigo stood up. "You're right. It's been a long day and we're all tired."

"We're not tired," Erdene-huu and Gamba replied.

Zorigo gently bumped his two boys' heads together. "We are going." Zorigo collected the bowls and left them on the cupboard. Lhxaa opened the door and a rush of cool air flooded the stuffy ger. The rest of the family followed him out.

"Sarhan amaarai—have a good rest," they said as they left. Bat could hear Zorigo's boys laughing and joking as they reluctantly returned home. They must be the only ones who weren't tired.

Altai turned to Bat. "Where will Bat sleep?" she asked, pulling off her deel and carefully arranging it on top of her bed. She took a brush and began tugging it through her knotted locks.

"Bat can lie next to Uvoo," said their mother.

Bat removed his deel and climbed carefully over his grandfather, who lay prone along the edge of the narrow bunk. Bat snuggled gently into his grandfather's back. His wispy hair tickled Bat's chin.

His grandfather shifted and groaned. "You're a good boy," he whispered. "Don't waste your opportunities."

"I thought you were asleep."

"Just resting."

Bat's father left to check that Erdene-huu and Gamba had given the animals enough fodder for the night. Tomorrow they would unload the carts, but for now the dogs would guard their possessions. His mother sat on the stool by the fire. With a rusted knife she shaved wood from a log. The lamps burned low; the oil was almost gone. The familiar smell of burned butter pervaded the ger and comforted Bat's sad heart.

"Good night," said Bat, letting his heavy eyelids close.

"Good night," his mother replied as she shaved strips of kindling.

The ger was still dark and cold when Bat woke. He shivered and wrapped himself tightly in his deel, aware that his grandfather was still sleeping. "Don't miss your opportunities," the old man had said. Bat wanted to speak to his grandfather about this, but it could wait, he thought, turning towards the ger wall.

Waking again sometime later, Bat leant over to touch the old man's face. He gasped; it was ice cold. Trembling, Bat pulled away, not sure whether the contents of his stomach would remain where they were. Easing himself over the old man's body, Bat stood. In the half-light his grandfather looked like a child. The old man's legs were drawn to his stomach, and his hands were cradled beneath his chin. In them he still held his beads, and Bat thought there was the trace of a smile on his grandfather's lips.

"He wanted to go. You need to be happy for him."

It was his father. Had he been awake or had Bat woken him? He didn't know. His father was standing beside him, putting his arm around his shoulders and comforting him.

Bat wanted to wrench himself away. He didn't need comfort. He just wanted his grandfather back. How could they leave him? *The two of them!* First his grandmother and then his grandfather...No! No! No! It wasn't right. It wasn't fair. How could Bat be happy? He stood as straight as the hitching post.

And then it was as if his grandfather were speaking to him, for somewhere in Bat's head the words sounded: "I'm free. Be happy."

Chapter 5

"Another funeral," said Monkho. "Perhaps I shouldn't have made him move his ger."

Walking back to the truck at the bottom of the hill, Altanbaatar frowned and, not for the first time, felt concerned. His wife was a worrier, and in the privacy of their ger, those worries could spiral into torment.

"Perhaps," Altanbaatar replied, "but it was better he was with us when he passed away. Just think if he'd been alone with Bat and he'd had to deal with his grandfather's death."

Monkho put her hand on Altanbaatar's arm. "You're right, that would have been too much for the boy."

They had laid Namdorj at the same place they had laid Altanbaatar's mother nearly three weeks earlier. The hills were sacred, and the wolves that would devour his body and fly him back to Tsenger lived close by. The lama said it was good to lay the deceased near the wolves' lair, as it shortened the distance the soul had to travel to reach Tsenger.

Custom dictated that bodies be laid at their final resting place before the sun rose. Hence the whole family had been up early and ready to accompany Altanbaatar's father to the burial spot. It was, Altanbaatar knew, unorthodox for women to come too, but his womenfolk had loved his father as much as he had, and he hadn't the heart to make them stay at home. Plus, he wasn't certain that he subscribed to the widely held belief that the grave spirits clung to women more easily than to men.

Altanbaatar smiled. His father was back in the valley that had become his own, touching the ground he loved, amongst the trees and birds, waiting for the wolves he'd spent his life shielding his flock from to carry him away. Altanbaatar bit his lip; his father had often spoken in defence of the wolves' ferocious actions.

"Tsenger is the father, the earth is our mother," he used to say. "And the wolves protect the earth from those who would harm her. That's how Tsenger ordered our world."

Monkho squeezed his arm. "What will people say?" she asked. "Will they think Tsenger is punishing us for hidden evil?"

He didn't answer. He helped her climb into the back of the truck. Naraa and Lhxaa, Zorigo and Soylomaa were already sitting with their backs against the boarded sides. Caught in their own thoughts, they sat quietly—all except Altai, of course, who wept loudly. Altanbaatar ruffled her hair and pulled her close.

He banged the roof of the cab, thankful that their neighbour, Bar-tuux, had been willing to drive them to the burial place. Bar-tuux turned the ignition, and the blue Russian truck coughed and rattled as the engine gathered speed and settled to a steady rumble.

Zorigo wiped his eyes. "I think Bar-tuux's engine needs some fine-tuning," he said as the black smoke cleared.

"You're right, it is a bit gruff," said Lhxaa. "But it got us here a lot quicker than an oxcart."

Zorigo agreed.

The local lama sat in the cab beside Bar-tuux. He'd accompanied them and stood at the graveside in his heavy red robe, mumbling prayers and reading Buddhist scriptures. Altanbaatar had stood next to him, but he found himself preoccupied with the cuff of his deel. He'd pulled it back and forth to peer at the second hand of his watch, which dragged its way around his watch face. The face was smaller, or perhaps his eyes were getting tired. He certainly felt tired. His knees creaked these days when he tried to get up from a squat, and the joints in his hands were becoming increasingly painful. The lama had stopped speaking, and Altanbaatar sighed. It was over.

He'd told Bat that Namdorj had wanted to go, that the boy should be happy his grandfather had passed on. But the lump in his own throat told him something different. His father was dead, and it felt like a piece of him had been torn away; nothing and no one could ever fill that space again.

Altanbaatar had always talked to his father, turning to him when the family was sick, or when they'd little food and the animals were dying. Whenever the worries mounted and threatened to sink him, he would quietly saddle his horse and ride out in search of his father. Invariably, he'd find him crouching on some hillside watching his sheep through his homemade telescope.

That telescope was another of his father's treasured possessions. Several years prior to the family moving to the province of Arhangai, his father and a neighbour had bought a pair of Komz binoculars from a Buriat trader, who said they'd belonged to a Russian spy. They were never sure about that, but certainly the binoculars were of good quality. After the trader left, the two neighbours separated the binoculars so that each could have a telescope to watch his flocks. His father kept his half wrapped in a brown cloth. The rough outer casing of the telescope was damaged, but the lenses were still as sharp as ever and made overseeing his herds much easier.

Spotting Altanbaatar, his father would wave, giving him the impression that the older man had been waiting for his arrival. As he got closer, his father smiled, a smile that lit up his whole face, reminding Altanbaatar of his father's joy when, as a boy, Altanbaatar returned from a term away at school.

They'd sit on the hillside together watching the sheep. Altanbaatar talked, and his father listened. Those conversations always lightened Altanbaatar's heart, although he couldn't ever remember his father giving him specific counsel. But the simple assurance that the suffering would pass gave Altanbaatar the courage he needed to return. His father's strange prayers to Tsenger, the god of the blue sky, also gave him comfort and hope. And his father was right, the times of hardship and suffering did pass.

But this agony, would it pass? The truck moved slowly over the bumpy ground. Altanbaatar looked at his children. Overnight, he and Monkho had become the family's elders. In a moment, the presence of wisdom had vanished. Now they were supposed to be the ones who gave wise counsel. How could they do that? Especially, thought Altanbaatar, since they didn't know where to find wisdom. Unlike his father, Altanbaatar didn't really know Tsenger.

Monkho was tugging at his sleeve. He turned to her. "He *should* have come with the rest of us in the truck," she shouted above the noise of the engine.

Altanbaatar shrugged his shoulders and peered through the gaps in the truck's wooden panels. What could he have done? Bat knew his own mind. This morning, saddling his horse, he'd told his father that he would not be going in the truck with them. Altanbaatar hadn't pressed the boy, but as they were leaving, he'd asked his son to ride there and back alongside the truck. Bat had agreed.

Through the panels, he could see the horse's brown body. His son's strong legs bobbed in and out of view as Bat moved in time with the horse's pace. Bat's foot, bare in a shabby shoe, was flat in the stirrup, and Altanbaatar knew that his son was standing to ride. *He's a capable rider.* Again, his father's words echoed in his ear. "That boy loves that horse," he'd said on one of those days they'd sat on the hillside, unseen, watching Bat gallop across the steppe. "It's like the horse is part of him," his father had added. "They're not just companions, but soulmates. They know each other so well that they're melded together."

The forest was becoming distant; they were nearly home. Bat's like me, or like I was, he thought. Wild and free, he was ready to take on the world. Altanbaatar smirked, wondering when his own invincible daring had disappeared.

As the truck reached the brow of the low hill, he stood to see their gers white against the lush summer green. Altanbaatar held onto the boarded side, and the truck chugged down the embankment towards the track that led to their door. Bat rode on ahead at an easy canter. He's no longer a boy, thought Altanbaatar watching his son. He's seventeen, and at seventeen I was married to Monkho.

A few people came to their ger. They'd heard of Namdorj's death, and they visited to pay their respects. Two days later, Namdorj's card-playing friends arrived. Monkho and Altanbaatar served them while the rest of the family finished erecting Namdorj's ger.

Exchanging snuff bottles with Altanbaatar, the trio sat on the bed on the right side of the ger while Monkho fed them rice and tea. Altanbaatar sipped tea with them and nibbled on hard curds. He felt the familiar disdain he always experienced around these rogues. Every few weeks, they'd visited his father to play Moshik, a card game they used to cheat the old man out of the few turgriks he possessed.

"Ax-aa—older brother this. Ax-aa—older brother that," they said, not one of them daring to speak his father's name for fear that they'd call his spirit back from its journey to its eternal resting place. Altanbaatar felt like shouting, "Namdorj, Namdorj," but he held his tongue. Their polite solemnness was a mockery to his father's memory. Standing to leave, they shuffled to the god-shelf Monkho kept above the family photos and bowed deeply, filling the moment with breathless silence. They were actors playing out a charade, and he felt the scene, like a frame snapped on his box camera, would etch itself on his memory forever.

Altanbaatar stepped outside. Bat and Zorigo were throwing the white covering over his parents' ger. The mourners followed Altanbaatar, and the family's guard dogs lurched on their chains. The oldest, a broad, wide-mouthed male dog, stood on his hind legs and roared like a lion, which caused the mourners to quicken their pace to the hitching post and their horses.

"I see you're erecting your parents' ger?" said one of the mourners, untying his horse. "Who's going to live there?"

Altanbaatar grinned. "We haven't decided," he said. He didn't want to give these men, who relished new words, a nugget of news to pass on to their family and friends. Altanbaatar thanked them for coming and waved them off.

"Conniving old wolves," he said under his breath as they rode away. Altanbaatar walked towards his parents' ger, reminding himself of the conversation he and Monkho had had last night while Altai and Bat slept.

"We need to give Bat space," Altanbaatar had said. "Living with his grandparents has made him more independent.

He's a young man, and we must treat him as one."

Fearing his next words, Monkho's hand flew to her throat, and she started to back away from him.

But he was adamant. "I've decided," he said firmly, "that Bat should continue living in my parents' ger."

"But he'll be alone," Monkho said simply. Altanbaatar moved towards her, kissed her brow, and told her to trust him. He hoped his advice had been wise.

Walking to his parents' ger, he caught the end of the rope Zorigo threw in his direction and tied it in place around the centre of the ger.

"An ail of four gers," said Zorigo holding a cigarette in the corner of his mouth. "Not sure that's good."

"What?" Altanbaatar shook his head. "Nothing wrong with four gers together, nothing wrong with even numbers," he said in answer to his eldest son's concerns. As if even numbers could bring bad luck to them.

Zorigo was bright and a quick learner who could turn his hand to anything practical. But sadly Zorigo wasn't a deep thinker, and his marriage to Soylomaa some ten or twelve years earlier had meant that an excess of superstitions had taken root in Zorigo's life. Altanbaatar sighed. Soylomaa was a good woman, but her fears were not a good influence on his eldest son, or on his own wife, for that matter.

Bat was pulling the second rope tight around the ger's middle as Altanbaatar reached him. His youngest son accomplished the task with ease, and Altanbaatar couldn't help thinking that Bat could make a good life as a herder. But...he stopped himself... that boy possessed a fine mind that was made for more. Even though the boy had lived most of his life with Altanbaatar's parents, his love of learning was clear to all, not to mention his ability to think through problems and find solutions. Just last year, Bat's school principal had caught Altanbaatar in the Erdene Mandal post office and told him that Bat should study beyond his school years. Altanbaatar had agreed, recognising that the principal was simply confirming what they, as a family, already knew.

But how should he proceed? He ran his hand through his hair, remembering the fire he'd seen in his youngest son's eyes when Altanbaatar's own frustrated anger had surfaced shortly after his mother's death a few weeks ago.

When crossed that boy can be as intransigent as a female camel, he thought. Even if Bat chooses to throw away his opportunities, I must hold my tongue and allow him the freedom to make his own choices.

Altanbaatar patted his son's back. "Ger looks good. Are you ready to move in?"

Bat smiled, "Yes, but it'll be strange without Grandfather."

"It will."

As Bat disappeared inside, Zorigo motioned to the metal bedstead that stood outside. "Help me move this." Altanbaatar picked up the other end of the bedstead, and together they manoeuvred the cumbersome frame through the door to the head of the ger. "These metal frames are so heavy," said Zorigo. "Wooden ones are much better."

"That's because you love working with wood. These metal frames last a lot longer," said Altanbaatar.

Zorigo shrugged his shoulders. They finished unpacking the oxcarts. The cupboards, table and stools were already in the ger. Monkho came to unpack the bowls and spoons, pillows and blankets. "Those three are as cunning as wolves," she said, cocking her head in the direction the mourners had gone.

Altanbaatar laughed. "I just muttered the same thing under my breath."

"They spend their time visiting the old and weak and relieving them of their money and treasured possessions," said Zorigo.

"Should be in jail. They're nothing but common criminals," Monkho added, opening one of the boxes. "Look! Your father's books."

"Burn them," said Zorigo.

"Burn what?" Bat asked, having positioned the small washstand in its place next to the door.

"These dusty old books," said Zorigo, casting a glance in the box.

"No! No," said Bat. "They were precious to Grandfather."

Zorigo shrugged his shoulders and moved on to the next bundle.

Bat grabbed the flaps and ripped the box fully open. Motes of dust spun in a shaft of sunlight coming through the open toono.

Zorigo coughed. "Grandfather hadn't looked at these books in years. I told you to throw 'em away."

"There's a lot of learning to be had from books," said Monkho, putting bowls into the cupboard. "One poet called books 'The eyes to the world.'"

"When I was a child," said Altanbaatar, "my father would draw that box out from under his bed and remove a single volume. For the longest time he'd stroke it, just like he was petting a new lamb. Eventually, pipe in hand, he'd settle beside the fire and open the book, reading until the candle grew low. Sometimes he'd tell us stories of our great history or stories that transported us to a world outside our valley that we knew nothing of."

Bat had already started piling the books on the table. "Look at this," he said, holding up an ancient copy of *The Secret History of the Mongols*. "You can buy this new in the village."

Altanbaatar took the book from Bat. It certainly was tatty; the back cover and several pages were missing. "Probably held sentimental value."

"*Chinghis Khan's Military Strategy…Birds of the Mongolian Steppe*," Bat announced, removing one faded volume after another. "D. Natsagdorj's *Short Stor…*"

"Aren't there any Buddhist scriptures?" Altanbaatar asked, knowing his father had once been a lama and, even after leaving the lamasery, had still respected the spirit world.

Bat rummaged through the box and pulled out a collection of pages. "There's just these," he said, handing his father the pages.

Altanbaatar turned them over. They were weightless, delicate, and as smooth as cotton, yet stronger than any paper he'd ever seen before. Bound together with thin black threads, the wrinkled pages had got wet somewhere in their history.

"Are they Buddhist writings?" Bat asked.

"I'm not sure…it's written in the old script."

"Can you read it, Father?"

Altanbaatar screwed up his eyes and traced each word with his finger. "Salix…the wind…blows where it wishes… and you hear…its sound…but you do not know where it comes from…or where it goes."

"Proverbs," said Monkho eagerly. "Let me have a look." She hastily took it from her husband. "…And so, it is with everyone who is born of the Spirit," she continued, thoughtfully pulling her long plait. "Don't think that's from our proverbs or the Buddhist scriptures."

"What's the book called?" asked Bat.

Monkho turned it over. "There is no title. It's just pages."

"Perhaps it's Chinese."

"Perhaps it is, Bat," replied Altanbaatar thoughtfully.

"But it's written in our script," said Monkho.

"Yes, that's strange," said Altanbaatar.

"Do you think your father knew more?" asked Monkho.

"About what?"

"The spirit world."

"Possibly," replied Altanbaatar, rubbing his forehead. "He was a devout man, dedicated to prayer, but not in the conventional sense."

Zorigo raised his eyebrows. "Why, because he didn't live in a lamasery?"

"Partly," answered Altanbaatar. "His relationship with institutional Buddhism was fragile. Your grandfather saw moral corruption in his lamasery, which shattered his trust in the system, leaving him estranged from traditional, Buddhist circles. Although, he acknowledged that many earnest monks truly sought higher levels of goodness and harmony."

"That's right," said Monkho. "Despite his disappointments, his generous spirit embraced all forms of spirituality."

"Embraced!" said Altanbaatar. "That word describes his attitude exactly. He held healers, bone-setters, and fortune-tellers in high regard. He called shamans masters of the spirit world." Altanbaatar held his hands before him, and then clasped them together, interlocking his fingers as one. "He understood that our beliefs are melded like an alloy; and that separating them back to their individual, unconnected roots of Buddhism and Shamanism is almost impossible. But...whether he knew more than that, I don't know."

Bat held up a finger. "He had a sense..."

"Of what?" asked Zorigo, folding the blankets and stacking them on top of the cupboard.

"I don't know exactly." Bat scratched his head. "He wasn't sure but he wondered whether there was a being bigger than Buddha, bigger even than Tsenger, who'd made and ordered everything."

"Everything?" said Zorigo.

"Yes, this world, the heavens, all creatures, and us."

Altanbaatar nodded; this was nothing new. He'd heard his father's musings before.

"Father's teaching is gold," said Monkho, unexpectedly quoting a line from a familiar proverb.

Altanbaatar looked at his wife with widening eyes. "Do you think his inklings were right?"

"I don't know, but I *do* think your father had times when he experienced real peace."

Altanbaatar put his hand to his mouth. "Mmm. There were certainly times when he possessed a tranquillity that seemed almost other-worldly."

Monkho placed the soft pages on top of the other books. "Do you think we can comprehend the spirit world?" she asked.

Zorigo drew a sharp breath. "Slow down," he said raising his hand. "Should we be trying to understand the unseen world?"

"I don't know," said Altanbaatar.

"Well, the spirits are all around us, touching our everyday lives, causing us to have irrational fears as we try to keep them happy," said Monkho, attaching the inner lining curtain to the ger walls.

"Pardon," Altanbaatar said, staring at his wife. He'd never heard her verbalise the emotion that controlled her desire to safeguard the equilibrium of the spirit world.

"I know," she said in answer to her husband's surprise. "It's a thought that's been going around my mind recently."

"And exactly which thought is that?" Altanbaatar asked, eager to fully comprehend Monkho's thinking.

"Whether there's a way to understand the visible and invisible world more clearly, so that knowledge can replace fear and, perhaps...give way to peace."

Zorigo pushed the empty boxes beneath the bed. "To understand such things, we need to become lamas or shamans."

They laughed.

"There must be other ways," said Monkho, finishing hooking the curtains in place.

"Perhaps we can understand life more fully through study and reading about the world and its workings," said Bat.

"Well, I ain't going to be doing no studying, that's up to you and Altai—you're the ones at school," Zorigo said, pointing to Bat.

"Me?" Bat sat on one of the low stools, staring at the stack of flabby-spined books.

"Yes, you son," said Monkho.

"Do you think I could discover the truth through study?"

"Maybe..." replied Altanbaatar casually, careful not to sound too enthusiastic.

Zorigo had already started splitting kindling for the stove, which was now in place in the centre of the ger. "Sure, you can," said Zorigo, laying the fire. "You've got a good head for learning."

Bat locked his hands together. "Before he died, grandfather told me not to miss my opportunities."

"Sounds like wise advice," said Zorigo.

Bat cocked his head to one side. "Do you think I should go back to school?"

Altanbaatar's mouth was dry. He sat on the bed, not daring to breathe.

"Sure, you're a clever kid," Zorigo said, striking a match on the side of the stove. He stirred the fire with a bent piece of metal rod that they'd fashioned into a poker. "I hated school," he said, "but you enjoy it. To me it was like a prison sentence."

Monkho chuckled. "You were only there four years, and that was simply because the education department insisted you learn to read and write. How old were you when you first went?"

"Eleven."

"Eleven!" Monkho said, shutting the cupboard door so firmly that the bowls rattled. Some of the lining curtain had slipped off the lattice frame, and she went to re-attach it.

"It was torture trapped in that building away from my herds and the open steppe for four years. I nearly died."

Bat pursed his lips. "I think I feel the same."

"Do you?" his mother asked.

He ran his hand up and down the books on the table. "I enjoy learning too, but I miss our countryside life."

"When the teachers told me to consider further education," said Zorigo, rolling another shabby cigarette and holding it in his lips, "I thought I'd suffocate."

He rubbed his dirty face, lit his cigarette, and took a long drag. He inhaled the smoke and pulled a bit of stray tobacco off his tongue. "But you," he said, pointing his finger at Bat, "are different. You can always be a herder, but Grandfather was right...you shouldn't waste your chances."

Bat twisted his lip. "Okay," he replied simply.

Altanbaatar sat still, gripping the blanket beneath him in his fist. Monkho straightened the blue curtains, finally pulling them taut to ensure that none of the lattice walling was showing. The curtains were old and in places torn. Monkho must have sensed he was looking at her because she turned her head slightly, and he saw that she was smiling.

The fire crackled, filling the ger with muggy warmth while Bat continued leafing through his grandfather's books. Namdorj's pipe laid on the table. Altanbaatar took it and stowed it beneath one of the roof poles. His father's beads were on the table too. Monkho had wanted to leave them with the body on the hillside, but he could not. Altanbaatar wasn't a praying man particularly, but those beads had been a part of his father, and he wasn't ready to let them go.

Bat sat engrossed in the books. He is a strange mix, thought Altanbaatar. His son was hot-tempered, yet the student in him was diligent and calm. Altanbaatar remembered his father's simple advice: "There's always a way out of the difficulties." He'd been right. Only Zorigo could have spoken to Bat about schooling and education. Zorigo, the least studious of their children, was the only one who could have answered Bat's question in a way that caused Bat to listen and think.

Chapter 6

Bat lay on his bed, watching the greyness fade through the open toono. The sky was turning soft blue. His heart ached, he tried to stem his tears as he pulled his deel closer. His grandparents were gone, and he couldn't bring them back. Sobs racked his body. Wiping his face with his deel, he pushed his arms into the sleeves, sat up, and swung his feet to the ground. He wriggled his toes in the brittle grass, its familiarity consoling him when everything else in the world felt foreign.

Everyone and everything were far away—his parents, brothers, and sisters and even his beloved horse. It was as if they spoke with muffled voices, and he couldn't reach them. If only life could be normal again, he thought, wondering how many times that plea had been on his lips these last few weeks.

He stood and moved to the door. After his grandmother's death, he'd been ready to stay with his grandfather and be a herder. They'd had a good plan, but his grandfather's death had put pay to that. Why did he have to go? Bat wound his orange belt around his hips and pulled his deel straight. If his mother hadn't made them move, perhaps his grandfather would have been okay.

He held the door handle, waiting to hear his father leave his ger. Over two weeks ago, Zorigo had told him that he thought it would be good for him to return to school. Ever since, Bat had been wrestling with the decision. Returning to school would be going back to something he knew, to a routine that was safe, and to learning, which he loved. Also, it was obvious that staying close to his parents would give him little chance to be a herder in his own right.

He must speak up. But telling his family would be like admitting that he had been wrong and that was terrifying. School started in two days and if he was going to go he needed to leave tomorrow. He stamped the floor. He would talk to his father.

A ger door swung open. Yes, it was the farthest away; it must be his father. Bat pushed his door open.

"You're up early, son." His father coughed, clearing his throat.

"I thought I'd help you move the cows."

Altanbaatar grinned and put his arm around Bat's shoulders. The cows, about twenty of them, stood lazily by the gers. The two of them walked behind the small herd, moving them forward by dints of whistles, clucks, and the gentle tapping of a stick. When the cows stopped to eat, Bat slapped their backsides. Overhead a buzzard circled and then settled on the bare branch of a nearby tree, eyeballing Bat. Bat shuddered. The predator was close, although the swans gliding gracefully down the river appeared unperturbed by its proximity.

The swans would soon leave for warmer climates and wouldn't return until the next winter had passed. Each autumn, his grandfather had told him that. Bat's chest tightened. His father guided the cattle to a sheltered spot in the middle of the trees and sat on the severed trunk of a fallen tree.

Bat sat beside his father, shivering in the early morning chill. The grass was heavy with dew and felt cold on his feet. He wished he'd worn his shoes.

"Hard summer, son..."

"I'm going back to school," he blurted out.

His father pulled his pipe from inside his deel flap. It was like his grandfather's, but it had a delicate jade mouthpiece that made Bat think it had come from China. His father filled it with tobacco, tamped it down and lit a match. The flame glowed yellow as he moved it over the pipe and inhaled gently.

"Is that what you want to do?" His father's question hung in the coolness.

Waking grasshoppers were just starting to chatter. By autumn, they'll be dead, thought Bat, although not before they'd buried their eggs in the ground ready for hatching next year.

Bat shrugged his shoulders. "I don't know. I want life to be normal again."

Altanbaatar sniffed. "It won't be."

Bat focused on a pair of swifts dancing before him. Their forked tails and swept-back wings silhouetted against the blue sky as they turned, banking hard left and then right. Bat envied them as they soared and dove with fluid, graceful movements.

"Life is never the same after those who have always been there suddenly leave," added his father.

Bat nodded. He was beginning to realise that. "But how do you keep going?"

"One day at a time," his father puffed on his pipe, "doing the work you have to."

"I love learning."

"I know you do, son," his father said, rubbing Bat's back. "I love learning too."

Bat closed his eyes. "Grandfather told me that you wanted to be a teacher."

"I did, but then your grandmother didn't want me to go to college." Altanbaatar tapped his pipe gently on the tree trunk, and Bat understood. His father didn't want him to throw away his educational opportunities.

"But I love this land. It's a part of me."

"Mmm," his father agreed. "I can understand that too. But this land will wait for your return."

Hadn't his grandfather said something similar? The cows tramped closer to the riverbank. "I have so many questions I want answers to," Bat said, wishing he could explain his longings more clearly. But he couldn't. "I want to understand life."

"You'll never fully understand life...but returning to school and getting an education is a good place to start."

The sun was climbing high in the morning sky. Its warmth comforted Bat.

"Zorigo's right, you have a good mind." His father stood and pushed his pipe into his boot, an action his grandfather had done a thousand times before.

"If you still want to be a herder, then come back after your studies."

"Can I?"

"Of course, we'll still be here." Snorting, the cows munched the riverbank's sweet grass. "We should get back so you can prepare."

"What about the cows?"

"They'll be fine."

They walked along the sandy bank, which was easier on Bat's unshod feet.

"You've made a wise decision. Living in denial of who you really are is one of life's deepest regrets."

"Denial?" Bat wrinkled his nose.

"One day you'll understand son."

His mother was alone in their ger when they entered. The falling sunlight lit up her brown face and made her gold earrings sparkle. "You were out early," she said to Bat.

He nodded.

"Pour yourselves a bowl of tea, and there's bread here," she said, pointing her knife to a pile of crusts and dried curds. Balanced on her lap was a bowl filled with sheep's blood, which she was carefully ladling into the animal's empty intestines. "I thought we could eat the sheep that was killed yesterday."

Bat's eyes widened. They were in for a treat. Everyone loved freshly slaughtered meat.

"Bat will return to school tomorrow," his father announced, sitting to pour himself a bowl of tea.

Splash! The bowl dipped between Monkho's legs, spilling blood and intestines onto her deel and the floor. Bat rescued the bowl from his mother and tried to scoop as much of the blood back into the bowl as he could.

"That's good news!" his mother cried, wiping her hands on her deel. "But tomorrow? Are your school clothes washed? Did your grandmother mend them?" She put a bloody hand to her mouth. "Do they still fit...? And what about pencils and exercise books?"

His father raised his hand. "Don't fret. Everything will be ready in time."

The ger door swung open, and Altai, the hem of her working deel hitched up into her belt, arrived carrying a pail of mare's milk. "Not much milk today," she said. "The mares know that the weather's cooler, and their foals need less. They won't give us much more this year. It's okay, though, there's enough for a full churn to store in the winter ambar for the New Year...Arhangai's airag really is the..."

Bat exchanged a knowing look with his father. His younger sister lived life at the pace of a galloping horse.

"What?" Altai said, pushing a stray hair out of her eyes.

"Have you ever tasted airag from other provinces?" Bat asked.

"No, but it's a well-known fact that our province's is the best. Our grass is soft and thick and tastes sweet and makes the..."

"Altai!" Her father raised his voice.

She stopped mid-sentence. "Yes, Aav aa."

"Bat will be returning to school with you tomorrow."

"Hoosh," she screamed, jumping up and down and turning a jig. "You've made me so happy!" She left her pail, flung her arms around Bat's waist, and squeezed him tight.

Breathless, Bat laughed. "Are you trying to crush the life out of me?"

"No, no, but I've been worrying," she said, looking up. "Who will do my homework if you're not there?"

Bat hooted. Altai loved school, but not for the same reason that he did. Lessons held no interest for her, and homework was a chore she rarely completed. But the fun and adventures she had with her friends outside the classroom made the rest bearable.

As suddenly as she had embraced him, she let go and dashed out of the door.

"She might be twelve," his mother said, drying her hand on a rag and leaving the intestines sitting in their bloody soup. "But she really is the baby. Are your school clothes in your grandmother's new avdar?"

"I think so," said Bat.

"Can't say that I'm impressed with that new avdar, though. Young fella calls himself a master carpenter. He used green wood on that cupboard, and anyone knows it must be seasoned. Door's so stiff you can hardly pull it off. The painting on the outside might be nice but it's no good if you can't get the door off," his mother complained heading to the door of the ger.

"Naraa! Naraa! You'll never guess what?" They heard Altai screaming.

His mother shook her head. "Yes, she's still the baby."

The door closed, and Bat saw that Naraa had quietly sneaked in. She sat at the table and poured herself a bowl of tea. Tall and willowy, Naraa was a beautiful Mongolian woman. She was of course much older than Bat, perhaps twenty-seven or twenty-eight. Bat wasn't quite sure, and he respected her too much to ask her outright.

"I hear you're planning to return to school," she said.

"Hard not to hear with Altai shouting," said their father with a wink.

Despite being a countryside woman, Naraa took care of herself. Her long black hair shone with a silky sheen. Her skin was smooth, and her teeth gleamed, a fact that had been a mystery to Bat as a boy. And then he'd seen her one day outside his parents' ger, brushing her teeth with a twig and soda. She'd told him that the soda helped keep her teeth white and healthy. Her knowledge had impressed him; he was proud of his wise sister.

She put her finger to her nose. "Just a minute," she said, leaving the ger. Bat looked at his father, who shook his head. A couple of minutes later she returned carrying a bag. "I bought these for the girls," she said, pressing the bag into his hand, "but they went to town and bought their own."

Bat opened the bag to find a collection of pens, pencils, and exercise books. "That's exactly what I need," he cried.

"Well, it should be enough to get you started."

"It will be," he replied, taking a bright pink pen from the bag.

"I'm glad you're going back to school." She paused for a moment, twisting her necklace between her fingers. "It takes a man to admit he's made a wrong decision."

Zorigo and his wife Soylomaa came and sat on the bed next to his father. His mother returned with Bat's school clothes. "Soylomaa, check whether there are any holes in these shirts," she said, handing her daughter-in-law Bat's white shirts.

"Naraa, check these trousers. Are they too short?"

Naraa held the trousers up. "They should last him another term," she said, without even measuring them against Bat's leg.

"They'll have to be okay as there's no time to buy anything new." His mother took the trousers from Naraa and rolled them up. "At least they're clean, but to start the school year without new clothes just doesn't seem right."

"It won't matter for one term," Bat's father said gently.

"Won't matter...! What will other people think of us?"

Bat was hot, which wasn't surprising as his mother was putting more wood on the fire. He thought of his horse, grazing contently on the new pasture that Zorigo had guided the herd to earlier this morning. He longed to call her and ride together into the coolness of the forest where only the birds and locusts disturbed the silence.

"You made the right decision," said Zorigo.

"Yes, the spirits have given you a good mind," said Soylomaa.

Bat cast his father a glance.

"Do the spirits give us our minds? Or was your grandfather right to wonder whether there is something greater than the spirits?" said his father.

"Surely the spirits are the ones who endow us with our minds," said Soylomaa, threading a needle to repair a hole in Bat's shirt.

"Perhaps," Altanbaatar replied.

Bat watched his sister-in-law. Her calloused hand moved swiftly, stabbing his shirt with a short, sharp movement before retrieving the needle from the back of the fabric and moving to the next stitch. She was smaller than Bat, with pronounced cheekbones and a pointed chin that left her looking as gaunt as a starved bird.

"Bat," his mother said, flicking the flies off the bowl of blood and intestines. "You need to start packing."

As he got to his feet, Soylomaa leant over and pressed a note into his hand. "For anything you might need." It was a hundred turgrik note.

"This is too much," he said, aware that his brother's family had little cash.

"Nonsense," said Soylomaa.

Bat thanked her and left the ger. Released from their chains, the dogs kept watch over the sheep and goats, although it was unlikely that wolves would attack during the day. Crows cackled as he walked to his grandparents' ger and the sweet-scented dung filled his nostrils.

Quietly closing his ger door, he sat on the edge of his bed, picked up his crumpled deel, and shook it. Light danced with the dust, and he pulled his coat over him and lay down.

Bat woke to a gentle knocking. I must have slipped the bolt across, he thought shaking himself awake. His father stood on the step.

"Have you been snoozing?"

Bat rubbed his eyes.

"I don't blame you," his father said, handing Bat his repaired school clothes.

Altanbaatar sat on a stool while Bat took his cotton sack from the avdar and filled his bag with his shoes, clothes, and newly acquired writing supplies.

"Your mother and sisters are cooking up a feast."

Bat laughed. "They're always cooking up a feast."

That night they crowded into his parent's ger, sitting on stools and beds around the fire. Bat's nephews, Erdene-huu and Gamba, sat on the floor. The candles burned brightly, lighting the food-laden table. Bat's stomach groaned. A large silver bowl filled with fresh boiled blood sausage, sheep's stomach and intestines, and other fatty delights steamed with deliciousness.

"Mutton is my favourite meat," said Altai, grabbing a slice of meat and dousing it with soy.

"You've just ruined it," said Zorigo. He drained his bowl of milk tea and knocked back a shot of vodka.

"Easy on the vodka," said Altanbaatar. "We don't want any drunkenness."

"We can hold our drink," Zorigo replied with a twinkle in his eye. "Anyway, the vodka sharpens our manliness."

Rolling his eyes skywards, Bat's father's sighed. "You boys..."

Altanbaatar sliced pieces of sausage, liver, and lung and stacked them into a meaty sandwich. Bat cut his own length of sausage and took a bite. Its rich flavour saturated his mouth. He cut a further length and devoured it like a hungry wolf gobbling up its first prey.

"You could be starting a new tradition," Naraa said, looking Bat in the eye.

"What do you mean?"

"You may be able to go to college. You would be the first in the family to go."

"I don't know about that," said Bat.

"Let's see," she said with gentleness.

Bat smiled, remembering the tale his grandmother once told him about his older sister's dreams. She'd wanted to be a secretary. At sixteen, she'd attended the local technical college where she'd learned to use a typewriter, but then she had become pregnant. The father of her child, a no-good sheep-stealer, had abandoned her. Left with nowhere else to go, Naraa had returned home. The child, a son, was given to the sheep-stealer's family to raise.

Naraa's hands moved like the swifts he'd seen earlier, rising and diving, swooping, and climbing as she related a story she'd read in the newspaper.

"In America, they say people travel by aeroplane. It is becoming the travel of today, and one day it will impact us."

"Not in my day!" Bat's father said.

Zorigo laughed and picked up a piece of wood he'd been fashioning into a horse-head spoon. His rough hands traced the shape of the head, paring the wood with practiced skill until it became a bold miniature.

"Planes are dangerous things," said Bat's mother. "Their engines stall, and they fall out of the sky."

Soylomaa agreed, gnawing a couple of rib bones down to the white. When she'd finished, she rubbed her greasy hands together and wiped them over her face. Zorigo sat beside her, and Erdene-huu and Gamba sat at their father's feet. The two were rascals. Bat's grandmother used to call them a double dose of trouble, as they left a trail of devastation wherever they went.

"Imagine being able to travel quickly," Naraa continued. "To be able to see more of this country, to get to Ulaanbaatar easily, to arrive and not be tired."

Lhxaa, Naraa's husband, sat to her right, laughing and smiling at her wistful dreams. Even to Bat, who knew little of girls and romance, it was evident that Lhxaa loved his wife. An Arhangai lad, he was older than Naraa (in Bat's estimation about thirty-five). He'd been married before, but his first wife had tragically died in childbirth. His dirty, blotchy face and permanent limp, the result of a local bone-setter's poor setting of a childhood break, meant that he was not a handsome man. But his deep, rumbling laugh, which seemed to start in the pit of his stomach, and his hard-working nature endeared him to everyone, making him as much as part of the family as any of Bat's siblings.

Naraa's face shone. "You could visit all the shops, the museums, and the theatres," she concluded. "It would be wonderful."

Everyone knew Naraa loved shopping. In fact, Lhxaa and Naraa's two daughters, Zyaa and Zola, were just like their mother. Leaving for school two days ago, Zyaa and Zola had ostensibly gone to settle themselves at Lhxaa's sister's home in Erdene Mandal, where they stayed during term time. But Bat suspected they were really spending their time mooching around the shops and market.

"Museums are boring," said Altai, snuggling up close to her father, who draped his arm around her.

"You can learn a lot from museums," Monkho chimed. "And on occasion," she added, smoothing her creased deel, "it would be nice to go to a concert."

Bat's parents' faces, etched with lines, smiled as they enjoyed the moment. His mother must have felt his gaze as she turned to him. "Have you finished your packing?" she asked.

"Yes," he replied simply.

Monkho got up and moved slowly to her avdar. As she opened the cupboard, the large carved photo frame that stood on top juddered. The photo frame was old, a wedding gift from her father, but it contained Monkho's most treasured possessions: their family photos. From inside the avdar, his mother removed a bag bulging with cheese and curds and, taking a handful of sweets from the table, she pressed them down into the mouth of the bag on top of the curds.

"Get that sewn up," she said, handing him the cloth bag. "Your arms reach the saddle straps; your legs reach the stirrups. Yes, my youngest son, are growing into a man."

Bat took the bag and quietly slipped out. The night was darkening. *My grandfather, are you tired from your journey?* He touched his mouth. Where had the unbidden words come from?

You think of me through a thousand moments of the day. The words were in his head. *I have given you all I know, taught you everything I have learned. Now it's time for you to learn from others.*

He stepped into his ger. *The path of thoughts is vague; the way of books is clear.* Was that a quote he'd learned at school?

Part 2

Chapter 7

Leaving his sister's ger early, Buyeraa hitched a ride with a nearby neighbour bringing sheep to market. It's been a good summer, he thought, holding onto his seat as the truck rumbled along the rutted track. He'd left school at the end of May exhausted, ready for the break.

The two months with his sister's family beyond Jargalant alongside the Zag River had been just what he needed. For the first week, he slept, waking only to eat meals and play cards with the children. After that, he began to feel better and was able to enjoy the beauty of the valley and its surrounding mountains. He'd helped with the chores, entertained the children, and spent his afternoons beside the river, reading and listening to the water tumbling over the rocks.

The truck pulled into Erdene Mandal just after eight. It was too early for any of the cafes to be open, so Buyeraa decided to head to school to see if he could rouse the night-watchman. After much banging on the school gate, the watchman appeared outside his ger.

"Who it is?" he asked.

"Buyeraa bagsh."

The watchman grunted and made his way across the hasher yard to release the lock and open the gate.

"Sairhan amaas uu—Did you have a good rest?" Buyeraa asked.

The watchman, a stooping fellow whom Buyeraa didn't recognise, nodded.

"Well, this yard is certainly very tidy and clean," said Buyeraa, scanning the swept hasher with its newly painted play area.

The watchman grunted again, broke the wax seal placed across the door and its frame proving that no one had entered since the cleaning and painting had been completed, and unlocked the door. Buyeraa thanked him and stepped inside. Gone were the grubby fingerprints and scuff marks, replaced instead by the caustic smell of fresh gloss that covered the walls and filled Buyeraa's lungs. We'll have to open the windows for days to rid the place of the smell, he thought, his footsteps echoing in the empty corridor.

He entered his room, opened the window, and lit a cigarette. The hasher was empty. No one else had arrived, but the new countryside pupils would be here soon, entering this foreign world of education for the first time. Few were ever ready, and many felt trapped by the new regime that kept them from their families and the life they loved. After their cosy gers, the cold walls and high ceilings of the school must feel like a prison. Some eventually embraced the changes and loved school, while others lived for the day they could escape.

He sighed. Stubbing his cigarette out in the thin metal ashtray. He pulled his sack onto the bed and sat. His bed was like a pit, the metal mesh beneath his thin mattress slack as a hammock. He rubbed his back and undid the knot that had kept his bag closed.

The door at the end of the corridor creaked open, the sound reminded him of an injured animal whining with distress. Were the first students arriving already?

"Just an older teacher." It was the voice of the watchman.

"That'll be Buyeraa bagsh. He's got nowhere else to go," a woman replied.

Buyeraa stepped behind his open door.

"What do you mean?" the watchman asked.

"His wife and young son were killed in an accident when they were moving to a new school. People say he had great prospects...would have been principal of his own school by now." The woman's voice grew louder. Buyeraa listened. "He's still a good teacher, and the students love him, but the sadness clings to his body like a curse to a snake."

Buyeraa took a deep breath as they came close and passed his door. Slowly he exhaled, grabbed another cigarette, and returned to his unpacking. On the top of his clothes laid a photo of his wife and young son. He touched their faces with his finger and placed the photo on his desk.

The words the woman spoke were true. When he'd lost his beloved wife, his joy had instantly been turned to sorrow. They'd been so excited, so happy as they planned their move from Jargalant to Undra-Ulaan where Buyeraa was to take up a new teaching post. It was a promotion. People had said he was too young to be promoted to head of the department. He and his wife Ganaa were both just twenty-six, but Ganaa believed Buyeraa could be a school principal or more.

He removed his shirts from the sack. Smoothing the creases, he ran his finger along the frayed collars. He really should buy new ones. He placed his clothes in the chest of drawers and closed the drawer.

Taking his new pencils, pens, and notebook out of his bag, he arranged them neatly side by side on top of his desk. The school in Undra-Ulaan had sent a truck to move them. It had been a warm August day, near the end of the month, he remembered. They'd decided to move a little earlier so that they'd be settled before the term began on the first of September. The nights were already getting cooler, and they'd even wondered whether it was going to rain, but it hadn't. By the time they'd finished loading, both the truck and the cab were full, so they'd decided to ride outside on top of their possessions between the beds and the blankets.

He drew on his cigarette and exhaled slowly, filling his small room with smoke that hung like a cloud on a windless day.

They should never have sat on top of the truck. He had sat on the left side, while Ganaa and their three-year-old son had sat on the right. And then...his memory was hazy.

The truck had swerved. He'd been thrown into the air and landed on the road like a ragdoll.

Gravel had embedded itself in his face and raw pain shot through his legs and side. He'd blinked. Where were his wife and son? Dragging himself to the edge of the road, he'd seen the truck lying on its side at the bottom of the embankment. Their belongings were scattered, and Ganaa and his son lay pinned beneath their furniture, motionless. His breath stuck in his throat; he had known they were dead before he reached them.

He'd wanted to jump out of his skin and run down the bank. But he couldn't. Painstakingly, he dragged himself to their sides, shaking Ganaa, willing life to return to her black eyes, but it would not. He'd cradled them both, howling like an ensnared wolf whose insides had just been ripped out. Eventually a passing driver and his wife had pulled him away.

Wiping a tear from his eye, he reached for another cigarette. The match shook in his hand. The driver of the truck, who had evidently been drunk, had survived. Injured but alive, he was holed up in some prison near Ulaanbaatar. The injustice of it all – him alive while his wife and son were dead.

"You're back early."

The school principal was tapping at his door. Buyeraa took a deep breath, letting the fire in his chest return to its home. Standing, he coughed and shook the principal's hand. In his early fifties, the principal wore a greasy smile that matched his greasy hair. His pot belly, allegedly evidence of too much drinking, sagged over the top of his trousers.

"I like to be organised before the children arrive," Buyeraa said as calmly as he could.

"Did you have a good summer?"

"Yes, spent the time with my sister's family beside the Zag River. And you?"

"We took a summer cottage on the edge of Hovsgol Lake—our children and grandchildren joined us. It was noisy, but restful too."

The corridor doors crashed open, and Buyeraa imagined them pinned back against the walls as children rushed in. The first wave was arriving. Suddenly the corridor filled with voices and laughter.

"Our fish were bigger than yours," one lad shouted above the rest.

"Never were," screamed another.

"You're a liar. Your whole family are liars."

"Come here and say that..."

Raising their eyebrows, Buyeraa and the principal looked at one another. "Trouble," said the principal quickly moving to the corridor.

Buyeraa followed to see two boys encircled by children. The shorter of the two advanced, driving the taller boy up against the wall as he pulled his fist back, ready to land the so-called liar with a punch flat in the middle of his face.

"That's enough!" the principal thundered.

The two boys stopped instantly. Dorj, the puncher, dropped his hand and released the other lad. Freed, the taller boy pressed his palm to his heart, knowing he'd just escaped a beating.

"My office..." the principal grabbed the boys' two heads and pointed them in the direction of his office, "immediately."

The crowd watched the two boys being marched down the corridor and through the double doors. Deprived of the pleasure of watching the first fight of the term, they booted their cloth bags along the floor.

"Pick them up," Buyeraa said, ushering the boys towards their dormitory rooms.

They scuffed their shoes along the freshly polished floors. Turning and twisting, they kicked their bags into the air and caught them like practiced footballers. Football had certainly caught the attention of these countryside lads, thought Buyeraa.

"Boys...please!" They weren't listening. He turned to go back to his room.

"Sain bain uu?" Altanbaatar stood beside his door.

Returning the greeting, Buyeraa invited the herder into his room. Buyeraa liked this man. He stood head and shoulders above most, and from the few conversations they'd had together, Buyeraa knew him to be an intelligent man. Altanbaatar had four children, as Buyeraa remembered, although only two were students now—Altai, his youngest daughter, who wasn't much interested in study, and Bat, a boy, who was a favourite of Buyeraa's.

Altanbaatar held out his hand. "Did you have a good summer?" he asked.

"Yes, and you?" Buyeraa replied shaking his hand.

Altanbaatar did not reply. Buyeraa met his eyes. The man's face was blank. There was no smile or twinkle in his eyes.

No frown or hint of anger. And the herder's shoulders were stooped as if he carried the burdens of the world on them. Buyeraa recognised the signs: this was his old friend, grief.

"Come in. Sit down," Buyeraa said, moving his only chair to the middle of the room. Buyeraa sat on the bed.

The herder shuffled in the seat and grasped his hands. "Can I ask you to keep an eye on Bat?"

"Of course," Buyeraa replied.

"The boy had a tough summer..." He stopped and straightened his deel. "His grandparents passed on."

Buyeraa pursed his lips. He never knew what to say because words never really brought any comfort.

"That's very sad," he said eventually.

"Unexpected," Altanbaatar said, shaking his head.

"That's the worst," added Buyeraa, remembering the shock of his own loss.

"They were old," Altanbaatar continued. "But they were gone in a moment."

Buyeraa nodded. "Life can change so quickly."

"Bat was very close to them. He'd lived with them since he was a small boy. He loved them dearly, especially his grandfather."

"And so did you," Buyeraa replied quietly.

Altanbaatar looked at his hands. They were the hands of a herder, Buyeraa thought, grimy and rough.

"Yes, I did. My mother was a natural meddler, but we loved her for it. Whereas my father never interfered, although he was the one I turned to for advice. And then suddenly they were gone."

The noise in the corridor was rising. The boys were shouting hello to their friends and sharing their summer stories excitedly. Buyeraa wondered whether he should tell them to be quiet to respect this man's grief. But he could not. As yet, their lives were untouched by the pain that he and Altanbaatar had experienced.

Altanbaatar wrung his hands. "I feel so old...and lost...like a part of me went with them."

"Life is never the same after the ones you love leave."

Altanbaatar's sudden laugh startled Buyeraa.

"I said the same thing to Bat."

"It's true, life is changed forever."

"I know," Altanbaatar said, suddenly getting to his feet and signalling that the sharing of confidences was over. Buyeraa walked to the door with the herder.

"So, you'll keep an eye on the boy?"

"Of course," Buyeraa said, patting Altanbaatar's back.

Altanbaatar raised his voice as he stepped into the corridor. "He loves learning and wants to do well."

"I'll make sure he gets every opportunity."

They shook hands again. "Altai wasn't as close to her grandparents so she'll be fine."

Buyeraa was just about to disagree when he caught sight of one lad thumping another. "Stop!" he shouted, pushing his way through the ring of boys that surrounded yet more wrestlers. "Stop!" he repeated, pulling the two apart. By the time the fight was averted, Altanbaatar had gone.

Buyeraa turned to the two would-be wrestlers. They faced one another, eyes blazing. The smaller of the two already had a bloody nose. The puncher must have struck him hard, as there was blood splattered on the freshly painted walls. The caretaker would not be pleased. Nord, the bigger boy, lurched forward. "You touch my bed, and I'll break your face!"

Quivering, the small boy yelled, "Bagsh aa—Teacher, he took my bed."

Buyeraa took the small boy's hand. "Show me," he said. Nord really was one of the worst bullies he'd seen in a while, he thought handing the smaller boy his handkerchief.

There were three beds in the boy's room, one of which was close to the window. Nord was already sitting on that bed with his arms folded across his chest.

"That bed is for a new student," Buyeraa said. "New students always have beds next to the window."

"Why?"

"Because new children are unsettled, and the window gives them the opportunity to see life outside." Buyeraa hated arguing.

"Babies!"

Buyeraa's face burned red. He picked up Nord's bags and walked out.

"Hoosh! Where are you going?"

"Follow me."

Nord dutifully followed. Buyeraa took Nord to the room next to his. "You will stay here for the whole of this term," he said, throwing the boy's bags on the bed nearest the door. Nord followed his bags, recognising that he was beaten.

Buyeraa pulled his jacket sleeves down over his wrists. If we can't change Nord, he'll be a bully for the rest of his life, he thought. Buyeraa climbed the staircase to the second floor. His leg felt heavy, and school had hardly started.

"Buyeraa." The history teacher motioned him into her room. "Have you heard?" she whispered with exaggerated movements of her mouth. "Batbold's grandparents passed this summer, and he nearly gave up school."

"Yes!" Word flew around the school quicker than a wolf seizes a lamb. He walked to the end of the corridor. Bat's door was open, and the boy was alone.

"It's good to see you, Bat," Buyeraa said, walking into the room. The boy stopped unpacking. Even dressed in trousers and a shirt, he still looked like a warrior. His long black hair, tied with a leather ribbon, hung like a tasselled mane, and Buyeraa noticed that although Bat wore shoes, he was not wearing socks.

"Sain bain uu, Buyeraa bagsh aa." Bat shook his teacher's hand. Bat was smiling, but his eyes, like his father's, were blank.

"Just spoke with your father. He told me about your grandparents. I'm very sorry to hear about their passing."

"Yes." Bat took the last shirts from his bag and placed them in the drawer, then sat on his bed and offered Buyeraa some curds. Buyeraa took a handful, they were soft with fresh sourness. "I'm glad you're back at school," he said.

"I'm glad to be back, sir." Bat got to his feet, moved to the desk beside his bed, and started straightening his colourful assortment of pens, pencils, and notebooks. The children were all required to keep their desks tidy and ordered.

"I want to learn, sir," he said, lining up the pink pens.

"I know you do, son."

"I want to gain knowledge."

"Study well and you will."

"I want to understand life."

"That takes time."

"I want to find the truth of this world," he said, holding his hands in a prayerful gesture. "And to find out if there is a god."

Buyeraa's shirt collar suddenly felt tight, and he wasn't sure whether he could contain his fire. He cleared his throat. "It is good to learn. It is good to gain knowledge. But your search for spiritual beings is futile."

Bat blinked. "What? Why?"

"Spiritual beings do not exist." He loosened the top button of his shirt. "Our world, and everything about it and us, is physical."

"But my grandfather, grandmother…"

"Misguided by legends and myths." How could this intelligent boy accept the folklore of his grandparents? How could he believe that legends had any connection with the truth of real life? "Centuries ago, our ancestors who knew no better worshipped creation and believed there were spirits on the mountains, in rivers and in fire. But now we know better."

"But the stories I've heard from my childhood…"

"Exactly…stories," Buyeraa said, waving his hand emphatically. "Today we know better. Science is showing us the way forward." Buyeraa stood. "We must study and learn scientific facts. They will give us knowledge and an understanding that will enable us to be better people."

Bat was biting his lip, but Buyeraa continued. "There are no gods." His throat burned as the words flew from his mouth. "Belief in supernatural spirits is based on fear and superstition and a lack of proper education. You are a part of a new generation living in the real world, not in a world that lives in people's imaginations."

"Religion isn't true?"

"No! I will teach you how to find the truth through learning. I will teach you how to grow as a man and become the best you can be using your own strength and power. The strength to be a good person is in you and not in some spirit!" Buyeraa punched the air. "You are in charge of your life. You're the one who makes the choices that direct your path to fulfil your future."

Buyeraa walked to the door. "Surely death has shown you that."

Chapter 8

No spirits? No religion? Could it be true? Buyeraa bagsh knew so much more about the world than Bat did. He held his shaking hands. Was science the only way to understand life? He moved to the window. The morning sun was climbing above the buildings on the main street. Outside the post office, the water cart had stopped, and people were gathering, ready to fill containers with their daily supply. The harnessed ox bucked, sending water over the side of the wooden butt and splashing onto the ground. The waterman slapped him, and the ox bowed his head contritely.

Herdsmen drove their cattle down the street. Standing in their stirrups, they gently nudged the sheep towards the market. Bat smiled. There was going to be some hard haggling with the traders today. When a fair price was agreed upon—although, of course the herders never felt a fair price had been reached—the herders would take their cash and buy flour, oil, and perhaps sweets for their children. Finding a few friends, they'd play a round of cards and swig vodka until nightfall. Sober or drunk, they'd then ride back to their families. Their lives never changed; they simply followed the rhythm of the seasons, doing what their fathers and grandfathers had done.

The post office truck pulled up beside the water cart. The driver had driven through the night to bring the twice-weekly delivery of post and newspapers to the rural post office. Sara-egch, the postmistress, descended the steps. Short and rounded with long, plaited hair, she reminded Bat of his mother. In fact, she and his mother were good friends and had been since they first met at school. Now in her forties, she'd been the postmistress for as long as he could remember and, according to his grandmother, had taken the job before she'd finished school.

The post driver got out and stretched. Sara-egch signalled for to him to open the van doors, but he shook his head; he probably wanted to sleep. Sara-egch said something, no doubt a sharp comment, Bat thought, because suddenly the driver was unlocking the doors and throwing the sacks onto the ground. Sara-egch often spoke harshly, although his grandmother had warned him that not everyone who smiles is a friend and not all who are angry are enemies.

Sara-egch pulled something from the side of her head—it was the pen she kept behind her ear. She bent to check the sacks. Bat couldn't see clearly, but he knew she was checking the labels and meticulously recording the details in her book. It was the same routine, every day of her working life.

She closed her logbook and reverently touched her forehead. Her father had been a lama who'd instilled the Buddhist ways into her life until every act and responsibility she fulfilled became infused with worship. Bat stared. No religion? According to Buyeraa bagsh, Sara-egch's beliefs were futile. The ancient traditions that were woven into her life, his family's lives, and those around him were mere myths and legends. He shook his head.

"Sain bain uu," Nadmid shouted, dumping his bag, and grabbing Bat from behind. Bat turned to face his old friend and sparring partner, who stood taller and broader than Bat did.

Locking their arms onto one another's shoulders, each pitched his might against the other. Bat pushed, but Nadmid pushed harder. Back and forth they tottered as they each battled to stay on their feet.

"Think you can defeat a champion?" Nadmid laughed.

"Champion, eh?" Bat took a deep breath.

"Elephant of Bat-Single sum." Nadmid grabbed Bat's belt.

"Champion of a countryside village?" Bat tried to shake Nadmid loose, but his opponent gripped him like a wolf holding a lamb between its teeth. He had to get him to the ground. "Aa...aargh," Bat cried, kicking Nadmid swiftly behind the left knee. Nadmid's leg buckled, and Bat pushed him down.

"Remind me," said Bat, raising his arms in the triumphant eagle dance, "how many people live in Bat-Single sum, four families? And aren't they all grandfathers long past their wrestling days?"

Nadmid stood and punched his friend in the back. Bat staggered and coughed.

"I let you win that one."

Nadmid towered a full ten centimetres above Bat. Bat grinned and with a quick ruffle of his hand tried to push the hair out of his eyes, only to have it flop forward again. "How was your summer?"

"Great," he laughed. "Yours?"

"Fine," Bat replied. "Did you see Buyeraa bagsh? He just came in."

"I saw him." Nadmid pulled his leg him behind in a dramatic exaggeration of the teacher's limp. "He was walking as fast as he could with that gamey leg and telling everyone off as he went."

Bat lay down on his bed.

"What did he want with you?" asked Nadmid.

"Just saying hello."

Nadmid shuddered.

"What?"

"He gives me the creeps," said Nadmid.

"Why?"

"The way he limps up and down the corridors like he's some monster."

"He's not a monster. His foot was crushed in an accident."

"I know about that accident."

"Everyone knows about that accident."

Nadmid opened his bag. Creased clothes and bent exercise books spilled onto his bed. He tried flattening his exercise books. "Impossible," he muttered, laying the books on his desk. He gathered armfuls of clothes and stuffed them into the cupboard, quickly shutting the door before they could fall out. "There, finished."

Bat shook his head. "If you folded everything and packed it neatly in your bag in the first place, then there'd be no problem."

Nadmid shrugged his shoulders. "There is no problem."

They'd been roommates for four years, and Bat still marvelled how his untidy friend could be a maths genius. Bat assumed that mathematicians, which was what Nadmid wanted to be, all possessed ordered minds and tidy lives.

"Educated in Moscow, my mum said."

"Who?" asked Bat.

"Buyeraa bagsh."

"Yeah...destined for great things according to my grandfather."

Still hungry, Bat took another dried curd from his bag and passed the rest to Nadmid, who helped himself to a large piece of soft, new aaruul. Bat pummelled his lumpy pillow.

"Never took his new job after his wife and boy were killed. His life was in ruins, my mum said."

Did Nadmid's mum know everything?

"Came home to Erdene Mandal, to the school he'd attended," Nadmid continued, "and became an ordinary teacher."

"Maybe he enjoys it."

"My mum says he's wasted here. He could have married again, had a family, got a new job, and got on with his career."

"Perhaps he's happy here," said Bat, beating his pillow again.

"Who'd be happy here?"

"Some people like the countryside."

"And you're one of them..."

"Maybe..."

Nadmid sat bolt upright. "Maybe? Not definitely...? Do I detect a change?"

"Perhaps..."

Bat had Nadmid's full attention. "You'd think of leaving this place? Of leaving your grandparents?"

Bat didn't reply.

"I thought you'd never leave."

Bat swallowed. "My grandparents have gone."

"Gone?" Nadmid's eyes were as round as dumplings. Tipping his head to one side, he pointed to the ceiling.

"Yes." Bat clenched his fists. "They both passed on this summer," he said slowly.

"Umm." Nadmid sucked on his aaruul.

All around them, cupboards slammed as their neighbours unpacked their belongings. Lacing his fingers behind his head, Bat closed his eyes. Despite the sparseness of their room with its two beds, two desks, chairs, and a shared cupboard, it was familiar and cosy.

"Will you go to university?" Nadmid demanded.

Bat forced his eyes open.

"You're clever, you could do it."

Bat rubbed his eyes. "Maybe."

"You must go!"

"I have been thinking about it."

"You need to do more than think about it. You need to make a decision."

"It's not urgent."

"Not urgent." Nadmid pinched the bridge of his nose and, leaning against the newly painted wall, let out a long sigh, "That's countryside people for you."

Bat frowned; wasn't Nadmid a countryside boy?

"If you want something, you have to chase it," said Nadmid.

Buyeraa bagsh had told him that the understanding of life only came through the study of scientific facts. Bat shuffled to the edge of his bed. A desire was growing inside him. He wasn't quite sure what it was, but it reminded him of the feeling that drove him and his mare to outrun the wind, to pursue its power until one day he hoped to beat it. Nadmid searched his face.

"Okay," said Bat.

"Okay?"

"Okay...I'll study to go to university."

"Really? As easy as that?"

"Really," Bat replied with a smile.

"Hoosh! Then let's celebrate," Nadmid shouted leaping to his feet, pulling two squashed cigarettes from his trouser pocket, and pushing one into Bat's hand. Bat didn't want it; he hated smoking. The smoke burnt his tongue and stuck in the back of his throat. But he accepted the cigarette anyway and let Nadmid light it. Officially, school rules forbade smoking, but the teachers turned a blind eye to any student caught with a cigarette in his mouth.

Bat took a long draw. "Do you think our legends and traditions are based on truth?"

Nadmid shook his head. "That's a strange question."

"Perhaps!" Bat flicked cigarette ash on to the floor. "Buyeraa bagsh told me our legends were just stories."

Nadmid scooted to the edge of the bed and eyed Bat quizzically. "Mmm…" he mused, as if he were preparing to apply his logic to some maths problem. "When I was a boy, I'd plead with my family to tell me the old stories…they were old friends and as real to me as my parents, brothers, and sisters." He leant forward, ripped a page from one of his new exercise books, and tapped his cigarette ash into it. "But today," he went on, tilting his head to one side, "I'm not sure. Times are different. We can study science and learn proven theories about the mechanics of life."

Bat stubbed his cigarette out against the side of the cupboard that separated their beds. He didn't want to be a smoker. "I remember my grandfather saying that the Russians wanted to educate us, to teach us all to read and write so that we could learn the 'right way' to think."

Nadmid nodded. "That makes sense." He drew two more cigarettes from his trouser pocket and offered one to Bat. Bat refused, but Nadmid perched another between his lips. "Perhaps through learning and knowledge, we can understand the old stories."

Bat rubbed his head. "I don't know."

"Neither do I, but we live in a time when learning and knowledge are the keys to power."

"Power? Where did you hear that?"

"On the television."

Bat had forgotten; Nadmid's family was one of the privileged few who had a television.

"Education gives meaning and direction to our lives and helps us become more efficient." Nadmid formed a large "O" with his mouth and started blowing rings of smoke. "Education gives you power."

Nadmid sounded like he was quoting propaganda. Bat opened the window. Small children chirping like merry birds played in the playground below. A motorbike screeched to the end of the road, and across the street a knot of women stood, their heads inclined towards one who was telling a story. Life in Erdene Mandal was predictable and, he realised, unlikely to change. Rooted in tradition, life on the steppe was also unlikely to change.

Bat closed the window. *Education is your best partner in life.* The teacher's words rang in his ears. Were they just ideals set on disturbing his perceived reality? Or were they truth? Could education really give him power?

Chapter 9

The sun, streaming through their curtain-less window, woke Bat. He clenched his muscles and pulled the threadbare blanket closer. The heating wasn't going to be on until the end of October which was another two weeks away. He would have to start sleeping beneath his winter deel.

He slipped his bare feet onto the floor, pulled on his trousers, and left the room quietly. The clock in the corridor said it was almost half-past seven; he had just thirty minutes before the breakfast bell rang. Hurrying to the empty bathroom, he splashed icy water over his face, remembering that his grandmother had always warmed his washing water when he was at home.

Nadmid was still sleeping when he returned but Altai sat on Bat's bed rubbing her hands together. "I'm freezing," she said.

"Sairhan amarsan uu—Did you have a good rest?" Bat asked, raising his eyebrows.

"Sairhan, sairhan, but I can't do my homework. I don't understand it."

"What is it?" Bat asked with a sigh.

"Maths." Altai thrust the book beneath Bat's nose.

"I'm no good at maths," he said, pushing the book away. "Ask Nadmid."

Altai cast a glance Nadmid's way. "He's still asleep. Besides, you're just as good as he is." This wasn't true, but her pleading eyes were melting the decision he'd made not to help her. "All right," he said, thrusting his hand out. "Give me the book."

She gave it to him and leapt from the bed. "I'm going to get dressed."

"Oh no, you're not." He seized her plait like he might grab a horse's mane and pulled her back. She sat, her bottom lip threatening a wobble.

"We're going to do this together."

"What's all the noise?" Nadmid pulled his blanket tighter and turned over. "It's still the middle of the night."

"It's just Altai and her homework."

"Can't she do her own homework?"

Bat opened her exercise book to the last page of scrawny numbers. Multiplication. He placed his finger on the page and began to explain, "You take the...."

"Just do it," Altai said impatiently.

"You should learn."

"I'm not interested. When will I need to do sums?"

"When you have your own ger and family and need to take care of your money."

"My husband can do that. Maths are so boring," she said, turning up her nose. "Stories are much more interesting."

Stories were interesting, it was true. But, as Bat was starting to learn, stories couldn't equip you for life beyond the steppe.

"The teacher will know you've had help," he said.

"I don't care."

Bat wrote the answers in her book, aware that Altai's lack of interest in education would take her right back home to his parents' ger. He closed her book. She took it, shoved it in the front of her deel and ran from the room as the breakfast bell rang.

Nadmid stirred while Bat pulled a warm jumper from his cupboard and sprinted to the dining room, overtaking dozy dawdlers. The hall was warm and thick with the smell of oily mutton. Bowls of soup stood on the counter. Bat collected one together with a meaty bone from the kitchen hatch and found a quiet place to eat.

The hum of chatter was rising, and a group of his friends sitting a couple of tables away beckoned him over. He waved, signalling that he'd soon be leaving. Shrugging their shoulders, they returned to their conversation. Last term, he'd have been sitting with them and chatting until the bell rang summoning them to their classes. But now, Bat preferred to return to his room to ensure that he was ready for the day's lessons.

The change had been effortless. Yes, he'd always enjoyed lessons, but he hadn't really taken learning too seriously, hadn't really thought that it could take him beyond Erdene Mandal, beyond the province of Arhangai. Of course, Buyeraa bagsh had given further direction to his aspirations.

A couple of days into the new term, the old teacher had called him into his room. Breathless, Bat had entered, wondering whether he was in trouble. But on the contrary, Buyeraa bagsh told Bat that provided he achieved good grades during this last year of schooling, the principal would put his name forward for a scholarship to study at university. Bat was amazed and left grinning from ear to ear, determined to get that scholarship.

Each day after he finished his chores, he'd make his way to the library, which before this term was a place he'd rarely visited. In fact, few students, it seemed, ever went there because Bat always found it empty. Mind you, the library's musty dimness welcomed no one, and the books, locked in glass-fronted cabinets, were guarded by a librarian with dragon-like fierceness.

The keys to the cabinets hung on a chain attached to the librarian's belt and they jangled as she walked. Her pinched face, small, pointed nose and permanently raised eyebrows struck fear into the faint-hearted. But Bat was not deterred.

His grandfather had told him that books were precious and contained a wealth of treasure. More recently, his mother, quoting a well-known author, had said that books were the eyes to the world. Bat wanted to see that world, although he doubted whether the librarian would allow him the freedom to read the books of his choosing. The cabinet keys never left her waist, and Bat was only allowed to take the books that she selected.

"Sit at that desk," she would tell him, peering over glasses perched on the end of her nose. Following her pointing finger, he would sit. "This must be returned at the end of the session, and under no circumstances whatsoever may this book be removed." It was the same threat every time.

Each evening, Bat worked through the volumes she gave him. He read about Mongolia's ancient history, the production of felt and the crafting of gers, the discovery of precious stones, and the establishment of new towns and villages. He read not only beneath the steely eye of the librarian but also with deceased authors, scientists, and poets watching over him. From their picture frames around the wall, he felt that they, at least, approved of his efforts.

A few days ago, he'd been sitting at the same desk poring over charts and maps that explained where the rich mineral wealth of the country lay. Seated in front of him, the librarian snored gently. Bat was contemplating whether he could remove himself and the book to a brighter light when the door suddenly swung open.

"I thought I might find you here," Buyeraa bagsh said.

"Shhhhh!" The dragon raised her head.

"There's no one else here," Buyeraa replied, lifting his hands.

"It's a library," she hissed.

Buyeraa beckoned to Bat. "Let's step outside."

Holding the book in his hand, Bat stood and moved towards the door.

"Leave it!"

Bat jumped, and the book slid from his hand. Hurriedly, he retrieved it, put it on the table and followed Buyeraa out, letting the door close on the librarian's fire. Buyeraa bagsh shook his head. "Must have been a general in her former life," he said. They chuckled and Buyeraa added, "If you're free after chores on Saturday, I'd like you to take a walk with me."

Bat pursed his lips. He wasn't in the habit of taking walks and wondered whether the teacher felt sorry for him.

They arranged to meet at the school gate after lunch. Bat had spent the morning washing his clothes and tidying his side of the room. Nadmid was nowhere to be seen, but Bat had long since stopped worrying about his roommate's untidiness.

Buyeraa was already at the gate when Bat arrived. In his deel and felt hat, carrying a wooden walking stick, the teacher could have been any local herder. Bat had never imagined Buyeraa bagsh wore anything besides his shiny black suit.

"Let's head to the hills," Buyeraa said, raising his stick.

They walked to the end of the tarmacked road on the edge of town and turned left towards a shallow hill. The sky, cloudless, bright, and blue, as it often was in the cooler months, warmed their faces, although the sun was already slipping beyond its highest point. The grass crunched beneath their feet, and all trace of summer flowers was dead and gone.

Buyeraa bagsh leant heavily on his stick as they headed uphill. The ground was stony and dry and their progress slow as the teacher placed his good foot firmly on the ground and brought his injured foot up to join it.

"My grandfather always said to tread carefully to show respect to the landscape," commented Bat.

Buyeraa stopped for a moment. "It's good to respect the earth."

Bat wondered how old Buyeraa bagsh was. Apart from his chronic limp, the teacher appeared fit and healthy. His brown face was smooth and almost wrinkle-free, and his eyes, magnified by the thick lenses of his glasses, were as clear as any young man's. People said he only got his shock of white hair because his brain had been stunned by the death of his wife and child.

They walked a little farther. "Let's sit here," said Buyeraa, pointing to a small rocky outcrop. They'd made it halfway up the hill. Letting his breathing slow, Buyeraa removed a small flask from the front of his bulging deel pocket. He took a swig and offered it to Bat, who rubbed his hands awkwardly.

"I don't drink vodka."

"Give it a try," Buyeraa said, nudging the flask into Bat's hand.

Bat grimaced. Shutting his eyes, he put the flask to his mouth, expecting the sharpness of vodka to hit his tongue. Instead, as the liquid neared his lips, he smelt the milky saltiness of tea and let it run down his throat. He handed the flask back to Buyeraa. "I was expecting something else."

"Life isn't always what we expect," the teacher said with a glint in his eye. "I don't drink vodka either."

They hadn't climbed far, but they could still look down on the town. It was quiet: the main street was empty, shops were shut, and Bat thought people were probably resting. Buyeraa pointed to a falcon circling above the hill beside them. Bat shielded his eyes against the sun and watched the bird bank high and fast. His tapering wings, silhouetted against the blueness, looked black. The falcon changed direction in a second, turning this way and that until, with pinpoint accuracy, he plunged to the ground to hook a tiny ground squirrel.

"Impressive," said Bat.

"Yes, it's amazing how each animal, each bird has adapted to its environment."

"Do you think that's what happened?"

"Definitely! Science is proving that our universe evolved to what it is today through natural phenomena."

"Natural phenomena?"

"Yes, Bat. Scientists have been discovering the pathways through which plants and trees, animals and humans have evolved from single-celled organisms."

"Hoosh!" Bat exclaimed.

"It is proven. The evidence is indisputable! Over hundreds of years...thousands of years...tens of thousands even single-celled organisms grew, multiplying and mutating into many forms of living organisms. Some cells became plants and trees, while others developed into creatures. But always," he said, moving his hands forward in a circular motion, "each evolving plant or creature adopted characteristics that fitted it perfectly to its environment."

"Is life still evolving today?"

"It is. New species of plants, trees, and animals are always being discovered."

Like one of Nadmid's maths problems, Buyeraa's explanation made sense. It followed a logical step-by-step sequence that Bat could understand. He was beginning to see how the world had grown and developed and how the changes had come slowly, little by little.

After all, he'd watched caterpillars grow until, shedding their cocoons, they became butterflies. He'd watched tadpoles grow into frogs. So the principles of growth and change that governed this earth were discernible.

"Creatures," Buyeraa repeated, "have all adapted to become matched to their environment and matched to the changing seasons."

Yes, it was rational. He could hold it in his head. But where did his grandfather's beliefs fit into the world's pattern? He scratched his head. "At the end of his life, my grandfather felt there was some sort of creator behind our world."

"I used to think like that. I believed in Tsenger, the god of the blue sky. I thought he controlled our destiny. I thought he was behind all life." Buyeraa's lips tightened. "But life's experiences have taught me differently. I tried to be a good person, believing that my goodness would bring fortune to my life, but it did not."

Bat loosened the stones beneath his foot and ground them into the thin earth. Below, a jeep skidded as it left the tarmacked road and bumped onto the sandy track. Swerving left, the driver straightened the wheels and headed off in a cloud of dust.

Buyeraa sat up. "Traditionally, we've explained the existence of this world through the eyes of a creator. Remember the story of Tsenger, the son who brought form to our shapeless world and through whom all creatures were made?"

"Yes."

"...and his evil brother, Erleg Khan the tempter, who introduced disease and mortality to our world?"

These stories were interwoven into the fabric of Bat's life, and he'd never questioned their accuracy."

"For centuries," Buyeraa said, tipping his hat forward, "we've lived our lives through the lens of these stories, legends, and proverbs. Hidden from reality, they gave our lives meaning and purpose, but they also blinded us to the truth."

The teacher struggled to his feet. "These rocks are hard," he said, rubbing his behind. He took Bat's arm, and they walked slowly down the hill.

"We have an opportunity to change," Buyeraa said. "The Russian way points us towards a world governed by facts, through education, discovery, and knowledge. We...you need to grasp this opportunity with both hands."

"I want to!" Bat's heart jumped with excitement. He imagined himself as a teacher, lecturing others. He could be one full of knowledge and wisdom.

"Of course, our stories are a part of our history. We must not lose them, but we must stop interpreting the world through our archaic beliefs."

Bat held Buyeraa's arm as they carefully retraced their steps. The light was just turning golden, and the air was sharp with a cool breeze blowing from the north. The sharpness reflected the clarity that was coming to Bat's mind. Science was the key, unlocking the knowledge that was beginning to open Bat's understanding.

"Will you teach me how to understand science more deeply?"

Buyeraa smiled and patted Bat's arm.

Chapter 10

The tea bubbled on the single electric ring that Buyeraa kept in his room. He removed the pan and gently blew on the milk to cool it, just like his mother had taught him over forty years ago. He'd been a child of eight or nine when she first gave him the responsibility of making the tea. It had seemed overwhelming, and he remembered hovering in front of the fire willing the wok of tea to boil. "Wait a moment," his mother used to say as he lifted the wok, ready to pour the tea into the flask. "Let the boiling pass and then pour." He stood, waiting, hoping he wouldn't spill any of the precious contents or drop the heavy wok. Thankfully, he never did.

He arranged the two chairs, one of which he'd borrowed from the dining hall, close to his single bar heater. The school was warm, although Buyeraa got cold when he just sat. He and Bat had been meeting for the past two months—no, he put his finger to his mouth—it must be three. October, November, December, he counted off, and now they were halfway through January. Yes, three months.

Initially, they'd walked out of the town and sat on a nearby hill, but it quickly became too cold for Buyeraa, and so he'd invited Bat to join him in his room. Buyeraa placed the flask on the small table. The orange paint was flaking, and some of the patterns had faded, but the table was still a treasured possession. It was one of the few things he'd kept from his home with Ganaa.

He picked up two bowls and wiped them with a tatty cloth. He enjoyed these talks with Bat. The boy had a hunger to learn and absorbed information quickly. One of these days, Bat's knowledge would exceed his own. Buyeraa spat on the rag and rubbed one of the bowls to remove a flake of dried porridge. He flinched, remembering the first time he'd offered Bat a drink. The boy had thought it was vodka, but Buyeraa was no drinking man.

No! He might have drunk a little before but since *that* day—he looked at the black and white photo of his wife and son standing beside his bed—he'd never let a drop of alcohol touch his lips again. No one had ever acknowledged that the driver of the truck was drunk, but Buyeraa believed he was.

Tap, tap, tap, tap.

Buyeraa straightened and turned to the open doorway. A young man stood leaning his head against the frame. Buyeraa looked again. "Bat?"

Bat nodded.

"I didn't recognise you with your long locks cut."

"I thought it was time to look like a serious student," said Bat, running his hand through his cropped hair.

A faint smile touched Buyeraa's lips. "Come in, come in," he said, motioning for Bat to sit on the nearest chair. Buyeraa poured two bowlfuls of milk tea. "Has Altai gone home?" he asked, handing him a bowl.

"Yes," Bat replied. "She goes whenever she can persuade our father to collect her."

"She is the youngest?"

"Yes. But she'll be thirteen soon."

Bat was right. She was growing up. Her chubby baby-face was changing, and she was becoming a young lady. Although you'd hardly believe it from the way she carried on, charging around with her over-excited friends. She was one of those students—Buyeraa had seen many of them—who simply tolerated school. She was intelligent enough, but she lived for the moment the bell rang at the end of the day, or better still when the holidays began.

Buyeraa noticed Bat's bowl was already empty. "You were thirsty," he said, uncorking the flask to refill it.

"I was." The boy wiped his mouth with the back of his hand.

The school was quiet as most children, like Altai, had gone home.

"What have you been reading this week?" Buyeraa asked.

"A book about the principles of communism."

"Interesting...did your reading lead you to draw any conclusions?"

"Not sure," Bat said, gazing into his bowl, "but the principles are good."

"Theoretically."

"What do you mean?"

Yes...the boy's intellect was greater than his own. Bat was already studying and processing information far beyond that which Buyeraa had been able to understand as a young person. But he was still young and inexperienced in life. Seated on the chair beside the fire, Bat waited. Buyeraa sighed and sat down. Was the boy ready to understand the immoralities that a system like communism promoted?

"Theoretically?" Bat repeated.

"The founders of communism had good intentions, perhaps. With the promise of common ownership and equality in society, they set up a regime that removed authority from the chiefs and placed common ownership into the hands of the state." Buyeraa swilled the last dregs of his tea around his bowl, savouring the saltiness on his tongue. Yes, good intentions, perhaps, he thought, but he knew the system was already unravelling. "But," he said, refilling his bowl, "it has been impossible to eliminate social classes."

"Social classes?"

"Yes, the structures by which people's economic background, education, and social network are defined."

"Ah," Bat said with understanding.

"Working together for the common good and the transfer of ownership of all assets and property to the state made us believe it was working."

"But it hasn't?"

"No, it hasn't. It was an ideal we embraced. As teenagers, we gloried in the communist teaching, believing that through it we could make a better world. Full of fresh-faced passion, we held meetings and vowed to change our country. We worked hard for the good of the economy, and the state provided us with all we needed. Life was simple. Life was good, and we were happy."

Bat knit his brow together. "What went wrong?"

"I got older," he laughed. "I got married, had a child and began to see the cracks."

Buyeraa twisted his half-full bowl back and forth. Thoughts chased each other around his brain like clouds on a stormy day. There'd been whispers. Always whispers. Of leaders who had been removed, repressed, and relocated. And then of over-zealous communist officials who had been openly shamed or agitators silenced. Initially he'd ignored it, pretended it didn't exist, until one chilling afternoon when reality had hit him squarely in the face.

One of his colleagues, Enk-Amaglan, an outspoken man who taught Mongolian history and wrote beautiful poetry, was arrested. As far as Buyeraa could see, Enk-Amaglan had done nothing wrong. But the secret police disagreed. Designated with the task of keeping everyone within the boundaries of the party lines, they'd visited the school.

"What cracks?" Bat asked.

It had been a windy, grey spring afternoon, and the entire school had assembled in the sports hall. Perhaps the police had been waiting for just such an occasion because brandishing truncheons, they rushed onto the stage, halted the annual singing competition mid-flow, and seized Enk-Amaglan from his seat beside the other teachers on the stage. Teachers and students all stood statue-like as Enk-Amaglan struggled to get free. The police hit him, knocking him to the floor until he whimpered like a child.

The headmaster had moved to intervene, but he got the butt end of a truncheon across his shoulders. Recoiling, he watched powerlessly as the police handcuffed Enk-Amaglan and carried him away. His family was moved to the city, and from that day on, no one ever saw or heard of Enk-Amaglan again.

It was then that Buyeraa truly realised that the ideals he'd held dear were a sham. Essentially, nothing had changed. The old chiefs had simply been replaced by new ones. There was no new egalitarian equality. The workers must still obey their masters.

"What cracks?" Bat's hand on his arm brought him back to the present.

"Cracks that exposed the decay." Buyeraa's cigarettes were on the table. He picked up the box, took one out, and lit it. "Cracks that showed that power was being wielded like a weapon in the hands of those with authority. They weren't thinking of the good of the country, or even for the good of their community. The state had become monstrous; a monolith, hoarding wealth and visiting tyranny on the working classes."

Bat's eyes, large and brown, searched Buyeraa's face. "But the ideology...?"

"Yes?" said Buyeraa.

"The ideology says the rules are for the prosperity of the people and the country?"

The boy knew the propaganda. "Yes." Buyeraa chose his words carefully. "But the leaders became tyrants who abused the system and the people." Buyeraa smiled. "Don't worry. It's not like that now." He poured himself another bowl of tea and offered the flask to Bat, who put his hand up to refuse. "People are more reasonable now," Buyeraa concluded, switching off the heater as the room was beginning to feel stuffy. The windows had already been sealed for the coming winter cold and the light was dimming. He turned the fluorescent tube above their heads on. It buzzed with shrill brightness.

"Were you controlled by the system?" Bat asked.

"I think we all were." Buyeraa looked into the distance, "But not anymore."

"What changed?"

Buyeraa placed his bowl on the small table. "Money," he said simply.

"Money?"

"Yes, Russia is running out of money. Sustaining an ideology and funding a satellite state that provides little real income is costly and in the long-term, untenable."

"And we are just one of the countries under Moscow's care."

"Exactly! For the last ten or fifteen years, Russia has been weakening her control over us. Slowly she has been withdrawing technical and financial support."

"Will the Soviet Union collapse?"

"That is a good question. If the Union doesn't collapse, then huge changes must be made." Buyeraa shook his head. "It's rumoured that Russians born in Ulaanbaatar and Darkhan are returning to their native country. And it's not only happening here. Other Soviet-controlled countries are pushing for change.

"A couple of weeks ago, I had lunch with one of my former students. He'd just returned from three years studying engineering in Poland. He told me his college in Gdansk boasts a student population that, alongside a growing number of ordinary workers, is campaigning for a new openness in politics and life."

Bat leant back in his chair. "So Russia is on the brink of bankruptcy?"

"Possibly..."

"Do we Mongolians want a new openness?"

Buyeraa smiled. "Some in Ulaanbaatar are pushing for political freedom and social justice. Have you heard of Sanjaasuren's son Zorigo?"

Bat shook his head.

"You are still a countryside boy," Buyeraa joked. "Zorigo is leading a group of students in Ulaanbaatar towards reforms. Some call him a dissident, but I think he genuinely wants to see change that will benefit our people...perhaps even see us become a democracy."

Bat's voice was eager. "Isn't democracy bad?"

"No worse than communism. There's always a danger that politics can be controlled by money and power. And one could argue that democracies are less stable than communist countries. But, at best, democracies are supposed to represent the views of the people and involve the population in the decision-making process of the country."

"Does it work?"

"It can," Buyeraa replied, standing and moving his chair back to his desk. He straightened the newly arrived newspapers. Reading through the Ulaanbaatar papers was one of his weekly rituals. Sara the postmistress, ensured that he had his copies by Friday so that he could spend his evenings reading the latest news from across the country.

"It can," he repeated. "Whether it will work in Mongolia, I don't know but one thing is certain, our country will change."

Bat picked up his chair, ready to return it to the dining room.

"One thing," said Buyeraa as Bat was leaving, "you will have to decide. Will you remain with the old, or will you be a part of the changes?"

Chapter 11

Bat shoved his trousers into the threadbare cloth bag that was a patchwork of repairs. Pulling the drawstrings closed, he tossed the bag aside and moved to the window. Jeeps and motorcycles, horses and oxcarts crowded the street below. Men with familiar faces carried freshly slaughtered sheep carcasses across their shoulders while others lugged sacks of flour to waiting carts. Women whose families lived in the valleys close to that of his grandparents stopped to chat. "Have you passed a good winter?" they'd ask one another. And, "Are your animals well? Isn't there a lot of work to do for the coming New Year?"

The winter had passed quickly, and Bat could hardly believe that Tsagaan Sar was just a few days away. Their father would already have left home and would be riding to Erdene Mandal to collect them. He and Altai would no doubt find him waiting, as he always did, in the school hallway close to the front door, shortly after lunch.

Bat moved his hand along the wooden sill; the cold made his fingers tingle. The thick layer of cotton wool between the double windows hardly stopped the draught. Tiny snowflakes were falling. Narrowing his eyes, he observed the distinct delicacy of each flake. Carried by the breeze, they bobbed and swirled their way earthwards.

It was all so familiar and comfortable. Part of him would have been happy to stay here but over the last few weeks, he'd noticed a change; the familiarity and ease felt claustrophobic. Was he outgrowing this place?

He put his fingers to the glass, wishing he could catch the snowflakes. He remembered the feeling of wonder he'd experienced as a boy when the first flake landed in his open palm, only to be followed by rapid dismay as, seconds later, it dissolved. In some ways, his newfound knowledge felt like that. This last term, he'd read so much, and talked long and hard with Buyeraa, and yes, he'd tried to listen. But somehow, he couldn't quite grasp it all; the facts just seemed to melt away.

"Glued to that window again," said Nadmid.

Bat jumped. "Watching people buy food for Tsagaan Sar," he said, clearing his throat. "I can't believe how quickly this term has gone."

"Can't go fast enough for me," Nadmid replied, pulling his shirts from the cupboard and stuffing them into his bag. Bat rubbed his nose: sour cigarette smoke clung to Nadmid's clothes. "Anyway, you've hardly been here," Nadmid continued, flicking his hand in Bat's direction. "You've spent all your free time in the library or with that old mule."

Bat ground his teeth. Nadmid had never liked Buyeraa. In fact, many of the students found the limping widower strange. But Bat had always felt differently. Buyeraa was a clever man, and this term Bat had understood more clearly that Buyeraa was a man to be respected.

Each Saturday, Bat had woken up early to complete his chores and get ready to go to Buyeraa's room straight after lunch. The afternoons they'd spent together huddled around Buyeraa's electric fire had opened Bat's eyes to a new world far beyond his experiences. Bat loved this new world, but he didn't know how to fully embrace it.

Bat had quickly learnt that Buyeraa was a man of routine. Arriving at the teacher's room, Bat would find two chairs carefully positioned facing one another. In between the chairs was a table set with a flask and two bowls. Bat would sit, waiting for Buyeraa to pour the tea. After they had taken their first sip, Buyeraa would ask him what he had been reading, and Bat would answer. It didn't seem to matter what subject Bat introduced, Buyeraa was always able to respond with great knowledge and understanding.

Most of the time Bat sat on his hands, leaning forward, trying to absorb as much information as he could. But there were moments when he just couldn't understand what Buyeraa was talking about, like when they'd spoken about politics. Buyeraa had spoken with such force that Bat's skull felt like it had been pummelled with stones, leaving Bat aware that he knew nothing of the political climate of his own country.

"Dreamer...! It's time to leave that window." Bat turned to see Nadmid throwing his half-packed bag back onto his bed and heading out the door. "It's lunch time," he shouted, disappearing down the corridor. Bat straightened his bag and placed his folded winter deel next to it.

"Are you coming?" Nadmid's head reappeared round the door.

"In a moment."

Nadmid shook his head. "Don't forget your friends," he said. "Even if you go to university you'll still need friends to have fun."

Bat rubbed his neck. Nadmid was intelligent, no one could deny that, but he didn't do enough work to gain himself a place at university. Not that he needed to do more; his parents were rich herders who owned champion racehorses, and that, apparently, made all the difference. Nadmid's passage to university, no matter what his school results were, was guaranteed. His parents were like celebrities. Not only did their racehorses earn them extra money, but Nadmid's parents also added additional prestige and honour to their village and, to hear Nadmid boast, to the whole province. To reward such favour, the local government officials sought to ensure that Nadmid's family were well taken care of and were given all the best opportunities.

Bat sniffed. The communist ideology, which advocated that all men live equally, supposedly abhorred such social and financial favouritism, but even Bat, with his limited knowledge, was learning that the ideals didn't always work in practice.

Perhaps they never do, he thought, remembering his conversations with Buyeraa. Opening drawers, he made one last check to ensure that he had packed everything. He dusted his hands and followed Nadmid to lunch. His roommate might have time for fun, but Bat did not: not if he was going to win a scholarship.

The crowded dining hall smelt of rotting socks. Cabbage in the soup again. Bat groaned. Having sat in the cellar since last summer, the cabbages were getting mouldier by the day. But the cooks insisted that vegetables were good for students, and so cabbage regularly appeared in the soup.

Bat joined the back of the lunch queue. "Hoosh," a short boy cried as another grabbed him. The two, a little younger than Bat, grasped one another's shoulders and started pushing each other back and forth. The queue quickly formed a circle around them and started cheering. Bat, enveloped in the excitement, shouted at the top of his voice as he willed the smaller boy to down his opponent.

"Stop!" The principal's voice rose decisively above the din, silencing the crowd and causing the wrestlers to spring apart.

"Back in line," the principal said, walking amongst them. "This is not a wrestling stadium. Get your lunch and sit down."

The queue reformed, and the principal walked its length. He came closer and stopped in front of Bat, who found himself gazing at the principal's chest and his shirt buttons, which appeared ready to pop. Despite his quickening pulse, Bat raised his eyes to meet the principal's blotched face and bloodshot eyes. In that moment, Bat wondered whether the rumours were true. Was their principal a drunk?

"Batbold, isn't it?"

"Yes..." Bat's throat felt dry. "Sir."

"I hear you've done well this term."

"Yes, sir," Bat straightened.

"And that you're aiming for a university scholarship."

"Yes, sir."

"Keep up the good work."

"Yes, sir."

The principal shook his hand in a gentleman-like fashion and moved back to his table to finish his lunch. The other students stared, but Bat didn't care. He took deep, satisfying breaths, letting his lungs inflate until he stood several centimetres taller. He was going to get that scholarship. He moved to the counter.

"Scholarship or not," said the cook, handing him a bowl of hot soup, "you need to eat your soup."

Bat obediently took it, picked up a wedge of steamed bread, and, balancing it on the top of his bowl, manoeuvred his way past the crowded tables. He sat alone, although Altai and a gaggle of her girlfriends soon joined him.

"So, it's true," she said spooning soup into her mouth, "You're off to university?"

"Maybe."

"I know you've been in the library reading the old books...I heard you've read them all."

Bat put his spoon down. "I haven't read them all...perhaps half. And don't forget, it's not a big library. There are probably fewer than a hundred books in there."

"That's still amazing. I've never read one whole book."

"Yes," Bat raised his eyebrows, "but I want to study."

Altai shrugged her shoulders. "Not sure what good all that learning does you. I've heard," she said, twisting her hair with a look of worldly wisdom on her face, "that too much learning can make you go mad."

"Perhaps I'm already mad," Bat answered.

"Perhaps," she laughed.

Altai returned to her friends and quickly became absorbed in lively conversation. Bat focused on his soup, avoiding the slimy strips of cabbage as best he could. Why had he said he was mad? He knew he wasn't, but over the last few months, his world had turned upside down, and he wasn't quite sure who he was. He wanted to be a part of the changes Buyeraa had spoken about, but how could he when he couldn't even formulate his own opinions?

"Oh Uvoo," he sighed, longing for his grandfather. "I wish you were here."

"What?" Altai asked.

"Nothing," said Bat.

"You said something."

"You are too nosey."

Altai clasped her hands. "Do you think Aav-aa will bring the camels?"

"You asked me that yesterday, and the day before, and last week."

"Bat," Altai said, half-closing her eyes. "These things are important."

"What? Camel, horse, motorbike, Jeep! Does it matter how we get home?"

"Yes, it does."

"Aav will probably bring the camels," he replied with a sigh.

"Yoo," she yelled, jumping to her feet and throwing her arms in the air so that her chair crashed to the ground. "Let's go...let's go."

Bat's eyes darted to the teachers' table. The teachers were toasting the end of the school year with a tot of vodka. Any other day, and Altai would have been given a stern warning and deprived of some privilege or other, but today, absorbed in celebrations, the teachers were oblivious to the commotion.

"Sssh," he said, putting his finger to his mouth. "He won't be here yet. Besides, you need to finish your lunch."

"I've had enough," she screamed, abandoning her friends.

"Sit down," Bat hissed through clenched teeth, but Altai was already halfway to the door.

At half past one, the bell rang, signalling that they were dismissed. Chairs scraped on the wooden floor, and the children pushed and shuffled their way out into the corridor like a stampede of horses. Bat felt an elbow in the small of his back pushing him forward. He arched and pushed back hard and then in an instant surged forward. With a sharp cry, the child behind him toppled forward. Bat didn't look back but instead elbowed his way through the crowd.

He reached the stairs, grabbed the metal rail, and bounded up them two at a time. Smaller boys squealed as he knocked them aside. Reaching the top, he saw that his corridor was empty. He was the first. A rush of warmth ran through his body as he raised his hands and did an eagle dance. He walked to his room, collected his bag, and retraced his steps.

The corridor was filling with boys all moving to their respective rooms. Above their bobbing heads, Bat caught sight of Buyeraa standing at the top of the stairs, staring straight ahead, and Bat wondered whether he was waiting for him. Eager to retrieve their bags and leave, children passed Buyeraa. Like the suit his teacher wore, the man looked sad and worn. The teacher waved, and Bat waved back. How had this man with his limp got to the top of the stairs so quickly?

"Have a good holiday," Buyeraa said, holding his arms out. Bat entered them and sniffed the teacher's cheeks as a respectful sign of their closeness. He stepped back Buyeraa's eyes were glinting.

"I'll be back next term."

"I know, I know," said Buyeraa sniffing loudly. "Off you go."

No longer in a hurry, Bat followed the rest of the children down the stairs. With her bag slung across her back, Altai was trying to wait patiently for him. However, as soon as she caught sight of him, she started hopping up and down. "Come on, come on," she mouthed.

Bat laughed. "I'm coming." As he put his foot on the last step, Altai grabbed his hand. He followed, twisting his hand in her vice-like grip as she dragged him further into the noisy chatter. And then, as suddenly as she'd seized his hand, she let it go.

"Aav-aa, Aav-aa!" Altai yelled, falling into her father's open embrace.

Their father stood in his usual spot close to the door where few others stood. Bat watched his father sniff Altai's hair and rub her back. It was only a couple of weeks since she'd been home, but you'd have thought it had been months.

Altanbaatar drew his daughter aside and opened his arms to his son. Bat hesitated—it had been five months since he'd seen his father for anything more than a fleeting hug and a brief exchange of words. Even during in the holidays, Bat had chosen to stay at school. His feet shifted back and forth. He hadn't been home for the whole term.

"Come on," his father beckoned. Bat walked into his open arms and buried his head in the thick silkiness of his father's deel. It was smooth to his skin and smelt of tobacco, woodsmoke, and sheep fat: smells that were as familiar to him as life itself and yet, for some strange reason, set him on edge.

Chapter 12

Bat felt broader, and perhaps, thought Altanbaatar, he was a little taller. Of course, his cropped hair made him look more grown-up. It had been five months since he'd seen his son properly. There had been the quick hellos when he'd come to pick up Altai, but, largely, Bat had avoided him.

Monkho and he had struggled with Bat's decision to remain at school over the weekends and particularly during the week-long October holiday. Monkho longed to have Bat closer and in her home.

"After all," she'd reasoned, "he spent most of his life with his grandparents. Surely now's the time for me to enjoy him."

Monkho had sobbed when Altanbaatar told her that they had to let the boy make his own decisions. She'd beaten his chest with her fists, demanding that he bring the boy back. But Altanbaatar had refused.

"We must give him freedom to make his own choices," he said.

"But we'll lose him."

Altanbaatar had taken her hands in his. "Better to lose him than see him live in the shadow of regret."

Holding Bat close, his heart ached. Monkho was right. In letting him go, they would probably lose him. They'd heard that Bat had studied hard during this last term. The teachers and Altai had told them. They were proud of him and had high hopes, but there was pain in releasing their son. Altanbaatar finally understood why, all those years ago, his own mother had refused to let him take up the scholarship he'd been offered.

"Did you bring the camels?" Altai was tugging at his deel. He released his son and nodded. "Why are we waiting then?" she yelled, banging the door open so hard that it shook on its hinges.

Bat caught it as it swung back, and they followed Altai out. Altanbaatar arched his hand above his eyes while Altai ran to the tethered camels. The dazzling sun was blinding.

"I'm glad it stopped snowing," Altanbaatar said.

"Do you think it'll snow again before dark?"

Altanbaatar turned his head towards the sky. It was clear, but the air was stirring again, bringing a light and moist breeze into the afternoon crispness.

"I think the snow is coming," he told Bat.

"Come on!" Altai yelled, releasing her camel.

"My-ix-tay—Show off," Bat muttered under his breath.

Altanbaatar heard Bat's tone. "She's just excited."

"Come on," she shouted again, jumping up and down and tugging the rope in an effort to make her camel sit down. The camel, refusing to obey Altai's command, flared his nostrils and started throwing his head this way and that. Altanbaatar quickened his pace. "Be patient, my daughter. Remember, camels are stubborn and easily angered."

"Stupid girl," Bat whispered, untying his own camel. "Don't you know anything?"

"Enough!" Altanbaatar reprimanded his son as he gently pulled Altai's animal downwards. The bull resisted. Coming closer, Altanbaatar tugged harder on the rope threaded through the camel's nose. "Tsuts, tsuts," he whispered, patting the animal's woolly mane. The camel jerked his head away, crying as the rope burnt his nostrils. "Tsuts, tsuts."

Altai hopped from one foot to another. This animal really was hers, although given the young male's temperament, Altanbaatar would not have chosen this camel for her. But he'd had no choice. When the calf was rejected by his mother at birth, Altai had become the calf's surrogate mother. Leading him everywhere by a rope and naming him Whitey, she'd barely left the animal alone until the calf grew enough to develop his own obstinacy.

"Tsuts, tsuts." Whitey quietly dropped to his knees.

"Get on," he said, handing the reins back, "and hold his head high." Altai obeyed, and the camel stood. Bat had already untied his brown camel and was sitting between its hairy humps with his bag slung across his shoulders. Altanbaatar smiled. Bat was an independent young man. His own camel stamped her feet.

"I know. We'll be moving soon," he said, rubbing her throat. She smiled, rolling back her lips to reveal yellowing teeth. "You're getting old," he said.

The camel snorted.

"But you're still my favourite."

She was the oldest and the first camel he'd ever bought. Years earlier, a group of traders driving their sheep and goats from Bayan-Uglii to Ulaanbaatar had stopped at his ger to buy supplies. Having no money to pay their bills, the traders left the young yellow camel as a guarantee that they would return. Months later, the traders came to redeem their camel, but Altanbaatar, Monkho, and their two small children were not willing to let her go. Tough negotiations and much tea drinking followed until a price was agreed upon, and the traders left, promising to return the next spring with a young male so that Altanbaatar could start his own herd.

People had raised their eyebrows when they'd heard. Arhangai people weren't supposed to be camel herders, but Altanbaatar had shrugged his shoulders and ignored their comments. He wasn't an Arhangai person, and what's more, camels were a part of his native childhood home.

That must have been more than twenty years ago, he thought. Since then, this old yellow camel had given birth to eight calves.

"Nuuuuuum, nuuuum." From the corner of his eye he saw Altai's camel shaking its head and trying to drop his shoulder.

"Hold the reins tight, Altai," Altanbaatar shouted.

"Eee-aah, eee-aah," the camel snorted, clawing the ground with its front feet.

"Keep his head high."

"I can't…" Altai's chin trembled. "I can't hold him."

"You can do it, my daughter," Altanbaatar continued more gently. Slowly he moved closer. "Tsuts, tsuts," he said, stroking the camel's mane. Pulling away, the camel whistled and screamed. "Don't relax your grip, and he'll soon realise who is boss."

Eyes on her father, Altai sat upright and set her jaw. She held the reins as high as she could in her clenched fists. The camel pulled left and right, jerking his head up and down, but Altai would not let go. Eventually the camel's agitation passed.

"Sit up," Altanbaatar said, taking Altai's hands in his. They were red and hot with rising welts. He guessed they were sore too, but Altai wasn't complaining. He rubbed her palms gently and winked. "Well done," he said, releasing her hands and slapping her leg. "Let's go home."

As he mounted his animal, he caught Bat's eye. His son's face was expressionless, and Altanbaatar couldn't guess what Bat was thinking.

The school was at the far end of the town close to the beginning of the black-topped road that ran through the town. They turned and started walking down the main street. Shoppers waved; everyone knew they owned camels, but the sight of them still turned people's heads.

"Are we going to the market?" Altai asked.

"No, we have to go to the post office."

"But I like the market."

"I know," said Altanbaatar observing the rows of rough tables standing cheek by jowl, close to the road. You never knew what you'd find hidden beneath the car parts and bras on the tables cluttered with a mishmash of merchandise

Pointing at the sellers, Altai laughed. "They look like sumo wrestlers."

"Sssh!" Bat put his finger to his mouth.

A faint smiled touched Altanbaatar's lips; his daughter was right. The sellers wrapped themselves in layers topped with fleece-lined deels, and they bulged like sumo wrestlers. Bat pulled his own deel closer.

"Are you cold, son?"

"No!" Bat said, sinking down between the humps.

Altanbaatar rode between his children. "How was the last term?"

"Good."

"I hear you've been reading lots of books."

Bat glared at Altai.

"What have you been learning?" Altanbaatar asked.

"That herders know nothing." Bat replied sharply.

Altanbaatar's mouth fell open.

"Altanbaatar," an old man called. Leaning on his stick outside the chemist, the ancient waved his free hand. Altanbaatar recognised him as a near neighbour who'd been an acquaintance of his father's.

"Sain bain uu ta?"

"Sain. Sain bain uu?" the old man returned. "Are you having a good winter?"

"Yes, yes, and you? Are your animals round and healthy?"

The man touched his head in mock salute, and they walked on, passing brightly coloured shop doors which, despite the cold, stood open to entice would-be customers inside.

"The flag's flying high," Altai said, pointing to the top of the government building.

The tattered blue and red national flag flapped in the wind. A black kite circled beyond, turning and changing direction with ease. Small clouds were edging their way into view. Altanbaatar gasped. The snow was coming.

Just beyond the government square, Altanbaatar could see Saran-Toya standing on the steps of her faded pink post office. How long had she been the postmistress? He couldn't remember. Monkho would know—she knew all those insignificant details. Sara, to use her shortened name, was Monkho's oldest friend, and according to his wife, the source of every morsel of gossip in the town or in the whole province, for that matter. Monkho often said, "If Sara doesn't know it, then it isn't true."

They drew the camels to a halt and greeted Saran-Toya with one voice.

She laughed. "Come in!"

Altanbaatar coughed. "Not today Sara, I want to get home before it snows."

"Is it going to snow?" She looked at the sky.

"It feels like it."

"I never was any good at reading the weather." She stamped her thick boots and disappeared through the wooden doors, saying, "Hang on there a minute."

"Do you think she's gone to get gifts?" Altai asked.

"Maybe…" Altanbaatar replied.

"You shouldn't expect things," Bat said.

"Why not? It's New Year."

"Because it's rude. And we are mourning the loss of our grandparents."

"Sara-egch didn't hear me." Altai protested, emphasising the respectful older sister address "egch" to draw attention to the fact that older people always wanted to bless children at New Year.

Altanbaatar shifted in his saddle. The street was emptying. He looked at his watch. It was already half past two.

"I want to get back before dark," he muttered under his breath.

Saran-Toya reappeared carrying a heavy cloth bag. She tried lifting it to Altanbaatar but couldn't.

He reached down.

"Hoosh! What's in here," he asked attaching the bag to his saddle.

"Just a few gifts for Tsagaan Sar. Have a good celebration. May all the beings in your vicinity be happy. May they be well, peaceful, and may they all be free." With a wave, she turned. "Oh, give my greetings to Monkho," she shouted, returning to her domain.

The tarmac ended as abruptly as it started, and the dirt track stretched out ahead of them. A row of shanty-like houses hidden behind high fences marked the end of the town.

"Hoosh, Altai," girls shouted, dropping their water churns and waving as she rode by. She yelled back, watching her friends collect water from the local well.

Once clear of the town, the camels quickened their pace. Altai headed out in front, and Altanbaatar was happy to let her lead. Her camel knew its own way home, and he wanted to keep pace with his son. The breeze was strengthening, and he held the reins tightly, knowing the change in weather could spook his camel.

He cleared his throat. "What makes you think herders are ignorant?"

Bat pursed his lips. "Because the real world is hidden from them."

Altanbaatar's eyes widened. "The real world? And what is the real world?"

"The world of education—of maths, physics, and science, of reason and logic."

"Do you imagine because countryside people do not live by science and logic that they are hidden from reality?"

"I think the world of legends and spirits obscures reason and logic."

Bat's serious face made Altanbaatar smile. "You are not wrong," he said gently. "The culture we grow up in does shape our view of reality."

"Not only that, but it conceals the truth," said Bat, twisting the reins between his fingers.

"But how do we define truth?"

"Through the objective sciences that govern this world."

"That sounds too simple, my son."

"What do you mean?" asked Bat, shuffling in his saddle.

"Science seeks to explain the natural world. But some things are beyond definition."

"Why? Surely science, logic, and reason clearly define life," said Bat, slapping the hump of his camel.

"Not all of life is so black and white. Some aspects do not fit neatly into categories or classifications. Take man, for example: science would analyse our bodies, our minds, and our actions, but how does it classify our experiences, our joy and sadness, our laughter and tears?"

"Oh, you mean emotions."

"Yes! Emotions, those intangible feelings that guide our everyday lives."

"Science can measure emotions," Bat replied quickly.

"Maybe it can. But I've yet to hear a satisfactory explanation. I remember Russian scientists dissecting human brains in an effort to locate the non-physical part of man."

"What did they find?"

"Nothing! They found nothing. Which leads me to believe that science offers a partial explanation of life, but something beyond man's ability to formulise gives identity to our world."

Bat rubbed his forehead. "Unseen principles give science its identity?"

"Yes, Bat."

"Are you saying that you believe in the spirits, that you believe in the gods?"

"It's certainly something I'm thinking about."

"Buyeraa bagsh said that the world is a closed system that runs by natural laws."

The north wind screeched, sending tumbleweeds cartwheeling across their path.

He speaks man's words, thought Altanbaatar, but there is no experience attached to them. His knowledge comes from books or from his teacher, not from life. "I remember reading about the closed system back when I was at school."

"Then you know that physics...astronomy...well, all the sciences," Bat shouted above the wind, "possess fixed operational rules that sustain the universe."

"Yes, I know. But I wonder, who composed those operational rules—who set them in place?"

"Are you saying you believe in a being behind the universe?"

"I think I am."

Slouched in her seat, Altai was still ahead of them.

"More than you, I was educated in the time of strong ideological beliefs, although your grandparents always believed in Tsenger, Buddha, and the spirits."

Altanbaatar watched his daughter's body follow the rhythm of her camel as she rested snug between her camel's humps.

He sighed. "But in recent days, Bat, I've been asking more questions."

"Buyeraa bagsh said some people believe that a possible supernatural being established the universe and its patterns, but once set in place, the universe was left to run itself."

Buyeraa bagsh, thought Altanbaatar feeling a twinge of regret. He was a good man and a knowledgeable man, but since the loss of his wife and son, it was a well-known fact that the teacher had shunned all notions of spirituality. At the beginning of last term, Altanbaatar had asked Buyeraa to keep an eye on Bat. Was Buyeraa the one now shaping Bat's young mind?

Bat hit his camel's back and the animal trotted on. Altanbaatar hung back, watching his youngest son come alongside Altai. Their gers were near, sheltered from the worst of the wind in their winter place close to the hill just around the next bend. They'd used that same spot since he and Monkho got married. It was part of their life's pattern, moving each autumn, no matter what the weather, on a day that Monkho said was auspicious.

Zorigo was guiding the cattle home. Gently nudging the stragglers back to the flock, he hadn't seen them yet.

He's a good son, thought Altanbaatar.

Bat was trying to wake Altai.

He's a good son too.

He sighed. He'd wanted Bat to return to school to continue his education. It's what he'd hoped for. Now the boy was embracing education and immersing himself in learning.

The greying afternoon pulled light from the day, leaving a heaviness that reached Altanbaatar's chest. Bat and Altai were nearly home. In the fading light, their images were becoming smudged.

"Bat," he whispered. "Oh, Bat."

The boy had a thirst for knowledge and scientific understanding. But Altanbaatar was starting to realise, perhaps a little late in life, that a man's quest for learning and knowledge were not enough to gratify the deeper longing that he was starting to recognise in his own heart.

Altanbaatar joined Bat and Altai at the hitching post. His camel dropped to its knees, allowing him to dismount. Altanbaatar's rough hand caught on the silk of his thick deel and he rubbed his chest, hoping to banish the hollowness.

"Father," he whispered, feeling the old man's presence close by. "Show me the way."

Chapter 13

The dogs bounced and barked, straining at the metal stake that chained them to the ground. By the time Bat and his father had hitched their camels to the hitching post, Zorigo had already led the cattle home and was feeding them.

He was a true herder, thought Bat.

Their four gers stood in a row close to the hill in their winter place. Bat knew the area, but he'd never lived here. Neither, he realised, had he been here for the move. Moving days were always days of anticipation as they prayed that the next season would be peaceful. His grandparents' ger, or his as it had now become, was at the far end of the row with Zorigo and Soylomaa next door. Naraa and Lhxaa followed, and his parents' ger stood at the end nearest the hitching post. Smoke from Zorigo's and his parents' chimneys circled, shifting ghost-like in the strengthening breeze.

His father shook Altai. "Wake up," he said, raising her head from the camel's hump and helping her down.

"What?" she said, standing reluctantly and rubbing her eyes.

"You're home."

The wind whipped the hitching post's rope wildly. "The snow's coming," said his father.

Bat listened to the howl of the northerly wind carrying on it the storm from the Siberian Plains.

The dogs' barking brought his mother and Naraa out onto the wooden step. "Were you asleep, Altai?" their mother asked wiping her blooded hands on an old rag.

"No. No!"

His mother raised her eyebrows and shook her head. "Of course not."

"What are you doing?" asked Altai.

"Cutting up the back leg of a cow we slaughtered before winter."

"Are you making soup?"

Monkho smiled. "Yes."

Altai let out a squeal. "Oh, the best."

"Za, come and say hello."

Leaping forward Altai flung her arms around her mother's ample middle. "When did I last see you?" Monkho asked.

"Two weeks ago." Altai said holding her as though she feared the wind would force them apart.

"Bolno, bolno—Enough, enough," their mother said, undoing Altai's arms and moving her to one side. "Bat." He stepped forward. She touched his short hair. "You've grown," she said taking him in her arms. He let her embrace and kiss him. She felt soft and warm and her wiry plait tickled his face.

"Sun shines on the golden earth," she whispered in his ear. "Wisdom shines on man. Sun gives light to the world and knowledge gives light to the nation."

His back stiffened. Proverbs! Another product of the outdated countryside life. She released him and he tried to step away, but she grabbed his hand. "You're cold. Come and have some tea before you help your father."

Naraa, looking trim and tidy in her work deel, touched his arm and smiled. She opened the door, and they entered. On top of the stove, a wok of bones seared and sizzled. The smoke caught in his throat, and Bat started coughing. Unwinding the sash from his deel, he wondered, why everyone insisted that the fabric be long enough to wrap around your body three times. He used the sash to wipe the sweat from the back of his neck, before tossing it, and his fleece-lined deel, onto the bed. He sat next to Altai, who slumped her head against his arm while their mother poured them bowls of milk tea.

"Have you been studying hard, Altai?" their mother asked.

"Of course," Altai replied, sitting upright and staring straight ahead.

His mother didn't ask him, but Naraa winked as she passed him a chunk of bread. The bread was as solid as a brick in Bat's hand, and he had to dip it in his tea before he dared chew. Bat drained his bowl and, slinging his deel across his shoulders, went in search of his father.

He shuddered; the temperature was quickly dropping, and in the dwindling light he couldn't see his father or

Zorigo. Guessing that they were near the animals, Bat headed towards the sheep and goats who were already munching fodder. Their twenty horses were softly nickering, and Bat took a moment to find his horse and put his arm around her neck. She nuzzled close to him.

"I've missed you," he whispered, pushing his head deeper into the horse's warm hide. The wind was quiet for a moment, and he listened for the sound of voices. His father and Zorigo were with the camels.

In the late autumn and winter, his father kept the camels in a corral beyond the other animals, as they were apt to wander far from home when food was scarce. Adjusting to the darkness, Bat made his way to the wooden fence. His father and Zorigo moved amongst the restless herd patting them and giving them fodder.

"Tsuts, tsuts," they repeated.

"Will those two camels," Zorigo asked pointing to two females standing apart from the herd, "give birth soon?"

"Probably."

"I didn't know you had pregnant camels."

"Bat!" His father jumped, and Zorigo let out a yell. "You're light on your feet."

Bat laughed. "How are the camels?"

"They're all good." His father was intensely proud of his herd. Many envied him, but no one had ever tried to buy a camel from him. Perhaps because, as Bat had recently learned, people were fearful. According to Buyeraa bagsh, the local officials confiscated all the Arhangai camels at the beginning of the Socialist era. When Bat asked how his father had managed to grow his herd, Buyeraa bagsh had winked and tapped his nose.

"All good!" Zorigo repeated, throwing fodder at the feet of the younger animals. "Although to my mind they're a miserable bunch—bad-tempered and stubborn. They'd kick you or spit on you rather than be your friend, and their breath smells like a rotting dog on a summer's day."

Bat chuckled. Zorigo was not wrong, and yet the camels had endearing qualities too. There were times when they were gentle.

"You'd miss them if they were gone," their father said.

"Tish-tay, probably would."

"They're majestic and mysterious animals. What do you think, Bat?"

"Yes…" He stumbled. "But why are the females pregnant so long?" he asked, voicing something that had bugged him for ages.

"A good question." His father came to the edge of the enclosure. "I've asked the same thing. Recently I've even wondered whether *someone* just had fun making them unique."

Bat's jaw tightened, and the blood in his neck began pulsing. "Or perhaps the camel is still evolving?"

"Perhaps it is," said his father.

Yoooooooo! Yoooooooo! The wind moaned. Zorigo set down one last pile of hay. "We need to get inside," he said, pulling the flaps of his hat down over his ears.

"Yes, I can almost smell the blizzard." Altanbaatar climbed over the fence. "Argh, my knees have seen better days," he said, dropping to the ground. "They don't support me like they used to." Bat caught his father under his shoulder and helped him up.

Stopping to pick up armloads of firewood and dung, they went into his parents' ger. Bat stamped his boots hard—his feet were numb with cold.

"Come in! Come in." The ger was full of family. His mother poured bowls of steaming tea and ushered them to sit. Bat took his gratefully. The wok of seared bones roasting on the fire had been replaced by a wok of soup. The sweet, fragrant meat, potatoes, and carrots made Bat's stomach scream with hunger. Altai and Naraa found bowls while Soylomaa unearthed more spoons. "Not often we're all altogether," said Solyomaa, spitting on each spoon before giving it an extra rub with a grimy rag.

Naraa stacked the bowls on the floor beside the fire and slowly straightened. "Lhxaa," she said curtly, "is doing business, and the girls are staying with his sister since they want to shop."

Bat saw his father raise an eyebrow but he made no comment.

"Bat!" His mother handed him a bowl of soup. Despite his groaning stomach, he cradled the bowl in his hand, letting its warmth defrost his painful fingers. Bat wasn't quite sure where to sit; there were just four low stools. Altai and his father were seated on two, and Zorigo sat on another, sucking his soup through the gap where his two front teeth had been. The last stool was empty, but that was his mother's. Bat moved to one of the beds.

Soylomaa shifted her small frame closer to Erdene-huu and tapped the space. "Come and sit here." Bat sat between his two nephews, Erdene-huu and Gamba. They smiled broadly, and their grubby faces perfectly matched their grubby hands. "Do you ever use water to wash?" he asked them.

They punched his leg.

"Careful," he shouted, holding his soup up high.

The boys withdrew their fists and looked at him with large brown eyes. These little rascals had always been a little afraid of him. He shuffled back on the bed and, leaning against the ger wall, started gobbling down the hot soup.

"Had trouble getting the sheep back this afternoon," Zorigo said. "They were as high-strung as a bunch of rabbits."

"They know the weather's uneasy with itself," Altanbaatar said.

The chimney clinked back and forth, ringing like a bell against the toono. Taking a small square of paper from his pouch, Zorigo filled it with tobacco, rolled it into an untidy cigarette, and tapped it on the table. With work-worn hands, he lit it and downed a slug of vodka.

Soylomaa clasped her small hands, her eyes darting from one person to the other. "Snow at New Year means we're in for a year of bad weather."

Bat's mother gathered her rotund body and returned to the stove. "Reckon we've upset the spirits, and they're going to punish us."

The wind roared like a tiger, making the ger shudder. "Don't mention the spirits," said Soylomaa.

Bat wrinkled his nose and looked at the roof poles that were set in the toono and reached to the ger's edge. Each pole looked comfortable in its place and unlikely to collapse.

He'd never really noticed them before and, if asked, would have assumed they were just orange, but now he noted that each pole was painted with soft scrolls and crests. Were these the work of one man, he wondered.

"...And the snow drifts were as high as any Khan," Zorigo said, raising his hand above his head. "It was up to the roof of the ger and stayed all winter..."

The family laughed. Zorigo's storytelling got taller with each narration. His father drew Altai closer. She leant into his chest and stroked the fleecy lining of his deel. His mother sat, pushed her hair out of her eyes, and began eating her soup. She looked tired thought Bat. Erdene-huu and Gamba noisily flicked knuckle bones across the floor while Naraa fussed as she collected bowls and cleared away the remnants of the meal. Bat pushed his back against the ger wall and watched.

Altanbaatar tried to see Bat, but in the flickering candlelight, the shadows hid his son's face. He'd been impressed by his youngest son's answers this afternoon. Bat was a thinker, his own man, and for that Altanbaatar admired him. But could Bat hold his new opinions with tolerance towards others?

Altai tugged at his deel, and he smiled into her soft brown eyes, "Tell us a story," she said.

"Not tonight, my daughter," he said, feeling suddenly weary.

In the blink of an eye, Erdene-huu and Gamba were at his side, pulling his sleeves. "Uvoo! Uvoo! Tell us a story, tell us a story," his two grandsons implored, nipping and picking at him until he relented. Pulling his pipe from his pouch, he lit it and settled into storytelling mode.

"A long, long time ago there lived an old man called, Boldoggui-bor, or as his friends called him, the Cunning Brown Man."

Erdene-huu and Gamba clapped their hands. "We love this story."

"Old Man Brown," Altanbaatar continued in low tones, "lived alone at the foot of a hill in a shabby shack made from scraps of wood and metal. He had seven brown sheep, which he kept on the steep hillside close to his home, and two grey horses. The two horses were very different. One was lean and swift and soared like a great eagle, and Old Man Brown loved this animal more than life itself. The other horse was short and stumpy and plodded along like a dumb mule."

Gamba, the smaller of his two grandsons yelled, "But he didn't keep the two horses together."

"Quiet!" Soylomaa placed a finger on her young son's mouth. Gamba's lower lip quivered.

"Come here," Altanbaatar said patting his knee. Gamba sat on his grandfather's knee.

"Now, where were we?" said Altanbaatar.

"Old Man Brown didn't keep his two horses together," Altai said.

"That's right. He kept one on the east side of his house and the other on the west. At lambing time, Old Man Brown took great care of his sheep because he hoped that one of his brown sheep," Altanbaatar held up one finger, "would produce a single, pure white lamb that he could give to Tsenger, the lord of the heavens. And do you know what happened?"

"One small brown lady sheep bore a spotless lamb," Erdene-huu said from his bed seat.

"That's right. One small brown female gave birth to a pure white lamb. Old Man Brown was overjoyed. He placed the lamb in a bag and put him on a high mound so that Tsenger could come and take it. In the meantime, Old Man Brown went off to care for the rest of his sheep."

Gamba jumped from his knee and returned to his mother's side. Altanbaatar tapped his pipe on his boot and filled it with fresh tobacco.

"Wind's dropping," said Zorigo.

"Probably snowing," said Monkho.

Through the dark toono, Altanbaatar couldn't make out whether it was snowing or not. He shuffled on his stool. His legs ached, and he felt uncomfortable. But it wasn't just his limbs that ached; his heart was uneasy too.

"Where was I?" he said, forcing himself to return to the story.

"Old Man Brown had gone to check on the rest of his sheep," shouted Gamba.

"Ah yes!" He inhaled the sweet smoke. "When Old Man Brown returned, he found that Tsenger had not taken the lamb. Instead..." He raised his hand. "An oily raven had torn the bag apart and ripped the lamb's eyes out." He let his hand fall onto Altai's back. She shrieked, and they all laughed.

"Fire burned in the pit of Old Man Brown's stomach. 'Why didn't you take my offering? Why did you allow that raven to destroy it?' he shouted at Tsenger and the gods. Letting his fury sweep him forward, the Old Man didn't wait for an answer. He grabbed his flying horse and he raced after the raven. He spotted the bird in the distance circling like some grand statesman high above the trees on the edge of the forest. Old Man Brown beat his horse, pushing him forward until they were flying. Standing high in his saddle, the Old Man reached above the trees and snatched the raven out of the sky. The bird screeched and clamoured, desperate to be free of the Old Man's clutches. But, filled with cold rage, the Old Man was not going to let the raven go. Holding him close, Old Man Brown plunged his thumb and forefinger into the bird's eyes and tossed the lifeless bird onto ground.

'How dare you kill the raven,' Tsenger thundered. 'You foolish, brainless Old Man, I sent the raven to bring your sacrifice to me. By bringing me the lamb's eyes, he was bringing me the very essence of the animal's soul.' Tsenger shot a finger of lightning to the ground. 'I will exact my revenge,' he said. 'I will destroy your treasure.'"

Erdene-huu's jaw dropped. He held his empty bowl tight, so tightly that Altanbaatar could see the whites of his knuckles.

"On his bed in the inky darkness, Old Man Brown heard the wolves howling as if they were planning an excecution. Old Man Brown tossed and turned beneath his blanket; they would destroy his treasure...his flying horse... 'I must save her,' he said.

"Shaking with fear, he pulled his deel close and stepped into the night. The sky was bright with a myriad of stars that lit his way. His horses were still tethered beside his shack, one on the east side and one on the west. With as much speed as Old Man Brown could muster, he switched the horses, moving the plodder to the east and his flying horse to the west side. Standing in the cold darkness, he held the reins of his flying horse tight, keeping her steady and quiet while his own nerves were as taut as a horse-head fiddle. The unnatural silence was suddenly pierced by a vicious snarl that stole Old Man Brown's breath. And then his plodder screamed, writhing as the wolves sunk their teeth into his body and ripped out his throat. The plodder thrashed in a turbulent but futile attempt to escape. 'Ssh, ssh,' Old Man Brown whispered softly into the ear of his flying horse. 'Stay quiet.'

"Beaten, the plodder let out one last moan. Motionless, he lay on the ground full of death. The wolves, their spirits high, their eyes burning red, tore the animal limb from limb, ripping his stomach apart. Crazed with the smell and the taste of blood they gorged themselves on the plodder's flesh as Old Man Brown waited for the frenzied feast to end.

"With full stomachs, the two wolves started for home. Old Man Brown mounted his flying horse and galloped after them. The wolves heard hooves in their ears, but with their meat-filled bellies, they could run no faster. The flying horse kicked the two wolves to the ground, and Old Man Brown plunged his knife deep into the wolves' stomachs. Tsenger and the gods watched with growing rage..."

Rubbing his chin, Altanbaatar stopped and pushed soft

new tobacco in his pipe's bowl. What had Bat said earlier? "The world of legends and spirits obscures reason and logic." Something of that rang true with Altanbaatar. These tales were a barrier to reality.

"Uvoo." Gamba was looking into his face, urging him forward. "Have you forgotten the story?"

"I haven't forgotten," said Altanbaatar, shaking his head.

"Are you feeling unwell then?" Solyomaa asked, wringing her hands.

"No."

Altai drew away from his side and stood with her hands on her hips. "Then what's the problem?"

Altanbaatar laughed to see his youngest daughter trying to act like a grown up. He turned his pipe over. Its jade mouthpiece was paper-thin. He should buy a new one, but this one was his comfortable old friend. The family was looking at him. What should he say? How should he answer? He heaved a sigh. "Since my father's death, your grandfather and great-grandfather," he said, patting Gamba's head, "I've been thinking. These stories of ours feel strange."

"Strange? Strange?" Altai repeated, blinking her eyes rapidly.

"Well…uncomfortable, flawed and," he paused, "perhaps untrue."

"Untrue?" Zorigo asked, pouring himself and Lhxaa another tot of vodka.

"I know! It's unsettling." Altanbaatar nodded. "I've grown up with these stories. I know them so well—they've shaped my life. But talking with Bat on the ride home this afternoon brought further clarity to my deliberations. Do you remember what you said, Bat?"

"Deliberations?" said Zorigo.

"About life, I guess."

"What did Bat say, my husband?" Monkho asked.

"Ah yes. What was it, Bat?" Altanbaatar asked, beckoning him to join the conversation.

Bat pulled himself forward. "That our stories, legends, and spiritual beliefs conceal truth."

"That's it exactly. Our stories and beliefs conceal truth."

Zorigo put his hand to his head and rolled his eyes. "But they are just stories."

"Indeed, they are, but the stories shape and reflect our view of the world, of heaven and earth. Just think of Old Man Brown trying to outwit Tsenger." Altanbaatar drew slowly on his pipe.

"But life is a fight between us and the gods," said Solyomaa, moving to the edge of the bed.

They stared at him, waiting for him to say more. The stirrings in the depth of his being were vague and hardly communicable. He took a deep breath. "But is there another way?"

"Another way?" Solyomaa's voice was edged with panic.

Altanbaatar stared at his calloused hands. He wished his thoughts were more ordered. "Our traditions and legends teach us that man is innately bad, that we are born flawed with weaknesses in us that we can never be free of."

"That's why we constantly have to work to placate the spirits," said Solyomaa hurriedly.

"But the work of placating the spirits is endless and impossible. We try, but we always live in fear that our badness will upset the spirits, bringing retribution and punishment into this life and the next."

He could hear the gentle whistle outside. The wind was calmer although it was probably still snowing. They all stared at him; their eyes wide.

"So, what are you thinking?" asked Zorigo.

"I am thinking that if there are gods, or even a supreme being, then they must possess an intelligence beyond ours."

"Of course," said Solyomaa.

Altanbaatar held his finger up. "But in their great wisdom they must also understand and accept our frailties."

"Impossible!" shouted Naraa, pounding her fist on the table.

"Why?" asked Monkho.

Naraa laced her hands and cracked her knuckles. "Because it's not our way," she said.

"Exactly, Naraa! But what if there is another way?"

A sudden gust lifted the skirt of the ger, sending a cold blast around their feet.

"Are you searching for a good spirit or a good god?" Bat asked.

Altanbaatar shrugged his shoulders. "Perhaps I am."

"What about the story, Uvoo?" asked Gamba.

"I think we'll leave the story for tonight," answered Monkho.

Chapter 14

Religion? Why was his father thinking about gods or a god? Bat had clearly told him. Education, science: these are the things that led to a correct understanding of the world and its closed system, not religion.

"Unbelievable," Bat said into the dark.

Had anyone heard him?

He lay on a bed in his parents' ger. The rest of the family had gone back to their own gers, but his mother had convinced him to stay with them. "After all," she'd reasoned, "your ger hasn't been used for months and will be icy cold." Complying with his mother's request, he'd thrown his thick deel on the bed and curled up beneath it.

On the opposite side of the ger, Altai's even breathing and his mother's snores told him that they were both asleep. His father lay at the head, but there were no sounds of sleep from his bed. Bat guessed that his father was still awake too.

Bat turned his face towards the ger wall. The coarse blanket beneath him scratched his face. He moved to the edge of the bed and felt the cool draught blowing under the wooden floor. Pulling his deel closer, he snuggled deeper into its warmth.

Consistent study based on facts and reality...not undefinable mystic theories...and science is the application of those facts in our daily life...his eyelids felt heavy.

Chrrick, chrrick, chrrick. Bat half-opened one eye. In the darkness he saw nothing, but he imagined his mother preparing kindling just as his grandmother had always done. He closed his eye; the rhythm of the knife shaving strips of wood comforted him.

"Bat, Bat!" Someone was nudging him awake. He opened his eyes to see his father standing above him. "Get up!" Bat rubbed his face and put his deel on. "The blizzard was hard." Just the mention of the word *blizzard* struck fear into the hearts of even the bravest herder.

The stove was humming. Altai slept, but his mother was gone. Bat went to the door, pulled his boots on, and followed his father outside. Blinking, he gasped. Their world had become a whitened landscape of pillow-soft drifts. He bent, scooped a handful of pristine snow into his hand and rubbed it over his face; its iciness quickly drove away the remnants of sleep.

"We need to find the animals," his father said.

Lhxaa stood at his ger door, pulling the flaps of his fur hat over his ears.

"You're back?" His father's breath billowed into the icy air.

"Got back late last night," he replied.

"What business took you away?"

"This and that," said Lhxaa, biting his lip. Bat's father shook his head and moved towards Zorigo's ger, muttering words that Bat couldn't hear. But before he reached Zorigo's door, his son came out.

"Did you have a good rest?" asked Zorigo.

"Fine! Fine!" His father waved his hand. "We must check on all the animals."

"The horses, cows, and camels are probably okay," said Lhxaa.

Shoulder to shoulder, they set out into the snow. After yesterday's winds, the air was still and the sky the palest of pinks. Lhxaa was right: the horses and cows were fine and had found shelter in the lee of the hills behind the family's gers, while the camels, standing nose to tail, all sported fresh white coats.

The four of them walked with care, scanning the horizon for any sign of sheep or goats.

"They must be buried," said Zorigo, voicing their fears.

"They'd have been trying to find shelter," Lhxaa added.

"Yeah, sheep get easily confused," said Zorigo.

"We'll split up," their father said. "Bat, you come with me."

Lhxaa and Zorigo turned north, while Bat and his father headed south into the undulating blanket of whiteness. "I reckon there's a good half metre of snowfall," his father said.

"Where do we start?"

"I don't know, son." His father sighed, shielding his eyes against the brightness.

They trudged, filling the eerie stillness with the crisp slicing of their footfall.

"Look," said his father, pointing to a patch of tightly packed snow ahead.

"Do you think animals are buried there?"

"That's usually a hollow."

Altanbaatar gingerly began poking his long stick into the mound. First, he did so with shallow movement and then, gradually, a little deeper. Prodding and sliding, he searched beneath the surface for any evidence of life.

His father fell to his knees, and Bat followed. "Here, son. There's something here."

With bare hands, they shovelled snow away. "You're right, there's something soft and warm," said Bat.

"Keep going, son."

Bat gently brushed the snow aside to reveal an ear and then a white face. They cleared the snow from the goat's body and pulled her free. She lay still.

"Is she dead?" asked Bat.

Altanbaatar put his ear to the animal's cold chest. "There's a faint heartbeat," he said, rubbing the animal's stomach and chest.

"Call Lhxaa and Zorigo."

Bat cupped his hands around his mouth and shouted. His voice boomed across the emptiness. Moments later, "Coming," echoed the reply, followed by their crunching footsteps as Zorigo and Lhxaa tried to run. But they weren't alone. Two vultures accompanied them, landing on the snowy ridge beyond them.

"Mangy predators just waiting to fill their bellies with death," said Lhxaa, watching the scrawny birds toss their heads nonchalantly.

"Ignore them," said Bat's father.

"We haven't found any animals," said Zorigo.

"Get digging," was Altanbaatar's breathless reply. "Dig."

Discarding caution, they sank to their knees and burrowed like rabbits.

"Here's one," yelled Bat.

"Here's another," said Lhxaa.

"They're all together," said Altanbaatar. "God, let them be alive."

What? The word thundered in Bat's head. *Could a god dictate whether an animal lived or died?* Using his long fur-lined sleeves, Bat swept snow away from the head of another goat he'd just uncovered.

"Bat! Run home! Tell your mother to brew a wok of strong black tea."

Pulling his sleeves over his cold, sausage-like fingers, Bat ran, tripping and trudging until he reached the ger door. He stood for a moment, holding his side and sucking air. Yanking the door open, he yelled, "Tea! Black tea."

"Already brewing, son," his mother said calmly, stirring the steaming contents of the wok.

Bat stretched his hands over the fire. "Aargh," he howled as the feeling started returning.

Ten minutes later, he was walking back with a heavy pail of tea and four bowls stuffed inside his deel pouch. By the time he reached the sheep, twenty animals had been uncovered. Some were lying down, some stood, but all of their black eyes were filled with fear.

Seeing the bucket, his father smiled wryly. "Your mother's a good woman."

They took one animal at a time. Altanbaatar and Zorigo held the sheep and goats' heads while Bat and Lhxaa poured tea down their throats. The animals were too weak to resist, and the warm liquid flowed into their stomachs and quickly began reviving them.

"Bat! Get more tea," his father said as they drained the bucket.

Bat picked up the bucket and was just preparing to return when a near neighbour of his father's rode by.

"Sain bats-gan-or—Hello everyone," Bilgay said.

Bat hardly knew the man other than by reputation, but his stout figure dwarfed his small horse, and his belly hung over his saddle like a sack of flour. Bat guessed Bilgay was in his fifties, although his purple, puffy face made him look older.

"I'm surprised to see anyone out this morning," said Altanbaatar.

"Like you, I'm checking my animals and those of my neighbours," replied Bilgay. "Any of yours dead?"

"Not sure," said Altanbaatar. "It's just the sheep and goats that got buried."

"Stupid animals," said Bilgay, dabbing the frost from his forehead.

"Snow buries sheep," said Lhxaa.

"I keep all my animals in the pen," Bilgay added.

"Humm" said Altanbaatar.

Bilgay rested his chubby hands on his belly. "This is a bad sign for the coming New Year. The gods must be punishing you for some bad deeds. You'd better put some ice in your doorway when Palden Lhamo visits tonight. None of us wants anymore bad luck."

"Thank you for your advice," said Altanbaatar. "But we must get these animals warmed, so we'll wish you a good New Year."

Bilgay wrinkled his lip and, turning his horse away, moved on.

"I'm amazed that horse isn't on its knees," said Zorigo when Bilgay was out of earshot.

Picking up the bucket Bat laughed sadly. Bilgay was a man without honour, thought Bat, pushing his shoulders back and walking to his parents' ger. Bat didn't know much, but he knew that Bilgay had been shamed and had lost his name. According to his grandfather, Bilgay had been a famous wrestler able to fell every opponent with lightning power. In his youth he'd been loved by the nation, loved by his family. He had been the unassailable hero of wrestling.

Those were the days of Bilgay's happiness, when his handsome features were still strong and defined, and his wife and children adored him. Those were the days before his dark side grew and he let fame and fortune ruin him. The days before he became a philanderer, an unruly drunk who'd been publicly abandoned by his followers. Destitute, his wife and children turned against him and, with nowhere else to go, he returned to the place of his birth.

Yes, thought Bat, Bilgay did not have a good name. He'd foolishly squandered his opportunities. The sun was warm on Bat's back. Clouds of steam rose from their ger roofs as the snow evaporated. Gripping the handle of his bucket more tightly, Bat determined that he would not waste his opportunities.

His mother had a second wok of tea waiting. He filled the bucket and made his way back to Lhxaa and Zorigo, who were rubbing the stomachs of the bleating animals. Holding his leg, Lhxaa straightened and took the bucket from Bat. His brother-in-law's limp seemed more pronounced, thought Bat, although he knew Lhxaa would never let a doctor examine his damaged leg again.

"How many animals have we recovered?" asked Bat.

"Twenty-two by my count," replied Zorigo.

"Still missing three," said Altanbaatar, combing through the snow carefully.

"Yes," said Lhxaa bending to dig again. "We're lucky the wolves didn't get them."

"The snow came too quickly," said Altanbaatar. "Let's find those last three, Lhxaa."

The last three were buried in a slack place away from the others where the ground had been grazed bare. Separated from the herd, they'd frozen and lay entombed in a white grave.

His father brought his shaking hand to his forehead. "Finish that pail of tea, and we'll move them back to the ger."

Lhxaa and Zorigo gently started pushing the ewes towards the gers, but the animals were reluctant to move.

"Run and get some fodder, Bat," Zorigo said.

Bat fetched a little fodder and scattered it in front of the sheep. One old ewe picked up the trail, and the rest followed in single file. By dints of calls and coos the three young men slowly drove the sheep and goats closer to home, while Altanbaatar carried one heavy carcass at a time on his shoulders to their cold store. They'd decide what to do with the three dead sheep another day.

Lhxaa and Zorigo filled the cart with fodder. The animals fell on the hay, gobbling furiously to fill their hungry stomachs. "Their full stomachs will help keep them warm," said Lhxaa.

"You're right," said Bat's father.

Tired of their imprisonment, the camels snorted, shrieking until their voices cut an eerie melody across the quiet steppe.

"Bad-tempered old drudges," said Zorigo.

"No!" said Altanbaatar, casting his herd a fond glance. "There's something regal, almost noble about camels."

Lhxaa and Zorigo pulled the empty cart closer to the ger. "That should be enough feed to keep them all going until tomorrow," said Lhxaa.

Bat rubbed his face. It felt strangely hot. He looked across at his brother, brother-in-law, and father. Their faces were red, scorched and burnt by the mirrored glare of the snow. Bat guessed his was the same too.

"Yes, they all have enough for the night," Altanbaatar said, making his way to their ger door. The sun was already sliding towards the horizon. Bat followed Lhxaa and Zorigo as Altanbaatar held the ger door open. Bat's footfall was heavy, his hands and feet cold to their bones. As he entered the ger, his father grasped his shoulder. "You did good work today."

Chapter 15

"Any dead?" asked Monkho as they entered the warm ger, unravelled their toe cloths and warmed themselves beside the fire.

Bat's father nodded. "Three—two sheep and a goat."

Bat's head felt strangely light as the realisation hit him: he was desperately hungry. His mother handed them each a bowl of noodle soup.

"I've left the three carcasses in the cold store for now," his father continued, taking the bowl of soup his wife offered him. "We can decide what to do with them later."

"It could have been worse," said Zorigo with a loud, satisfying slurp.

"It could have been," Altanbaatar agreed. "But I hate losing animals like this."

"There's no time to linger over your soup," said Monkho,

wiping the plastic table cover with a rag. "There's buuz to be made."

"We aren't celebrating New Year this year," said Zorigo, lighting a cigarette. "Our neighbours all know that we've had bereavements, and they won't come to greet us."

"Well, a few may come," said Monkho casually. "In which case I want to be ready."

Bat saw his father frown. And was that a wink his mother just gave Lhxaa?

She cleared away their bowls, and Bat groaned. He'd never been a part of the family buuz-making effort. In their ger, his grandmother had always made all the New Year's dumplings.

"We're exhausted," said his father with a sly smile.

"We've hardly been idle either," his mother replied, handing Naraa a large pot of minced beef and onions. "While you were out rescuing animals, we've been preparing meat."

"Tomorrow is New Year's Eve. Or had you forgotten?" asked Altai.

Her father hit his forehead with the palm of his hand. "The blizzard took it from my mind."

Altai laughed. "It will be strange not to greet our neighbours."

"It's the tradition," said Naraa, bringing the large batch of dough to the table.

"Yes," continued Altanbaatar. "It's a time for sadness, not celebration, as we remember those who've left us."

"And there'll be another year to look forward to," said Naraa.

"Have you men washed your hands?" their mother asked.

Bat's father spat on his hands and, rubbing them together, pronounced his clean.

Monkho shook her head. "Wash them!"

Moving to the washstand, Bat ladled water into the tin basin and the four of them washed in cold water. "Satisfied?" his father said, showing the women his hands.

His mother inspected them and nodded. "Let's get started," she said, handing Naraa one of the rolling pins and placing the wooden board on the table. Giving the dough one last knead, she broke off a chunk for Altai who began dividing it into small balls, which she lined up along the edge of the table.

With swift movements, his mother and Naraa rolled the balls into thin circles. Naraa's long plait moved in rhythm with her rolling pin. On her lips she wore the faintest touch of red.

Altai passed a circle of dough to her father. "Fill the first buuz, Aav-aa." He took the round, placed a spoonful of meat in the middle, pinched the edges together and handed it back to Altai.

"What do you think?"

"Not bad, Aav-aa,"

He gently cuffed the side of her head. Pushing his hand away, she placed their first dumpling on the large metal tray. "Just nine hundred and ninety-nine to go."

Lhxaa passed Bat a thin circle. It stuck to his hand, wrinkling as he tried to straighten it. With his tongue between his teeth, Bat carefully placed a spoonful of meat in the middle, pinched the edges together, and slipped a splodge of a dumpling onto the tray beside the others.

Altai, who'd been put in charge of counting, spotted it immediately. "What's this?" she asked, holding up the misshapen dumpling.

Bat's cheeks were hot. "I'm a bit out of practice."

"Don't worry, you'll be an expert by the time we've finished," said Zorigo, placing a perfectly formed one next to his.

Naraa's and their mother's rolling pins moved up and down the wooden board in unison. Suddenly Naraa stopped. "It's at times like this that I wonder where my son is."

Bat knew that Naraa had an older son, the result of some teenage romance. But he was rarely mentioned, or if he was, it wasn't in Bat's hearing.

"He must be sixteen or seventeen by now," his mother said without missing a stroke.

"Yes, quite grown-up," Naraa replied.

Lhxaa moved to her side and touched her hand. "Perhaps you'll meet him again," he said with a tenderness that surprised Bat.

"Yes, perhaps." She took a small tissue from her deel belt and dabbed her eyes.

The ger door rattled with heavy thumping.

"You locked the door?" his mother asked.

"I was trying to keep the cold out," replied his father.

Zorigo undid the string and let his wife in.

"You're locking us out now?" said Solyomaa, stamping her feet on the old towel that had become a doormat.

"Of course not," replied Altanbaatar.

"It's a dark, cloudy night, although there's no wind." She placed a large bowl of potato salad on the cupboard.

"The storm has passed, and tomorrow will be warmer and brighter," Altanbaatar said, finishing another dumpling.

"Hopefully, the cattle will survive," said Zorigo.

"Hopefully…" said Lhxaa massaging his damaged leg. "But there's little food on the ground and the animals are weak."

"Coming out of winter, it's always the same," said Zorigo.

Solyomaa let out a gasp. "So, we must keep the spirits happy."

"And how do we do that?" Altanbaatar asked.

Solyomaa's eyes darted between Zorigo and his father like those of a frightened squirrel. "By our prayers, and the prayer flags, our good deeds, and getting the lama to read the scriptures."

"It sounds exhausting," said Altai. "Aav-aa, what do prayer flags do?"

"It is exhausting, my daughter. You've seen prayer flags."

"Of course, I've seen the bright squares of cloth flying from people's gers, or on mountains or holy places. But what do they do?"

"Well, you've probably seen the writing on them too."

"I have," said Altai, sounding knowledgeable.

"The writing consists of prayers and mantras that flap in the wind, supposedly spreading harmony and compassion into the area around the flags."

"Can a piece of fabric spread peace and compassion?"

"I doubt it," said Altanbaatar.

Monkho handed Solyomaa a spare rolling pin. Bat noticed his sister-in-law's lips were pressed hard together. She took the rolling pin and joined her mother-in-law and Naraa.

"But it's our way." The words shot from Solyomaa's mouth like bullets from a gun. "And after all, we are, as you rightly said last night, Father, born in this place with its rituals and traditions."

Solyomaa pushed an imaginary hair from her eyes and returned to her dough-rolling with vigour.

"Yes! Everyone is born into the world inside a place that defines its beliefs through its long-held customs," added Zorigo in support of his wife. He stubbed his half-smoked cigarette against the stove and let the butt fall to the hearth. "Besides, we don't know another way to keep the benevolent spirits on our side and to appease the wrathful deities."

"We have no choice. Holier people than us established our rites. We should be active in prayer," said Solyomaa. "We should pray to Tsenger, solicit the lamas' intercessions, and entreat the shamans to bring messages from the gods or our ancestors."

"Mind you," said Lhxaa with a laugh, "you'd be hard-pressed to find a shaman these days. In my grandfather's day, they were resident in every town and village."

"Oh, they're around," said Bat's mother. "It's true, the Communists tried to eradicate them, but they couldn't destroy our ancient ways that easily."

"Isn't it a mix anyway?" asked Bat, placing his dumpling on the tray. He was starting to get the hang of this.

"A mix?" asked Solyomaa her cold eyes flashing Bat a glare.

Bat took a breath. "Yes, our so-called way is a mix of religions."

"What do you mean?" said Solyomaa.

"Well, our people believe that spirits and souls live in animate objects. We pray prayers to gods, or the lamas pray for us. We look to the shamans to read our future or get wisdom from the spirit world. We seek enlightenment, while believing that every part of our lives is linked with all that happens in the spiritual world."

"You've been reading well, my son."

"I have Father. I've read the *Secret History* and the few religious books that weren't destroyed in the 1930s purges. They speak of a mix of beliefs, of Buddhist practices forging with the ancient ways of the shamans and Tsenger."

"It's true," said Altanbaatar. "Shamanism and Buddhism have become a strong alloy bound to the fabric of our souls."

"But we live in this place," said Solyomaa, banging her rolling pin on the side of the table. "How can we separate belief from our heart's home? We can only believe what we know. Besides," she said with a sniff, "our beliefs are precious to me."

Altanbaatar patted his daughter-in-law's back. "We are only talking."

"I know, but it's talk that fills me with fear," said Solyomaa, taking her rolling pin and resuming work.

"Don't be afraid. We are just talking out our thoughts," said Bat's mother gently.

Lhxaa placed a generous spoonful of meat into a dough case. "What do you think Aav-aa?"

"About what, Lhxaa?"

"Living to please the spirits."

"I think," said Altanbaatar, placing the unfinished dumpling on the table, "that it's like trying to walk on your hands."

Solyomaa held her hand to the amber bead that hung at throat. "But how else will we escape the fire of hell and reach heaven?"

"I don't know," said Altanbaatar. "But let me ask you: have your efforts to please the spirits and be a good person succeeded? Have they removed that nub of evil, which we all feel lodged in our hearts?"

Solyomaa dropped her head forward. "No."

"I thought not. Our own efforts to be good or right are never enough."

Altai rubbed her forehead. "I don't understand."

"This week," he paused, taking his pipe from one of the roof rafters, "you women have all cleaned each ger from its toono to its wooden floors. You washed all our clothes, threw out the old ones and cleaned away all dirt and dust. And you've made us all new deels for New Year's Day."

Altai's finger lingered over the rows of buuz. "But that's what we do at New Year. Everything must be clean and new—it's a *new* start."

"Yes, Altai," her father replied. "You are right. We work hard to clean and renew everything on the outside. Appearances are what count. Dirt is seen as something shameful. But all that cleaning doesn't change us on the inside."

"New Year should also be a time of forgiveness and restoration, which gives us peace on the inside," said Lhxaa.

"That's right," agreed Naraa.

"But do we really forgive and let go of our grievances?" asked Monkho.

"No!" said Naraa, quickly rolling dough circles. "All we do is store them in a tiny cupboard in our hearts and unlock the cupboard to let them out when we are hurt or offended again."

Monkho straightened, holding her rolling pin like a baton. "But by storing up those wrongs, those hurts become a seed of anger that quickly turns bitter, leaving us sicker than the person who wronged us."

"Sicker than the other..." Bat's repeated the words.

The candles on the table were mellow. The oil was low, and the light would soon be gone. Bat wondered where this conversation was heading.

Zorigo and Lhxaa had an efficient production line going. Lhxaa, his hands grubby beyond the cleaning properties of any soap, stuffed dough rounds with meat while Zorigo crimped them closed.

"Sickness. Maybe not sickness," said Altanbaatar, studying the pipe in his hand. "Perhaps *inner torment* would better describe it."

"Describe what?" asked Altai, squishing her eyebrows together.

"The desire I have to be better than I am and yet my inability to be that better man."

"But can anything help us be better on the inside?" asked Solyomaa.

"I think education can help us," said Bat. "Education gives us knowledge from which comes understanding and the opportunity to make ourselves better."

"That is a very good point son. Education is helpful, although in my experience, it only highlights our deficiencies. It cannot change them."

Monkho placed two more logs on the fire. They crackled, sending sparks flying out from under the ill-fitting lid. It was getting late, although there would be no stopping until all the buuz were made. Hair escaped from his mother's plait, and she stopped to pull the stray ones back into line. Bat thought that he caught the faintest hint of a smile on her lips. Was she enjoying this conversation?

"But Father, you must have some thoughts," said Naraa, who'd stopped rolling to let Zorigo and Lhxaa clear the growing pile of dough rounds.

"Yes, I have some thoughts, but they are jumbled."

"Tell us!" said Altai, standing with her hands on her hips. They laughed.

"You know, I used to sit with your grandfather on the hill when he was watching his sheep and goats. We'd often talk about life and its struggles, but we also talked about the world around us—the blue sky and the warming sun. Or at night, we'd marvel at the moon and trace lines of stars that sparkled brighter than any jewels."

"We all love and revere the vast sky of our homeland," interrupted Zorigo.

"I know we do, but towards the end of his life, your grandfather started asking me to look beyond our natural world, beyond the order of life and the rhythms of our seasons."

"The scientific rhythm of life," said Bat, suddenly recognising something in this bizarre conversation.

His father smiled. "Yes, son. Science has identified the rhythms of the seasons, but they are not mechanical. The land is alive with more than robotic cycles. Think of the wonder of a newborn lamb, or summer's vibrant flowers growing thickly beneath the trees, or the pure coolness of the mountain spring. There is beauty in nature that is fresh and constantly being renewed with cleanness and purity."

"You sound like a poet," said Altai, arranging the buuz in rows of twenty. "Two hundred and fifty-three," she concluded.

"Perhaps," he said.

"No...definitely two hundred and fifty-three."

They laughed. "I didn't doubt your counting, Altai. I just meant that...perhaps I'm a poet."

Altai looked confused.

Monkho handed him a fresh bowl of tea. Altanbaatar gently blew on it until it was cool enough to take a slow sip. Placing it on the table, he continued, "Whether we looked at the sky or at the nature around us, it didn't matter. Your grandfather always asked me the same question: 'Do you think there's a loving being beyond our land, beyond Tsenger? A god whom we could know and who could make us clean and new like our natural world?' I always shook my head, not knowing how to answer. But since he's gone, I've begun to wonder."

"Yeah," said Zorigo. "No matter what evolution says, I think we all believe that a greater power than us created this world."

His father placed his finger to his lips. "So, my question is, if there is a creator, how can we know him?"

"That's two questions," said Altai.

"So it is," replied her father with a smile.

Monkho, Naraa, and Solyomaa continued working their rolling pins expertly up and down the wooden board. With their free hands, they turned the dough until it was just the right shape and just the right thickness.

Bat held his head in his hands. If it hadn't been dark and snowy, he'd have grabbed his horse and ridden for the hills. Instead he stayed, watching his father twisting his jade-stemmed pipe between his rough fingers. His grey hair was thinning, and in the shadows his father's face appeared more deeply scored than by day. He was a good man, wise and genuine, a man whom Bat had respected.

Altai was counting again, and Bat wondered why she'd been asked to keep tally since her maths were so poor.

"Less than three hundred," she said. "We need to go faster."

"You're right, Altai," her mother replied. "Some of us need to talk less and work more."

"Of course," said Zorigo, taking another piece of dough. "But I have a thought."

They looked at him expectantly.

He shrugged his shoulders. "If we believe that there is a creator or a god, then perhaps we should ask him to find us."

"Perhaps we should," agreed Naraa.

"Mmm!"

"What is it Mother?" Solyomaa asked.

"I've heard that Tseren-ax, the storyteller, has an old book about the creator of this world. Perhaps we could visit him tomorrow."

"Why not?" replied Altanbaatar.

Bat's dumpling fell from his hand. He quickly picked it up, tried to reshape it, and placed it on the metal tray.

Handing it back to him, Altai cried, "Reject!"

Chapter 16

Monkho rubbed her neck as she pulled herself upright. The last couple of days had been exhausting. Yesterday they'd hoped to visit the old storyteller's home but having abandoned the making of buuz the night before last, they had to finish them yesterday. Of course, they had to sample a batch of dumplings, and by the time they'd done that, it had been too late to go out.

The buuz sat on large metal trays under their beds, waiting to be steamed if visitors arrived. She was not expecting many but you never knew. Most friends and family would respect their year of grief. But a few might come, so in a modest way they were prepared.

Monkho put her hand to her forehead and pushed her head backwards to stretch her aching muscles. Like Altai, she would miss greeting their visitors with the exchange of kisses and wishes of peace.

Altanbaatar, Bat, and Altai slept soundly. Monkho criss-crossed logs in the stove around crumpled paper and struck a match. The fire burst into life. She filled the wok with water and placed it above the flames. Last year had been a strange year.

Learning to live without her husband's parents was like learning to live without one of her limbs, which was surprising given that she'd long held a grudge against her mother-in-law (or as Naraa had so aptly described it, had held onto a nub of bitterness). Why she'd held onto it so long, Monkho had no idea, other than that it had become a habit. She sighed. It was too late to change it now.

And as for her sweet-natured father-in-law, she missed him deeply. Her father-in-law's musings had certainly prompted her husband's recent questions. Although, it was odd to be questioning their traditions; it felt like they were trying to move the lattice that kept their home shaped and upright. Their children had been equally uncomfortable when Altanbaatar spoke his thoughts. Poor Solyomaa, she'd been jittery ever since.

She scattered tea leaves in the water and replaced the lid on the wok. Those few pages, the smallest fragment of a book that they'd found amongst Namdorj's possessions after his death, had certainly sharpened their curiosity. Even though the pages confusingly spoke of a new birth, a door, and a road to a different life through a special saviour, all of which seemed incomprehensible, they had at least opened their eyes to the possibilities of a new way.

A wry smile touched her lips. Had Zorigo had his way, her father-in-law's box of books would have been burnt. Thankfully, Bat's protests had halted Zorigo's ideas. And the pages had found their way into their home, where they'd been read over and over. They didn't understand much, but Altanbaatar felt that the words shone a path to a way of hope.

Monkho added milk to the tea and let it gently simmer. The others still slept. She yawned, feeling weary herself but knowing that there would be no chance of rest today. It was first day of the New Year, and they were going to visit Tseren-ax's ger.

Monkho rubbed her stomach, grateful that the pains of indigestion were lessening. It was the same each year, she thought, remembering how she filled her stomach with meaty dumplings and then groaned her way through each New Year's Day. Next year she would eat less. Monkho laughed, aware that she'd made herself the same promise for the last twenty years.

After their visit to Tseren-ax, they would come home and have their first family meal of the New Year. She hoped this year would be a good one. Her hands quivered, not with her familiar companion, fear, but with a kind of anticipation.

Bat lay curled up beneath his deel. Since his grandparents had gone, she'd nursed hopes of getting closer to him. She sniffed.

"Peaceful, peaceful," her husband said quietly.

Monkho wiped her nose on the sleeve of her old deel. "I thought you were asleep."

"Come here," he said.

She abandoned the tea and lay down again beside Altanbaatar. In the half-light, his eyes were tender, and he stroked her back like she was one of his beloved camels.

"Bat's distant, and I don't know how to reach him."

"He's young and full of new ideas."

"But I'm his mother."

"Ssh! Just sleep."

Monkho must have slept because when she turned over, Altanbaatar had gone. She drew her deel close and slipped to the edge of the bed. The floor was cold and the fire barely alive. Raking the cinders, Monkho added another log. She was glad that the worst of the winter was over and that she wouldn't need to get up so early.

Altanbaatar stamped his boots outside and opened the door. "The animals all seem fine," he said, putting his hat on the peg and pointing to their children's motionless bodies. "I see Altai and Bat are still asleep."

"They're tired."

"That's as may be, but it's time they got up."

Altanbaatar roused his two youngest children, who both groaned and turned away. Monkho handed him a bowl of milk tea. He took it and sat rubbing his hand across his face. The skin beneath his eyes was starting to sag, and his grey hair would never be black again. Like herself, he was aging, although he'd always be the dashing, young rider she'd fallen for nearly thirty years ago. He's a good man too, she thought, thinking of some of her friends' drunken, womanising husbands.

The water in the wok was boiling. Monkho bent to lift it off the fire, but Altanbaatar was there before her. "Let me," he said placing the wok on an upturned stool. She smiled. Yes. She'd caught herself a good man who knew how to handle life. Even in this time of confusion, there was something steady about him. She shook her head.

"What?" he asked.

"I was wondering what possessed me to suggest we visit Tseren-ax's ger."

"Wisdom?"

She tipped her head to one side. "I'm not sure about that. I was just thinking about that dratted book of his—you know, the one about some foreign god."

Altanbaatar smiled. "When do you want to leave?"

"After breakfast."

Getting Altai out of bed was like moving a stubborn mule. She'd clung to her blanket, refusing to let it go. Bat got up more easily and brought in firewood and dung, although he'd glared at his father when he realised that they were expecting him to accompany them to Tseren-ax's ger. His father tapped him lightly on the shoulder and told him that he might learn something. Bat had turned away, but not before Monkho saw the coldness in his eyes.

"Come, help me saddle the horses," said Altanbaatar, pushing Bat towards the door.

Monkho pulled her fur hat hard over her ears. "Altai, get

your deel on," she said, seeing that her daughter was still not ready to leave.

"Why do we have to go so early?"

"It's not early."

Altanbaatar stamped the loose snow from his boots onto the old towel. "The horses are saddled," he said, propelling his youngest daughter out the door.

Monkho followed, aware that none of them had thought about the direction they should leave the ger. Usually she would solicit the lama's counsel, but she'd completely forgotten. She hoped it wouldn't be a bad omen for the year. She said a quick prayer, to whom she didn't know, in the hope that they'd be protected.

Bat was already on his horse and Altanbaatar was pulling Altai up to sit, snugly, in front of him. Zorigo and Naraa waited at the hitching post.

"Eej-ee, let me give you a leg up," said Zorigo, bringing the horse to her. Monkho gripped the saddle while her son pushed her up. There was a day when she'd have jumped onto the bareback of any horse. She shuffled, trying to get comfortable in her saddle. It was a while since she'd ridden.

"Enjoy your visit," said Naraa, handing her mother the reins.

She smiled. "Buuz are on trays under our beds."

Naraa nodded. "I know."

"I was just saying in case any visitors arrive."

"It is New Year's Day, and few people will be out this early."

"We're out visiting."

"That's different!"

"Some will want to make an early start."

"But most people know that we're not greeting this year."

"That won't stop some," said Monkho.

"I know. But they'll understand."

"Is this a good idea?"

"What?" Naraa asked, rolling her eyes.

"Visiting Tseren-ax?"

"Of course! They have no family, and they'll be glad of your visit."

Naraa was right. Tseren and Nina had no children. Poor Nina. People had said that there was badness in her and that the badness prevented her from bearing children. Others said she'd offended the spirits. Mind you, she'd maligned Nina in much the same way herself. She tightened her stirrups and pulled the horse's head around.

"Eej-ee," Altai called. "We need to go."

"Okay." Monkho waved, squeezing her legs against the horse's sides.

The sun was climbing in the clear sky. She shielded her eyes against its brilliance while basking in its warmth. After the roughness of the last few days, it was good to see the prayer flags hanging limp at the horses' hitching post.

Bat led them down through thc shelter of the trees to the riverbank. The snow was less deep and shone in the sunlight. Beside their path, newly formed, minute prints ran down to the frozen river. Maybe they belonged to voles or mice. The river, brushed with the lightest dusting of snow, glistened like a million diamonds. It was the most beautiful place on earth, thought Monkho. Only the soft thud of their horses' hooves and animals' snorts broke the silence. Surely there's no stillness like the stillness of our place under snow.

Altanbaatar and Altai followed Bat. Now fully awake, Altai chattered like a ground squirrel. Altanbaatar let her talk, and her singsong voice rang out across the river and beyond. She'll never leave us, thought Monkho. Once she finishes school, she'll come right back home and marry someone local—unlike Bat.

She sighed. They'd all recognised Bat's intelligence, and they wanted him to go to college, but the learning would turn him away from them. Monkho gripped her chest. Yes, she wanted to draw him close into the family. Zorigo was near. Even Naraa, with her grand dreams of a more sophisticated life, was close. And Altai, well, she was their home bird. But Bat, he was different.

She watched as Bat moved his head from side to side, searching for the new path close to the river's edge. He knew the land so well, and yet Monkho feared he would turn his back on it. The ice creaked. Beneath the river's frozen surface, the thaw was coming. One foot in the wrong place, and horse and rider could plunge through the weakening layers. Monkho knew of many who had perished in such iciness.

Bat turned away from the river and headed north onto the uneven ground amongst the trees. The trees stood like frozen skeletons, and Monkho pitied their nakedness. But come spring, they'd be bursting with new life again. She tugged the reins, and the horse halted. Could her husband be right? Was there a creator god, and if so, could she know him?

"Monkho?" Altanbaatar was beside her.

"I'm fine," she said, answering the question in his voice.

"Good," said Altai with a bright smile. "Because we're nearly there."

Monkho smiled. "I know. I hope no one arrives at home while we are away."

"Naraa and Solyomaa can look after any visitors, and Zorigo is there too," said Altanbaatar, trotting alongside her as they headed towards the clearing. "Although where Lhxaa went to so early this morning, I've no idea."

"I'm sure he's fine," said Monkho.

"Fine," her husband repeated. "He's hiding something."

Monkho bit her lip, knowing Altanbaatar was imagining the worst. But Lhxaa didn't seem to care. He'd made Monkho swear. He had been so serious, so earnest that she'd agreed and, with all her willpower determined not to breathe a word, not a single word, not even to Altanbaatar. But keeping this secret required all her strength.

"Bat's waiting," she said, pointing to the clearing ahead where Bat had stopped.

Reaching him, they picked their way to the solitary ger crouched hard by the hill. Smoke curled in rings from its short chimney. They tethered their horses and dismounted. Monkho pulled the large round of cream that she'd kept frozen in their store from her saddlebag. She was sure Tseren-ax and Nina would enjoy this treat. Cream was good for the heart, and it brought such cheer to a piece of bread in the cold months. Monkho patted the round, remembering warmer days when the darkness hardly touched the day.

"Give me your arm," Altanbaatar said. She linked hers in his, and they walked together to the orange door. Bat and Altai followed. Tseren-ax sat staring into the fire, his bony hand wrapped around his black pipe.

Nina, a tiny woman with a shock of white hair, was putting food on the table. "I thought we'd have early visitors," she said. Tseren-ax didn't move. She punched his arm.

"What?"

"We've got visitors," she shouted.

"Ah...ah! Why didn't you tell me?"

"You're going deaf as well as blind."

He rubbed his ears. "I am not! Come in. Come in," he said, stumbling to his feet.

Altanbaatar and Monkho moved to the centre of the ger.

"Give me that cloth, woman," said Tseren-ax.

Monkho's eyes widened. Had Tseren-ax forgotten that Altanbaatar's parents had died in this last year? She opened her mouth but then caught sight of her husband giving a quick shake of his head. She understood and closed her mouth.

Nina handed Tseren-ax the new blue cloth. Standing as tall as he could, he cradled the piece of silk in his two hands. Its blueness was as pure as the eternal sky and a symbol of the respect between them. Altanbaatar stepped closer and, clasping Tseren-ax's bony elbows with both his hands, kissed the old man's cheeks. "Amar sain uu—Good peace to you," they said to one another.

Tseren-ax extended his arms to Monkho. Leaning forward, she let his papery face touch hers as he planted toothless kisses on her cheeks. Tseren-ax beamed, delighted to greet such early visitors. There can't be many storytellers left, Monkho thought, remembering the days when a storyteller would turn up unannounced at her parents' ger or at some other neighbour's and spend the whole night eating, drinking, and telling the old tales. Often, he'd still be going as the morning edged its way into their gers. It's a shame the old ways are disappearing, she thought.

"I love your deels," said Altai, stroking the smooth silk of Tseren-ax's sleeve. "Are they new? Where did you get the fabric? Was it expensive?"

"Altai!" said Monkho, pulling her daughter towards a stool.

Nina laughed. "Nothing wrong with genuine curiosity," she said, smoothing imaginary creases from her rich purple coat. "I might not be the storyteller but there hangs a tale to these lovely costumes."

Her husband heaved a sigh. "Okay woman. Get the tale told."

"Well, we once saved a child from drowning in that river," she said, pointing in the river's general direction. "Tseren, when he weren't hard of hearing, heard a child screaming. The lad was just a little one, standing no higher than a lamb. Well, he must have been playing on his own and fallen into the water 'cause we heard him shouting. The poor mite. So Tseren runs." She raised her eyebrows. "That was in the days when he could run. Anyways, he jumps right into that river and pulls the little lad out. The boy was freezing and shivering, but we brings him in and wraps him in blankets and gets the fire going. His parents were that grateful, they thought Tseren was a holy man."

Tseren shook his head.

"Yeah, I told them you wasn't," she said, putting her hand on his shoulder. "But they never believed me. Anyway, ever since, they've gifted us with beautiful new deels ready for the New Year. And you're right, Altai, the fabric's always top quality."

Tseren-ax thumped the table. "Where's the tea, woman?"

They laughed. Monkho removed her hat and handed it to Bat, who placed it on top of the cupboard with the others. He winked, and for the first time she caught a glimpse of the old Bat.

Nina, her twig-like hands shaking, passed out bowls of tea. Monkho cupped the bowl in her hands; tea always brought such comfort. Tseren-ax passed his snuff bottle to Altanbaatar, and Altanbaatar offered the old storyteller his. Slowly the two men loosened the coral stoppers, took a sniff, nodded, and returned their snuff bottles to one another.

Altai looked Tseren-ax in the eye. "I always wondered why you do that."

"Altai!" Monkho's face glowed red. Did her daughter not know the reason for the exchange of snuff bottles?

"That's a good question, young lady." Tseren-ax said graciously. "You might think this is just an old man's tradition, but it isn't. In the days of our great Empire when we ruled swathes of this globe," the old man traced a large arc with his hand, "our fearless warriors would ride thousands of kilometres on their sturdy horses. Arriving at a stranger's home, they needed to know whether relations with their hosts were going to be amicable or not. The exchanging of the snuff bottles and the return of it with a nod revealed an ally."

Nina plonked a platter of potato salad on to the table. "That's enough! There's no need to lecture the poor girl."

"I was just answering her question," said Tseren-ax, looking sheepish.

"It's good to tell the young ones where our traditions come from. And Bat loves history, don't you?" said Monkho.

"I do, Ax-aa."

"Can I help you, Tseren-ax?" Altanbaatar asked.

"Just wanted to get to the god-shelf."

The shelf, in the place of honour at the back of the ger, was littered with gods. Amongst them Monkho spotted Drolo, the suppressor of demons, and Variocana, the white father who transformed anger. She shivered. Once she believed that those statues held great power, but today all she saw were lumps of metal. Tseren-ax had several tiny golden lanterns and a pile of Buddhist writings. A large package wrapped in a worn brown shawl stuck out, too big for the shelf. Tseren-ax tried to lift the package.

Monkho tapped Bat's knee, and like a young deer, Bat leapt to his feet.

"Ax-aa, let me get that for you," he said, handing the package to Tseren-ax.

Nina put five bowls brimming with buuz onto the table. Already feeling like a stuffed marmot, Monkho groaned inwardly.

While they ate, Tseren-ax caressed his precious package. "Altanbaatar," he said clearing his throat. "There's talk."

"What sort of talk?" her husband asked.

"That you're asking alarming questions that cast doubts on our traditions and beliefs. People think you're losing your sense of reason. They say you think there's a god who created this world."

Tseren-ax always was a plain-speaker, thought Monkho. Not only that, but how on earth had news of her husband's questions reached the old story-teller's deaf ears, especially since as far as Monkho knew, the discussion had only been amongst their family? Was Tseren-ax provided with supernatural powers?

"You're right, Ax-aa," said Altanbaatar, wiping his mouth and placing his bowl on the table. "I have been questioning."

"What are you searching for?"

"Truth!"

"You don't think our beliefs and traditions are true?"

"I have my doubts," said Altanbaatar, popping a dumpling into his mouth.

"Every man has doubt."

"Have you experienced doubts?" Altanbaatar took a spoonful of salad.

"Of course, I have, and I still do."

"Are you comfortable living with such uncertainties?"

"Comfortable or not, it's how life is."

"Is it?" Monkho heard the despair in her husband's voice. He wanted solid answers. "Surely beyond all the spirits, the gods, and even Tsenger, there must be something that is certain."

"I think knowledge can help us find solid answers," added Bat quietly.

"That is a good point, Bat," replied Altanbaatar.

"Yes, son, your father's right; your answer has merit," said Tseren-ax. "But you will find that life is more complex than mere learning."

Bat let his eyes fall to his bowl. With his short haircut and silver deel, he looks so grown up, thought Monkho. His words sound wise, yet they have no life experience attached to them.

"So, Altanbaatar," Tseren-ax said, offering his guest a shot of vodka. "Is that the reason you came to my ger today?"

"Partly." Altanbaatar took the glass and brushed it to his lips before placing it on the table. He was no great drinker, although he did not wish to offend his host. "We wanted to offer our greetings for the New Year, but we also know that you possess a rich understanding of life and its wisdom."

"You flatter me."

"Perhaps...but I am sure you have something to share with us."

Tseren-ax smiled, "You know I have this book." He patted the package. "It's been in my family for two generations." He undid the knot that held the shawl in place to reveal a shabby red tome with faded gold lettering. "This book came from my grandfather, although there's some dispute as to whether he truly was my grandfather."

"Not really your grandfather?" said Altai scratching her head.

Tseren-ax tapped his nose with his knobbly forefinger. "Yes. The man I knew as grandfather was a lama, a devout man who was tricked into sleeping with a prostitute. Shamed in front of his fellow lamas, he was forced to leave the lamasery and make his home in a simple ger on the edge of the desert beside the herders. He knew nothing of the existence of a son until my father turned up at his door. The old lama was shocked but embraced the boy, and the two of them lived together until my father met my mother and I came along.

"By the time I was old enough to remember my grandfather, he was frail and bent double. I used to sit on his knee, and he'd tell me stories of the white-faced foreigner who'd walked into his ger one day."

"A foreigner?" said Altai.

"Yes, a foreigner. Until that day my grandfather and his friends had never seen one. When the yellow-haired man walked in, they thought him a spirit. But when he tried to speak our language, they realised he was no spirit."

Altai rubbed her hands together. "Were they afraid? Was the man a warrior trying to make war on our land?"

"U-gui, gui—No, no, my child, it wasn't like that at all. Only one came to my grandfather's ger, although there were others in the country. Even though they were tall, they didn't come to fight us. They weren't made for battle. Their hands were too soft."

"Where did he come from?" asked Bat.

"From Europe, Scotland or Holland. I can't quite remember."

"Why did they come?" asked Altai.

"They came to bring us news, news of a saviour my grandfather had never heard of — a saviour they said could change our world. Word has it," he snuffed, "that our people didn't receive their news. The foreigners had little understanding of our great history and the pride we have in it."

Tseren-ax took a few mouthfuls of potato salad. "Neither did they know that our hearts are not easily changed."

"The yellow-haired man came for many summers. He wasn't strong enough to live through our winters. He learned our tongue and learned to ride a horse too. He travelled the desert by horse or camel visiting herders."

Altai laughed. "He must have looked funny: a long man riding one of our horses."

"He must have," said Tseren-ax, beckoning his wife to refill his tea bowl. "Yet despite his strangeness, he was loved and welcomed into people's homes. Apparently, he visited hundreds of families, but I think the foreigner enjoyed a special friendship with my grandfather."

"Why?" Monkho asked, thinking it peculiar that a Mongolian should be friends with a foreigner.

"Because my grandfather's ger was the first home he ever visited."

"Do you remember his name?" Monkho asked.

Tseren rubbed his forehead. "Something to do with trees."

"Trees?" said Altai.

"Yes. His name meant trees or forest in his language. Ed-forest, or Ed-wood…?"

They laughed.

"He visited many families, selling books and giving remedies for people's ills. But he always returned to my grandfather's home where, smoking their pipes, they talked late into the night."

"Did your grandfather accept the foreigner's religion?" Altanbaatar asked.

Tseren-ax shook his head. "No, but the man had a good heart and my grandfather respected him for that."

"Your story sounds like a legend," said Bat.

"You're right, it sounds unbelievable. But I have no reason to doubt my grandfather's words, especially since I hold the foreigner's book of translated stories and wisdom in my hand. On one of the yellow-haired man's last visits, he gave this to my grandfather."

Altai inhaled quickly. "Tseren-ax can I look at your precious book?"

"Carefully," said Tseren-ax, passing it to Altai. It was big in her small hands, and she let it fall into her lap. She fingered the pages. They were thin and yellowed, and Monkho could see that they were written in the old script.

"Eej-ee, what does it say?"

Monkho took the book and, starting from the top of the page, traced the words with her finger. "The wind blows where it wishes...you hear its sounds...but you do not know where it comes from...or where it goes."

"We've read those words before," Altanbaatar said. "Yes—we've read those words before."

"It might just be a coincidence," said Bat.

"It might," replied Monkho, aware of a warmth in the pit of her stomach. "What," the words stuck in her throat, "makes you think that this book could be true?"

"Because," Tseren-ax touched his forehead reverently, "*that* book talks of the god who created this world and made us."

Chapter 17

Altanbaatar's pulse thudded like a drum in his ear. Is this how an explorer on the verge of a new discovery felt? Was he going to be disappointed? Or were his questions finally going to be answered? He wiped his brow.

Monkho was shaking his arm. "Did you hear Tseren-ax's question?"

"What?"

"Would you like to hear a story from this foreign book?" Tseren-ax repeated.

"Yes," Altanbaatar replied simply.

Altai drew her stool closer. Her eyes wide with expectation, she nestled her head under Altanbaatar's arm. Bat sat on the other side of the table, fiddling with the navy edging of his new deel.

"It's an intricate book," Tseren-ax said, running his finger the length of its seam.

"Intricate?" said Altanbaatar.

"It is not just one book, but a collection of different books written by different authors over many centuries. Some parts are exciting. Some are full of wise words, while others are unfathomable. There are stories of the world's beginnings, of kings and wars, of captivity and exile, and finally, there's the story of freedom. This book speaks of a freedom that brings new life to all men."

Altanbaatar raised his eyebrows. "Sounds like you're very familiar with that book."

"On cold nights, I like to read the stories."

Altai laughed. "That's because you're a storyteller."

Tseren-ax smiled. "Although the stories are different, a common thread does run through each one: all the writers knew the creator god and believed he was real and near."

"Do you believe in the god of *that* book?" asked Altai.

Altanbaatar caught Monkho's eye and winked. She was bold with her questions.

"The god of this book," Tseren-ax tapped the volume with his knuckles, "could be a part of the truth. There may be many paths to eternal happiness. But our beliefs are the truth to me; they are the touchstone of my identity, anchoring me to this place and its community."

"Perhaps all the stories fit together," said Altai.

"Perhaps they do," said Monkho. "But sit quietly and let Tseren-ax begin."

Altanbaatar looked to the open skylight. A new blue cloth hung from the toono, and the sky beyond was cloudless. *If you are there...if you're the real god, then speak to us,*

Altanbaatar prayed silently. *We want to hear your voice.*

Nina filled tiny glasses with shots of vodka and pulled her stool close to the fire.

"This story is an adventure," said Tseren-ax, putting the book aside. It was evident that the old storyteller had made this story his own.

Altai clapped her hands. "An adventure is good."

Monkho put her finger to her lips.

"It's about a young man called David, or in our tongue, Dav-it. He wasn't of high birth. He was like us, a shepherd and herder. Dav-it had a good heart, a soft heart. He believed in the god of his people, the Israelites, and he always wanted to follow his god's words and way. Later his god chose him to be king, but *this* story happened before that."

Nina threw another log into the stove that sent the fire into cackles of delight and left Altanbaatar fighting to loosen the buttons on the collar of his new deel.

"Dav-it's a favourite of mine. His story reminds me of our brave warriors, the magnificent Khans who conquered new lands and established our great Empire." Tseren-ax took a sip of tea, followed by a swig of vodka. Altanbaatar raised his glass to toast the old man but the bitter liquid did not run past his lips. Nina refilled her husband's glass and added another drop to Altanbaatar's.

"Drink up," said Tseren-ax, emptying his glass and wiping his mouth on his deel sleeve.

"That's your new deel!" his wife said.

Tseren-ax shrugged his shoulders. "Dav-it was the youngest son of the family," he continued, ignoring his wife's comment.

"His brothers thought he was the tail, the one left behind, the one who had to care for the animals while the others got on with the important business of fighting their king's enemies."

"He doesn't sound like a great Khan," Altai said, placing her hand under her chin.

Altanbaatar patted her head. "He sounds like a Mongolian boy."

"Now!" Tseren-ax raised a finger. "The enemies of the Israelites were giants, hairy and fat. And there was one in particular—an ogre of a man—who was the enemy's undefeated champion. His name was Goliath, and he was a fearful sight. In fact, whenever the Israelites heard his thunderous voice calling them to the fight, they'd scurry back to their tents and dive under their bedcovers."

Altai giggled.

"It's true," said Tseren-ax. "Even the Israelite king Saul, clothed in his grand armour and standing head and shoulders above his people, feared the giant."

"He must have been some monster," said Bat. Altanbaatar noticed his son was no longer fiddling with the edging of his deel but was leaning forward.

"He was a monster of a man," said Tseren-ax. "One day when the soldiers' food supplies were low, Dav-it's father sent for his son. 'Dav-it, leave your sheep in the care of another shepherd and take a donkey, loaded with food, to your brothers.' His youngest son did as his father asked and started the long walk to the battlefield. As he neared the open plain, much like our steppe country, Dav-it wondered where the battle cries were. Surely, he reasoned, he'd be able to hear shouting and the clash of weapon on weapon. But he heard nothing.

"Arriving at the Israelite encampment he found soldiers loitering by their tents, playing games, cleaning their armour, and polishing their swords. Dav-it tied up his donkey and went in search of his brothers. Eventually he found them huddled in their tent. 'Are you afraid?' Dav-it asked.

"'You have an evil tongue,' his older brother Eliab yelled raising his hand. An agile young man, Dav-it dodged the blow, and Eliab's hand just crashed against the tent's wall.

"'Ignore him,' said Shammah. 'The Philistine's champion is a giant of a man with a head the size of a chariot wheel. His eyes are black and filled with hatred...And for forty days he's been devouring our best soldiers like tasty ants.' Shammah shook his head.

"Dav-it put his hand on Shammah's arm. 'Who is this giant to defy our God? Let me go and kill him.'

"Eliab laughed. 'Who, you? You're just a boy.'

"'You can't go,' said Abinadab, another of Dav-it's brothers. 'He'd kill you in a moment.'

"'His armour is as heavy as you are, and the handle of his javelin is as thick as a hitching post,' said Eliab.

"'Yeah,'" added Abinadab. "'And he's been a man of war since his youth.'

"'But I've killed lions and bears and defended our father's sheep from all kinds of predators. This Philistine is just another godless bear to slay.'

"Eliab shrugged his shoulders. 'Let the lad go.'

"Dav-it left the tent, and Abinadab went to tell King

Saul. The King rushed to meet Dav-it. 'This giant has been threatening us for forty days,' said the noble king.

"While the king was speaking the giant came out onto the plain. With each footstep, the earth shuddered."

Tseren-ax thumped his hand on the table, and Altai's hands flew to her mouth.

"The giant, his eyes wild with fury, roared, 'Send me someone to eat, or an Israelite dog to slay. But if you fleas have the skill to kill me, then we mighty Philistines will become your servants.'

"Dav-it was shocked. 'Who's this foreigner to defy the armies of the living God?'

"King Saul looked at the small lad in his shepherd's cloak. 'You are just a boy.'

"'But the living God is with me.'

"'Yes. But if you are to fight this giant, then you must wear my armour.'

"Dav-it placed the king's helmet on his head. It flopped over his eyes, hitting his nose. 'I can't wear this. Let me go as a shepherd.'

"King Saul nodded. 'Okay. But go in God's strength.'

"Dav-it picked up his staff, went to the stream, chose five round smooth stones, put them in his shepherd's pouch, and approached the giant.

"Goliath's armour bearer moved in front of the giant. When Goliath saw Dav-it, he laughed. 'Are you playing games with me? I will crush you like a twig and toss your bones to the vultures. You and your god are nothing and nobodies.'

"Dav-it held his sling in his hand. 'You come at me with your powerful sword and heavy spear, but I come to you with a more powerful weapon—I come in the name of the Lord of hosts, the God of the armies of Israel. Today the Lord will give you into my hands, and I will chop off your head. And then everyone will know that it is the Lord who saves a man, not the sword or the spear.'

"Goliath roared, 'You think your god is more powerful than me. I am stronger than words, stronger...'

"Dav-it ran forward and, taking a smooth stone from his pouch, loaded it into his sling, swung it above his head, and let the stone fly. Thud! It hit the giant square on his brow. With a mighty crash, the giant hit the ground, flat on his face. Dav-it grabbed Goliath's own sword and chopped the giant's head off."

Again Tseren-ax thumped the table, and Altai screamed.

"When the Philistines saw that this shepherd boy had killed their champion, panic gripped them. They flung their hands in the air and ran to the hills."

"Then Dav-it became king?" asked Altai.

Tseren-ax picked up his pipe, lit it, and took a long draw. "No, not then. Dav-it had more battles to fight, more growing up to do before he was ready to be king."

Altanbaatar tapped his fingers on the table. "It's a good story," he said, wondering what he'd been expecting. "But it's no different than our own stories about giants and heroes."

Monkho nodded. Were they both thinking the same? Had he—had they—pinned their hopes on a myth? Was Bat right?

Altanbaatar looked at Bat and felt his own stomach tighten. What were they doing here? Why had he brought his family? Bat returned a thin smile. Was science the answer? "No," a voice protested in his head.

The horses tied to the hitching post outside neighed with restlessness.

Altanbaatar took a breath, reached for his bowl, and sipped his tea. It was cold. "What makes you think this book could be true?"

"I never said it was true. But you are asking questions, and this book might help you," said Tseren-ax, caressing his pipe. "Read the stories about Dav-it. Read his songs."

"That man was a songwriter too?"

"Oh yes," said Tseren-ax, exhaling a slow stream of smoke. "His songs are deep and searching, honest and…" Tseren-ax picked up the book abruptly. His hands shook as he offered the volume to Altanbaatar. "Take it."

"I couldn't," Altanbaatar whispered.

"Why not?" The old man's eyes beaded with tears.

"It's too valuable. And besides, it's been in your family for so long."

Nina stirred the fire. "Then it's time someone else discovered its secrets."

Altanbaatar glanced at Monkho beside him. Should he take it? She nodded. He extended his hands, and Tseren-ax placed it upon Altanbaatar's outstretched palms. "May the words contained in this book answer your heart's questions."

The heavy volume was stained and faded. Turning the pages, he caught the sweet, woody scent of age.

Rubbing his bulging knuckles, Tseren-ax said, "We have no children. No one who might be interested in a foreign religious book. But, you my friend, I think you will read it, and perhaps uncover its mysteries."

"Do you think that book contains *the* truth?" Monkho asked.

"I think there's truth in it."

"I thought you didn't believe in the foreign god," said Altai.

"Oh, my young friend, I'm too old to change my ways, too old to leave the stories that have formed me. I read about Dav-it and others in that book, and I see that they knew their god. Dav-it lived to follow god. Many times he failed and did wrong, but every time he returned to his god wanting to grow and change."

Altanbaatar bit the inside of his cheek. "How could he want more if he already knew god?"

"Because that book's in two parts." Tseren-ax grinned as though he held a secret. "And Dav-it wanted his god to do something for him that wasn't possible until the second half of that book." He tapped his pipe on the side of the table, letting the ash fall to the floor. He added more tobacco, sucked, and held a fresh match over the pipe's chamber. Once the pipe was burning, the old storyteller looked Altanbaatar in the eye. "Dav-it asked his god to make him *clean on the inside*, and that," he said, lowering his voice, "reminds me of you."

Altanbaatar gasped. *Clean on the inside*. The words pounded in his head. Tseren-ax understood; he had seen into Altanbaatar's soul. Perhaps the old storyteller felt the same.

Perhaps he too recognised the futility of the endless prayers and rituals, their merit-making efforts and the interminable pressure to keep the spirits happy. Perhaps, Tseren-ax knew that no ritual could ever remove the hopelessness that lurked at the bottom of a man's heart. Altanbaatar stroked the book. Maybe it would give him the answers after all.

"We ought to be going," said Monkho, getting to her feet. "Bat, pass me my hat."

Bat reached for her hat, put his own on his head and moved to the door.

"Do we have to go?" asked Altai.

"We do," said Monkho. "Thank you for your hospitality and for this special gift."

By the time Altanbaatar grabbed his boots and pulled them on, Bat was already outside and heading to his horse. He sighed, unsure how to guide his son forward.

Leave him to me.

"What did you say?"

"Nothing! We're just waiting for you," said Monkho.

Someone had spoken, he was sure of it. Altanbaatar looked at Tseren-ax and Nina. They smiled, patiently waiting to bid them goodbye. Was he losing his mind? He shook their hands. "Thank you again," he said, stowing the volume in the front opening of his deel. The book's heaviness felt mysteriously soothing against his chest. He patted it. "I will find the truth."

"I know you will," replied Tseren-ax.

Chapter 18

Bat followed the river home. Beneath the ice, rivulets trickled. His bay mare, sensing his mood, walked slowly, her heavy hooves falling flat in the snow. The others followed in silence. Tseren-ax had given his father that religious book. Why was his father trailing after a foreign religion? Bat rubbed his mare's mane; her winter coat was coarse and thick, protecting her from the worst of the cold. As the warmer weather came, she'd soon start shedding her coat.

Bat rocked in his saddle. What was he to do? His father wasn't listening to him. If only Bat could explain more clearly, get him to understand that learning was the key to understanding truth. But it seemed impossible.

Bat turned away from the river and squeezed his horse's sides. She quickened her pace to a trot. Bat squeezed harder, and she began to run. The sun was warm, but the cold air stole the breath from his lungs.

Ahead of him a thin plume of silver smoke rose, twisting and curling like ghosts in the breeze. He shuddered. Ghosts! They weren't real. "Oh grandfather," he whispered, longing for comfort. "I wish you were here."

There were two new horses tied to the hitching post when he reached the gers.

"Visitors," his mother shouted from behind. "I knew someone would arrive," she rasped, dismounting.

"It'll be fine," said his father, ensuring that their horses were securely tethered. "Naraa or Solyomaa will be entertaining them."

Bat's mother shook her shoulders. "I should have been here—this could bring us bad luck."

"That's enough of that," said his father as Altai dropped to the ground and raced to the door.

Bat entered last to see two of his cousins, Hurlin and Moujic, seated at the table chewing slices of roasted meat. Hurlin and Moujic rarely passed this way, except at New Year when the brothers travelled north to visit older members of their family.

Beside Hurlin sat a young man Bat didn't recognise, although he looked similar in age to himself. Bat thought the boy flinched as they came closer. Naraa, on the other hand, was serving their guests with a bright smile plastered on her face that the sun would have been hard-pressed to beat. Lhxaa too appeared happy. He sat on the other side of the unknown young man with his mouth set in a lop-sided grin.

Naraa placed her hands on the young man's shoulders and paused. With a brief cough she said, "I'd like to introduce you to my son, Dash."

"What?" Bat father's eyebrows rose a notch or two.

And his mother let out a great shriek. "Come here! Come here, my child!"

Dash cleared his throat and walked towards his grandmother who, by comparison with him, was a rounded barrel. Dash bowed his head to let her cover him with kisses. Bat's father's open mouth quickly assumed a broad smile as he joined his wife and started patting and rubbing the boy's back. Naraa stood by her son, her lashes heavy with tears. Her nose was beginning to turn red as the tears flowed. Lhxaa moved to his wife's side and quietly slipped his hand into hers.

Altai, meanwhile, was hopping and whooping. "You have a son? I have a new nephew—a nephew who is older than me."

And Bat, running his fingers through his clipped hair, wasn't quite sure what to do.

"How did you find him?" his father asked.

Naraa patted Lhxaa's hand. "My husband found Dash. He found the family, and he's been meeting with Dash for the past few weeks to arrange this visit."

"Ah," Bat's father replied, putting his finger to his nose. "So that's why you kept disappearing."

Lhxaa nodded.

"When did you find out about Lhxaa's plan?" Altai asked Naraa.

"This morning when they arrived on Lhxaa's bike."

"Were you shocked?"

"My heart nearly stopped, Altai. But I am so happy."

"I'm amazed you were able to keep it quiet, Lhxaa."

With a mischievous grin, Lhxaa winked. "Well, there was one other person who knew my plan," he said, pointing to Monkho.

"Never!" Bat's father said, placing his hands on his hips. "My wife could never hold a secret."

"She can, and she did."

"When it's important," Monkho said, "I can." Her eyes were bright, and Bat thought that she'd soon be sobbing too. "Anyway, there'll be plenty of time to talk later; now we need to serve our guests. Pass me your bowls," she said, holding her hands towards the two nephews who stuttered and stammered their apologies. "Nonsense! Nonsense!" Bat's mother protested as Moujic and Hurlin tried to leave. "You must stay and have some fresh tea and eat with us as we celebrate the arrival of my grandson."

The two cousins looked from one to the other. With a nod, they passed their bowls to their aunt, who filled them with tea, while Bat's father gathered his new blue silk cloth. "Our New Year has just become a time of joy." Extending his arms, he added, "I think we should greet our visitors. Amar bain uu? Peaceful, are you?"

"Amar bain uu?" they replied, placing their arms beneath Altanbaatar's extended ones and kissing his cheeks.

The two boys returned to their seats, and Lhxaa passed them more meat, which they ate happily. Bat shook hands with Dash, and the two shifted awkwardly. He looked a little like Naraa, thought Bat, although his long, overhanging fringe made it difficult to be sure. Naraa dabbed her eyes with a square of white cloth. Lhxaa had already disappeared outside while Bat chatted with the cousins. Bat filled a small plate with salad and, listening to them talk of their cattle's fatness, pushed cubes of potato around his plate.

Placing the wok above the flames, his mother raked over the fire. "Dash, fill the wok with water."

Dash rose, collected water from the butt beside the door, and filled the wok.

"Bring me a tray of buuz from under the bed," she said, settling herself on an orange stool next to the fire.

Dash retrieved a tray of buuz and held it steady as his grandmother filled another trivet with dumpling. His mother was enjoying directing Dash.

"Altai, refill the potato salad bowl," his mother said.

Giggling, Altai heaped more potato salad into the bowl. The buuz hummed merrily, filling the ger with fragrant meatiness. And Altai, completely enamoured with her new nephew, insisted on calling him her younger brother, even though he wasn't.

Those who came to pay their respects to Bat's grieving family found themselves greeted with peace and caught up in the happy reunion between Naraa, Dash, and their family. Seeing the joy in them all, their visitors quickly approved of Altanbaatar's decision to celebrate this New Year. News of Dash's arrival raced around their neighbours like a wildcat chasing its prey.

"So often death opens a door to new relationships," one of their neighbours said.

Bat stiffened; he wasn't sure about that but he couldn't deny the lightness that had returned to the family.

From morning until evening, their ger buzzed with activity as buuz were steamed, bowls of tea drunk, and roast mutton devoured. His Altanbaatar, Zorigo, and Lhxaa had greeted every visitor, ensuring that they were comfortable and that each one left with a small gift. Amid the busyness, Monkho had managed to introduce each person to Dash and explain how this was an extra special *new* beginning for the family.

Several times Bat overheard Naraa telling their mother that Dash would return to his family after the celebrations. Naraa's remarks were met with a, "That's absurd! He's with his real family now."

Most visitors came to their parents' ger, although a few visited Zorigo and Solyomaa's home. The buuz they'd prepared just a few days earlier were all quickly consumed. Any leftovers were happily gobbled up by the dogs, who lay with full stomachs, powerless to raise a bark to any passing stranger.

Taking his share of the jobs, Dash quickly became absorbed into the family. Bat liked Dash. They hadn't talked much; there hadn't been time. Bat had wondered whether his nephew felt overwhelmed, especially since his mother insisted on parading him before every visitor. But Dash took it all with a good heart, bending his tall, slim frame to greet all those who came through their door. Behind the long fringe, Bat noticed a cheeky grin. In time he and Dash could become good friends.

Bat's arms and back ached. He'd cut, sawn, and carried countless blocks of ice from the river to their gers where they'd melted them to provide the endless litres of water needed to wash all the dishes and keep their gers clean. Bat had muscles growing in places he never knew existed. At the end of each day he collapsed on his bed, content in weariness, happy that there was no time to think about anything other than serving their guests.

Today, the last day of their two-week holiday, just four distant neighbours had visited them. As the light faded, their visitors started homeward. For the first time in more than ten days, the family was alone.

"Solyomaa, Naraa," Monkho said as they washed and dried up the last of the bowls and spoons. "Bring any food you have to our table, and we'll eat together."

Bat's sister and sister-in-law nodded and headed to their gers.

"We'll go ensure the animals are ready for the night," said Lhxaa as he and Zorigo pulled on their boots.

"Bat, Altai...Are your school bags ready?"

Altai wrinkled her nose.

"Then get them packed."

Bat slipped quietly out. The sky was already greying as he ran to his ger at the end of the row. The door creaked with stiffness. He shivered; his fire was dead in the hearth. Finding a candle and match, he lit the thin wick, and the flame immediately cracked the gloom, spreading cheer around his tent. He pulled his cloth bag from the avdar and stuffed it with clothes and the new exercise books that had been gifts from his family. Drawing the strings together, he knotted the bag shut, extinguished the candle, and returned to his parents' ger.

Soft candlelight spilled onto the low food-laden table. Slices of meat stacked on plates sat next to salads, and the tower of oil-less cakes was decorated with blobs of cream, cheese, and sugar lumps. His mother's large blue and white china pot was filled with the last of their airag, and a bowl brimmed with Russian sweets. There was no strong alcohol at this meal. His father had toasted their New Year's guests with vodka; although having no desire to encourage drunkenness, he reluctantly refilled his guests' glasses. Bat knew his father never worried whether his guests thought him stingy or not; he'd rather they left sober than drunk.

"A man loses his dignity when he's drunk," his father said.

Zorigo and Lhxaa both liked a glass of vodka or two, but generally amongst the family, his father never served anything stronger than airag.

"I've seen too many lives broken by enslavement to alcohol," he said.

Bat counted thirteen of them in the ger. His father and mother sat at the table alongside Altai and Zorigo, while Solyomaa sat on the bed on the right side. Her two boys, Erdene-huu and Gamba, sat on the floor playing knuckle bones with Dash. Amidst loud shouts, the two young boys were trying to cheat their way to victory, but Dash was already skilfully beating them.

Beside Altai on the left-hand side of the ger, Naraa, Lhxaa, and their two girls, Zyaa and Zola, sat on the bed. Zyaa, the oldest and the bossiest, was carefully plaiting Zola's long hair. Both sisters' mouths moved in rhythm as they chewed gum that someone had given them. Bat rubbed his jaw, remembering the rubbery texture of the gum he'd once had at school.

"Here," said Solyomaa, handing him an empty bowl.

He took it, not sure he could eat another morsel, although he slid a slice of mutton into his bowl.

His father held his unfilled bowl in his hand. "Altai! Pass me *The Red Book*."

Altai groaned but fetched the book from its new home on the top of the cupboard beside the bowls and plates anyway. His mother had declared it the only high place of honour in their ger.

His father opened it, and Bat clenched his fists. Twice since they'd returned from Tseren-ax's ger, his father had read from *The Red Book*, and twice Bat had felt a nub of anger rise in his heart.

"Bring the candles closer," his mother said.

Solyomaa and Lhxaa placed three candles near Altanbaatar. Bat had conceded that it was plausible that some of *The Red Book* could be true. Perhaps a higher being had made the universe and planets. But the rest, well, it sounded a lot like a Mongolian legend.

"…was more cunning than every other creature," his father was already reading. "The snake came to the woman and asked, 'Did God really say that you could not eat the fruit from that tree?'"

It's just a fairy story. Bat pushed his back further into the ger wall. The lattice framework hidden behind the felt and the curtain dug into his back.

"...discarding the commandment God gave them not to eat of the fruit of the tree of knowledge of good and evil. The man and the woman took and ate. As soon as the fruit entered their bodies, their eyes were opened, and they saw that they were naked."

"Folklore, just foolish folklore," Bat whispered.

"...In the cool of the day, their God walked in the garden. When the man and woman heard him, they hid themselves. God asked them, 'Did you eat of the forbidden fruit?' The man said, 'The woman gave me the fruit.' Their God cursed them and put them out of the garden where they lived..."

"Was the garden the only place where their god was?" Altai asked with a frown.

"I am not sure," her father replied. "But it was the place where the man and woman walked with their god."

"So, they could no longer be close to him?"

"No! Their wrongdoing put a wall between them and god that broke the intimacy of their friendship with him."

"The man and the woman must have felt bad on the inside," said Altai, massaging her stomach.

"What makes you say that?" asked Bat, gripping the metal bedframe.

"Because they hid themselves when they heard god walking in the garden."

"They did. Every one of us knows what it feels like to cover up our wrong. We know the shame of disobedience."

Bat's mother ran her finger along the edge of her lower lip while the family waited for Altanbaatar to continue. Altanbaatar tapped his finger on the book's hard cover.

"After the man and woman ate the fruit and felt the shame of their wrongdoing, their children and children's children and all mankind were born carrying that same sense of shame, knowing that none of their efforts would ever enable them to properly overcome the barrier that stands between them and god."

A flush of heat rushed through Bat's body. "Barrier that stands between them and god." The words shot from Bat's mouth like an arrow from its bow. "It's just a legend."

Altai drew closer to her mother, and Bat saw Naraa place her hand on Lhxaa's knee.

"Perhaps it is, Bat," said Altanbaatar evenly. "But it's the first book I've read that attempts to explain where the shame that lurks in my being comes from."

"What because someone in a story thousands of years ago disobeyed an order from their god?"

"Yes," his father said. "Because the man's and woman's disobedience separated them from god, like our wrongs separate us from one another."

"Too simplistic. It is not logical, not rational, not plausible." Bat struggled to remember the things that he and Buyeraa bagsh had spoken about.

"Why?" his father was asking.

"Because gaining knowledge and learning about the science that explains the world will enable us to live rightly."

"Bat, you speak of gaining knowledge, whereas I speak of something that lies at the heart of man."

Bat's fist crashed down on the table. "You live in a hidden world, lost from true development while the rest of the world follows science and logic."

"But what about the presence of god?" his father asked.

"There is no god." Bat's heart pounded in his ears.

Altai snuggled closer to her mother. Was that a smile on Zorigo's lips? What did he know? He was just an uneducated herder who could barely read. They were smiling at him—all of them. They didn't understand. Buyeraa bagsh had told him that Mongolia was changing, and he was beginning to see it. Buyeraa had told him to find his place, and he was going to do that. But one thing was clear: it was not here with his family.

He left his family in the ger, pulling his deel closer as the night's blackness enclosed him, soothing his soul and hiding his flaws. He forced himself to breath slowly. They were fools; simple countryside people resisting truth, persisting in their world of make-believe spirits and ghosts. But they didn't know what he knew—they weren't getting an education and changing.

The ger door scraped softly against the shallow step. His mother came and stood beside him.

"No stars tonight?" she said, linking her arm in his.

"No," he replied.

Hearing them, the horses nickered softly, and the camels shifted in their corral.

"We'll have two new camels soon, and there'll be the lambs and kids to care for too."

She gripped his arm, pulling him down as she leant her weight on him. Once she'd towered above him, but now, he was a good twenty centimetres taller than she was.

"Spring is always busy and caring for those camels is the trickiest of all…Never know whether a mother will reject a calf or not. It takes a wise herder to ensure that a calf survives."

Bat nodded, remembering the times he had watched his father and grandfather gently coax a mother into accepting her calf.

"Your grandfather used to play those haunting melodies on his horse-head fiddle that touched the mother's heart, but it was only as she wept that she'd allow her calf to feed."

His chin trembled, and the tears slid down his face. "I can't stay," he said.

"I know. You'll return to school and then go onto the city. We understand. But don't leave us in anger because raw anger inevitably turns to bitterness." She patted his arm. "And left to grow, it becomes a fire that will capture your soul."

Bat kicked an imaginary stone.

"The soft eats the hard as right defeats wrong," she said.

For once, he agreed with her. Right would…eventually defeat his father's wrong.

Part 3

Ulaanbaatar
31st May 1995

Chapter 19

It must have been after eleven when Bat heard the clunk of the Russian key turning in the lock. He switched the bedside lamp on and sat up. Restless since ten o'clock, he'd tossed and turned, trying to work out why his wife was so late coming home. Now he would find out. Amaraa closed the front door quietly and came into the bedroom.

"The university's head of literature has asked me to judge the Children's Day poetry competition," she said, her face flushed with smiles.

"Good evening," he said curtly, wondering how Amaraa could still look as fresh and neat as she had this morning. They'd been together for more than six years, and, if it was possible, she was more beautiful than the twenty-year-old girl he'd first fallen for at college. "Have you forgotten we promised to take the children to the Children's Park tomorrow?"

Amaraa waved her hand in that dismissive way she had. "You can take them."

"I can," Bat replied, feeling the back of his neck prickle with heat. "But we were going to go as a family."

She twisted her lips and dipped her head. "Bat. This is important. Influential people will attend the competition, people who will notice me. It will be good for my career."

"What about what's good for our family?" The words shot from his mouth. There he was again, shooting her down when all she wanted him to do was share her excitement. Why couldn't he rejoice with her? After all, it was partly her strength and drive that had drawn him to her in the first place. He had admired her ambition, been energised by it, but now all it did was stir his anger.

"Promotion will give me a better salary, and that will benefit our family."

"Our children have enough. They need you."

"You've always resented my career."

"I have not." He took a breath, trying to rein in his annoyance as he watched the pleasure drain from her eyes. "I do not. But our children need their mother here too."

"You can't control me," Amaraa snapped, walking to the bathroom.

Bat thumped his leg. He'd hurt her, but he could not take the words back. He could not apologise.

A few minutes later, she returned wearing her long silk nightgown. She sat at her dressing table, uncoiled her hair, and started brushing it with sharp, short strokes. Bat waited, hoping against hope that she would change her mind and accompany them to the Children's Park. But when she turned her face to him, he saw that her lips were as thin as a pencil.

"I am no countryside woman to conform to your infernal nagging."

Bat smiled. It was evident Amaraa knew nothing of countryside women, as none he'd ever met would let themselves be battered by a man's nagging.

She pulled her hair back into a ponytail, tied it with a thin strand of scarlet ribbon and proceeded to smooth moisturiser over her face and neck. The thick white cream looked nearly as cold as the coldness between them. Removing her slippers, she slid into bed beside him, arranged the covers over her body, turned off the bedside light, and lay down.

The light was already streaming through the thin green drapes when he woke. In sleep, Amaraa looked as innocent as a child. He shook her shoulder, and she opened her eyes lazily.

"Will you come to the Children's Park with us?" he asked.

"I made no promises," she said, climbing out of bed and making her way to the bathroom. She closed the door gently, and he heard the water running. Pulling on his dressing gown he shivered and walked to the window and drew back the drapes. How had they grown so far apart?

The grey sky was bursting with menacing clouds that hovered above the hills surrounding Ulaanbaatar. Once, Amaraa had made his heart sing. Like the wind beneath the steppe eagle's wings, she'd encouraged him to soar, encouraged him to achieve his goals. He'd followed her and achieved success, but it was not enough.

Bat licked the acid bitterness from his lips. It was Children's Day, and he was going to be cheerful. He would take the children to the park and make the best of it. The children would be disappointed that their mother was not accompanying them, although they probably wouldn't be surprised. He punched the window frame causing the panes to shudder. How many times had Amaraa broken a promise to him, or more importantly, to the children? Too many times to number. Her drattcd career: it always came first.

He'd dressed in casual slacks and an open shirt by the time Amaraa returned to the bedroom wearing a pale green suit he'd never seen before. The suit fitted her petite figure perfectly, touching her body and accentuating its every curve. For a second the air caught in Bat's throat; she was bewitchingly beautiful. She combed her black hair into a smooth chignon that shone and rubbed scented cream into her hands. Her freshly polished nails were the same shade of red as her lipstick.

"I made no promises," she repeated quietly. "Do you have a cigarette?" she asked, walking from the hall to the bedroom.

Bat lifted his eyebrows. "I thought you said smoking was a filthy habit."

Picking up her handbag, she stood waiting for his approval. Bat kept his mouth firmly shut. She would receive no compliments from him. Amaraa shrugged her shoulders, put on her black patent leather shoes, and left the room. Bat returned to the window. Moments later, he heard the thud of the apartment's door as his wife let herself out.

"Where's Eej-ee gone?"

Bat turned to see Garna, their six-year-old daughter, fresh from sleep, standing in the doorway chewing her lip.

"Your mother has to work today," he said brightly.

Garna's shoulders slumped. "She promised…"

"I know, but her work is important."

"It's always important…more important than us," she said, lowering her head.

Bat scooped Garna into his arms. "Her work is never more important than you." She wrapped her legs around his waist and clung to his neck. "Chu, chu," he whispered wishing he could banish all her unhappiness. He pulled her closer, thankful that no barriers ever stood between him and his love for their children. In fact, Garna's birth had opened a new book within him, a book filled with unfamiliar language. Though he was inexperienced in its grammar and syntax, he'd found that it quickly gave expression to the love that filled his father's heart.

How had they managed to create something so remarkable? Garna was the two of them combined— Amaraa's beautiful face with his smile. And yet she was fully herself, inquisitive but, to her mother's dismay, not the least bit studious.

"You're getting heavy," he said releasing her and letting her stand. "Go and get washed and dressed."

She stood unmoved. "I don't want to."

He placed his hand on her head and propelled her

towards the bathroom. "I need to get Jargal up so that we can go to the park."

Garna let out a scream of delight and skipped into the bathroom with a carefreeness that reminded him of his younger sister, Altai. Crossing to his son's room, Bat felt a stab of pain pierced his stomach. How was Altai? He'd attended her wedding four years ago, but since then he hadn't visited the countryside. Apart from his father's monthly phone calls from the Erdene Mandal post office, Bat hardly kept in contact with his family.

Jargal's door was ajar, and his bedside light still on. Fearful of the dark, their son was a little worrier, a fact his mother deemed unreasonable. Jargal lay sprawled on top of his bed covers.

"Jargal, Jargal," Bat said, rocking the boy gently awake. His son took one of his chubby fingers, stuffed it in his mouth and curled up.

"Wake up! We're off to the Children's Park."

Jargal screwed his face up and rubbed his eyes. "Too early," he said.

Bat pulled the curtains open and the dull light filled the room. He took his son and lifted him off the bed.

Jargal squirmed. "Don't want to go."

"You don't want to go on the merry-go-rounds, see all the animals, have ice cream and sweets? Come on, we'll have the best day."

Jargal opened one eye. "Can we have ice cream?"

"Of course!" Bat laughed. "It's a holiday."

His pot-bellied son loved food and his particular favourite

was ice cream. However, Amaraa had banned such delights from their apartment. "Jargal is too fat," she'd said throwing a tub of Russia's finest into the bin.

Bat had shaken his head. "He's just a boy. By the time he's Garna's age, he'll be fine."

Promises of ice cream spurred Jargal into action, and the three of them were out of the apartment in less than half an hour. Bat took them to a local café for breakfast. It was a shabby place, with bars on the outside of the windows and lengths of tape securing the broken panes. In the corner of one window, Bat spotted a faded but easily recognisable blue and white poster. After the peaceful revolution of 1990, Russian communism had relinquished its power and the poster was everywhere. Depicting an icy window, the word "democracy" had been penned by a finger on the inside of the glass. Beyond the frosted opaqueness, stood the unmistakable image of Chinghis. Bat smiled. The Russians had tried to erase Chinghis Khan and much of Mongolian culture from public memory, but now, thankfully, people were reaffirming their national hero.

"Is it open?" asked Jargal.

"I'm sure it is," said Bat, opening the door to let them enter. The floor was sticky, and the strong smell of mutton and cabbage instantly returned Bat to the school dining room of his youth. I must try to go home this summer, he thought. They stood on the rucked lino, not sure where to sit, until a rotund grandma pushed her way through the beaded curtain that separated the kitchen from the eating area. A once-white overall covered her bulk. Balancing a flask and three bowls on her stomach, she motioned for them to sit at the table by one of the windows.

"Where are you going?" she asked, running her greasy hand through Jargal's spiky hair.

"To the Children's Park," he replied.

"You'll have a grand time, although it may rain," she said, glaring through one of the windows.

"Egch-ee! Older sister! What's on the menu today?" Bat asked.

"Huushuur."

"Then we'll have a plate of huushuur."

"It's like the countryside," said Garna taking the stopper out of the flask and carefully filling their three bowls with milk tea. She cupped her bowl in both hands and blew gently, rippling the tea's surface as any herder would have done.

Bat winked at Garna. Countless times she'd begged him for countryside stories, all of which had to include a meal around the ger table with flasks full of piping milk tea.

The waitress, although Bat thought that title a little grand for this old grandma, returned with a plate stacked high with golden fried huushuur. Jargal grabbed a pasty and bit into its thin crust. Meat juices ran down his face as he mouthed, "Yummy."

"I wish we had these at home," said Garna.

In no time at all they'd demolished the plateful, and Bat was opening his wallet to pay the bill. As if by magic, the grandma appeared at their table. "Put your wallet away," she said. "It's Children's Day."

Bat tried to force the money into her hand, but she refused to take it. "Use it to treat the children at the park," she said. Reluctantly, Bat returned the notes to his wallet.

"Thank you, thank you," said Garna, flinging her arms around the grandma's middle. "They're the best huushuur I've ever tasted."

The elderly waitress held Garna. Letting her go, she wiped a tear from her eye. "You have a beautiful daughter."

Bat nodded. "I know."

Jargal offered the grandma his hand, and they shook politely. Then Bat and the children walked out onto the street.

The pavement was already filling with people. Girls in meringue-white dresses and boys in tiny suits and ties held their parents' hands as they headed to Sukhbaatar Square. Bat was thankful Garna and Jargal needed no such finery today. They threaded their way through the crowds; Jargal hung on to his father while Garna forged ahead. They stopped at the crossroads, weaving their way through the halted traffic until they reached the pavement.

An amplified recording of children singing boomed across the Square. Jargal skipped alongside Bat, fascinated by the opportunities to have his photo taken with a stuffed bear, a red racing car or a giant plastic palm tree. At the end of the row Jargal paused. Three hairy camels tied to a post shuffled impatiently in front of a young photographer who tried to coax Jargal onto the back of one of the majestic animals. Jargal plugged his thumb into his mouth.

"Do you want your picture taken on the camels?" Bat asked.

Garna and Jargal shook their heads. "Too scary," said Garna.

Bat chuckled. He'd told them too many horror stories. "I am sure these camels will be very well-behaved."

Garna and Jargal looked at him through narrowed eyes.

Walking on ahead, Jargal caught his first sight of an ice cream seller. "Ice cream," he shouted, pointing to the small freezer standing on the square.

"You've just had breakfast," Bat said.

"But I'm hungry for ice cream."

Bat bought three tubs and handed Garna and Jargal one each. Jargal ripped the paper lid off his tub and, grabbing the tiny plastic spoon fastened to the underside of the lid, started shovelling the delicious dessert down his throat.

"Slow down," said Bat.

"It tastes so good," said Jargal between mouthfuls of creamy sweetness.

"Yes, it does." The Russians certainly know how to make ice cream, he thought Bat, thinking it one of the more pleasant legacies of the Communist era.

They crossed Peace Avenue, and Bat took them down the crowded, narrow alley that led to the Children's Park. Jargal's hand tightened in his. "It's okay," he said, pushing his son in front of him. Garna was lagging as she'd stopped to gaze at a seller's table filled with pretty stones and jewellery.

Jargal twisted and shouted loud above the noise. "Hurry up Garna, or we'll go in without you."

Garna reached them as they joined the press of families waiting to pass through the turnstile.

"It's like a sea of people," said Garna.

"Are all these people going to the Children's Park?" asked Jargal.

"They are."

"Lift me up."

"You won't see anything more," said Bat, hoisting the boy onto his shoulders.

Garna stood on tiptoes. "What can you see?"

"People!" shouted Jargal.

Shuffling forward, they moved through the turnstile, bought tickets, and joined others waiting to ride the merry-go-rounds.

Bat looked at his watch. It was three o'clock; they'd been in the park for four hours. No wonder his feet ached. They must have ridden every ride and walked the entire length of the park he thought, watching Garna and Jargal wave the flags the painted clowns had handed them. They'd eaten American-style hot dogs on a bench close to the trees on the southern edge of the park. As they ate, Bat had tried to get them to scan the woods for signs of deer hiding in the quietness, but their noisiness had ensured the deer's concealment.

On the way back to the fun fair, they'd ridden horses led by a young herder. Unaccustomed to harnesses, the horses snorted obstinately and the children begged to get down. But Bat assured them the horses were simply longing for the open steppe, which prompted Garna to ask when they could go to the countryside. As usual Bat gave her the rather vague reply of, "One day."

"One more ice cream," said Jargal, raising his chunky finger and looking his father in the eye.

Bat grinned and removed his wallet from his pocket. "And then home."

Garna's eyes widened. "Just one more ride."

"Aren't you tired?"

"No! No!" they shouted.

Finishing their ice creams, they grabbed his hands and pulled him to his feet. His knees ached as they dragged him back to the merry-go-round. The ride was stopping, and children were getting off. Garna and Jargal raced to bag themselves a horse each. Bat sat on a thin metal bench close by. Loving every moment of this day they'd never once mentioned their mother or grieved her absence, but Bat wished she'd been here with them enjoying the simplicity of being together as they used to do.

The ride was filling up and the operator told everyone to hold on tight. Jargal, his stocky legs not yet reaching the stirrups, clasped his hands around the horse's head. They were off. Shrill and tinny, the music rang louder and louder as the ride gathered speed. Jargal's mouth was moving, commanding his golden horse to go faster. Backwards and forwards Jargal pushed the wooden animal until, bravely, he raised one hand above his head in triumph.

Bat closed his eyes for a moment, remembering the rush of adrenalin he'd felt as his own bay mare raced across the steppe. Sensing the horse would soon be flying, Bat had raised his hand above his own head, and hollered in triumph. His then long hair flew like a flag in the wind. His bare feet clung to the rounded sides of his horse as she ran hot with sweat, and the sun roasted his shirtless chest. Reaching the top of a hill or a mountain pass, they surveyed the land below them; he and his mare belonged in that place.

But Bat had left, and the bay was gone. His father had told Bat that he had to shoot her when she became diseased and old

Bat cleared his throat. The music was slowing, and the ride was coming to an end. He walked to the merry-go-round.

"Again, again," Jargal cried as Bat pulled him off the ride.

"We must go home."

"Do we have to?" squealed Garna.

"We do." He took their hands and led them through the metal turnstile as they followed other families making their way home. With one hand, children clung to their parents while in their other they carried plastic cars or dolls.

Bat felt the first spots of rain on his forehead and hoped that they'd be able to get home before the deluge came. Amazingly, the dark clouds had held their water all day.

"Can we come again?" Garna asked.

"Perhaps," said Bat. The rain pitter-pattered on the pavement, and then, as if someone had fully opened a tap, it started falling in sheets. They covered their heads, but the rain hammered harder, soaking them from head to foot.

"Let's get a bus," shouted Bat above the noise of the rain.

Dodging puddles, and people, they made their way to the bus stop, where the crowd huddled silently. Garna and Jargal held on to his legs and shivered. Their clothes clung to their small bodies with translucent wetness. Bat smoothed their shiny hair, wishing he'd at least brought an umbrella or raincoats with him, but in the rush to get out the door this morning, he'd forgotten.

"I'm cold," said Jargal.

"I know," Bat replied. "A bus will be along in a moment."

Bat wriggled his toes in his black leather shoes. His socks were sodden. Amaraa would call him a countryside lad, ill-prepared for city life.

The bus approached, spraying dirty water over the waiting passengers. The battered yellow bus had seen better days. It slowed, and the crowd, en-masse, started walking even with the doors until the driver opened them, and they all scrambled aboard. Jargal squealed, and Bat tried to hoist him above the crush, but he couldn't. Grandparents sat on the seats with little ones on their laps while the rest, standing cheek-by-jowl, steamed in the stifling humidity.

"Not far now," said Bat.

"My trousers are sticking to me and I can't stop my teeth from jumping up and down," Jargal said.

"At least we're not in the rain," replied Bat, pulling his children close.

Ducking and bobbing between the passengers, he tried to see through the misty windows. They were just approaching school number five. "Ours is the next stop." He took the children by the hands and pushed his way to the door. "Just a short walk and we'll be home," he said, pulling them off the bus.

They stood on the pavement for a moment. The sky was brightening, and the rain would soon pass. Foaming brown water, pooled at the edges of the road as it tried to escape down the drains.

Garna tugged his hand. "Not far now," she said.

Bat smiled. Garna sounded like a grown-up. "No, we're nearly home."

Turning at the corner, they passed the statue of Lenin; whose darkened features seemed sharper in the wetness. Their feet squelched on the flooded pavement, and the swaying trees showered them with beads of rain.

Bat shivered. "When we get home, you two get those wet clothes off and jump in a hot bath while I steam some buuz."

Forgetting his jumping teeth, Jargal squealed with delight. "Oh, my favourite," he said, studying his father's face. "Do you think there's any more ice cream?"

Chapter 20

Amaraa was not at home when they arrived, and for that Bat was grateful; she'd only have scolded him for the mess. Bat collected their discarded clothes from the bathroom floor and put them in the washing basket, hoping that Basan-Jav would wash them before Amaraa noticed. Although it was more likely that the children would tell his wife what had happened.

Garna and Jargal quickly demolished a mountain of buuz and then headed to the lounge while Bat washed the dishes. A few minutes later, he entered to find them curled up, asleep on the sofa. Bat picked up Jargal and carried him to his bed. Pulling the covers over his son's podgy body, he squeezed his hand, but Jargal was already fast asleep. Bat turned Jargal's bedside lamp on and left.

Garna stirred as he lifted her from the sofa. "It was the best of days," she muttered, snuggling into his chest. Her freshly washed hair tickled his chin. He tucked her into bed, musing on the strangeness he still felt at the fact that his children slept in their own rooms. If he'd had his way, they'd have slept together in one room.

Leaving their bedroom doors ajar, Bat walked to the kitchen. The clock above the table read just passed seven. He opened the Russian fridge and took a cold beer from the door. Amaraa wasn't keen on his beer drinking, but an American had introduced Bat to the habit, and it had become a ritual for him at the end of each day.

Ryan, the American, had been an English teacher at Bat's college. A bizarre meeting in the college corridor had led to an unexpected friendship with this Californian and his family. Neither of them knew the other's language well, but Ryan had an openness that kept drawing Bat to his apartment. There was a contentment in Ryan's and his wife's company that reminded Bat of his countryside home. When they left three years ago, Ryan had handed him an English book as he'd tried to explain something about the god he believed in.

Bat missed Ryan. He sat in the lounge looking at the big windows and high ceiling. They were on the third floor of the five-storey building which, according to Amaraa, was the best. "Not too hot in the summer," she said. "And not too cold in the winter." Bat had no idea what was best; he'd simply signed the lease agreement. Everything else, including the choice of décor and furniture, was Amaraa's decision: carpet, couch, and chairs, all had to match apparently.

But to Bat, the orderliness and the pale green walls were as sterile as a hospital ward. Even with two children in the house, there was hardly anything was out of place, although that was largely due to Basan-Jav, who came each morning after the family left. Bat told Amaraa they didn't need a cleaner but Amaraa had disagreed, and, as always, he'd conceded.

The chilled beer was full of crisp sweetness that reminded him of summer grass drying under the hot sun. He placed the bottle carefully on the glass-topped table and sat back on the couch.

Frozen winter covers mountains with snow and ice,
Sparkling, sparkling with crystal brightness.
Summer's sun opens flowers and leaves to blossom.
Birds from afar come to sing their songs in this place.
This is the country of my birth: beautiful Mongolia.

Natsagdorj's poem described this land eloquently. The poet's photo was amongst those of Mongolian heroes that had hung high on the wall in Bat's old school library. In his last school year, Bat had spent many hours reading his way through the library's meagre collection. In moments of boredom, he'd studied the faces of those writers and poets. Natsagdorj was, naturally, a dashing young man. It was a tragedy he died at such a young age, thought Bat, wondering what further treasures a longer life might have enabled the writer to give his country. People spoke of him as the founding father of modern Mongolian literature, and his work was certainly well-loved.

That last year at school was a year of decision for Bat. His old teacher Buyeraa, who, according to Bat's father, had recently become the principal of the Erdene Mandal school, had pushed Bat forward. Nurturing Bat's ambition, Buyeraa bagsh had helped Bat learn how to think and encouraged him to go to college. He'd also challenged Bat to be a part of the changes that would shortly overtake Mongolia. And Bat had.

In 1989, his final year of college, Bat heard a young man called Zorig speak. Bat had then been newly married with a chubby toddler, and things between him and Amaraa had been sweet.

As a recent graduate of Moscow's State University, Zorig was expected to teach scientific socialism at the State University. However, he'd come home believing it was time to see Mongolia transformed from a nation ruled by a single party to a democracy.

Zorig and a handful of young intellectuals spoke with a passion that seized Bat's imagination, causing him, despite Amaraa's protests, to join the herders, miners, and academics demonstrating each Sunday in Sukhbaatar Square. From their red-fronted edifice, the communist leaders observed the protests with growing alarm. And on the ninth of March 1990, the government quietly stepped down.

Victory had been announced right there in the Square, and Bat was jubilant. Amaraa was less so, warning him that there would be trouble. But Bat couldn't see it; all he saw was that the oppressors and their system had been removed and that the way was clear for a new beginning, for freedom of speech and for economic and civil liberties. Full of zeal, Bat had been ill-prepared for the war of words and rhetoric that followed. Allegations of corruption quickly emerged as the newly elected government sought to move forward.

Amaraa begged Bat to walk away from his political connections, but Bat refused. Until last year, he was all for throwing over his career in education to go into politics. But then an unthinkable atrocity had occurred that broke Bat. Zorig, the golden swallow of democracy, as the people called him, was murdered in his own home. From that moment, Bat walked away from politics. Amaraa had tried to comfort him, but he could not receive her comfort.

He drained his glass and wiped his mouth with the back of his hand. Since Zorig's death, he'd determined to enjoy the good things in his life: his children, his job, and his wife.

Amaraa was beautiful, talented and, to the countryside boy he once was, sophisticated. He'd first caught sight of her walking through the lobby of the university when he was registering for a dormitory room in his second year. Dressed in jeans and a tight-fitting T-shirt that accentuated her curves, she'd caught his eye, and his gaze had followed her up the lobby's wide marble staircase. Reaching the top, she'd turned and coyly winked, and his heart had somersaulted.

A couple of days later, she'd sat next to him at lunch, and they started talking. Amaraa's questions were endless— she'd never met a herder before. She eagerly corrected his grammar and accent, assuring him that she'd help him fit in.

They quickly became lovers. She wanted to experience the roughness of the countryside, and he was more than happy to gratify her desire. It had been intense and totally intoxicating. He gazed at the apartment's picture-less walls, trying to recall the last time he'd looked at her as though she were amazing.

Two months after they met, Amaraa had announced that she was pregnant. Her parents were horrified, calling Bat every disgusting name under the sun but determined that no daughter of theirs would have a termination. They insisted that he marry Amaraa, which, of course, Bat was thrilled to do.

However, the wedding had been a disaster. His parents came from the countryside. Dressed in their best deels, they looked like a pair of gypsies beside Amaraa's parents. Amaraa's mother, smoothing her perfectly coiffured hair, wrinkled her nose at his mother, who had worn every piece of jewellery she possessed and had let her own grey hair hang loose. Amaraa's father shook hands with his own father, but afterwards Bat saw her father wiping his hands on his handkerchief. But worse than all that was the smell. Mutton fat and wood-smoke clung to his parents like gum to a shoe. These were the smells of countryside life, but in the city, in that posh hotel, they were completely incongruous.

Six months later, Garna was born. Bat had thought her a miracle with her minute fingers and toes, and he cooed over his daughter endlessly. Amaraa, it turned out, was less maternal. She hated Garna's grizzling and the way she craved milk. Within a month, Amaraa had passed the child to her recently retired mother and returned to college.

Finishing their degrees, Amaraa and Bat both graduated top of their classes. With his new father-in-law's influence, Bat got a job teaching in the history department of the university. There'd been muttering amongst the teachers, but Bat had ignored them, only to offend the teachers further by receiving a series of rapid promotions. He'd worked hard, he reasoned; he deserved it. Just recently the principal had told him that he would likely make head of the social history department by the end of the year. At nearly twenty-seven, he was doing well, grasping his dreams, and pursuing them to their conclusion.

His beer finished, Bat threw the bottle in the bin and went to the bedroom. The rain pattered against the window, and he imagined the flooded road below. In the darkness, he undressed and climbed into bed. He was tired and longed for warmth; the apartment was cool since the state-controlled heating had been off since the middle of May. No amount of heating would remove the chill in his heart. He thought of his parents. In the rain, their ger would be warm: the wood-burning stove humming as it burned, the family crowded around it, chattering, disagreeing, laughing and drinking lashings of tea.

Chapter 21

Bat shook himself awake. The telephone was ringing. Light filtered through the curtains as he pulled himself up to switch on the bedside lamp. His alarm said it was ten to six. Amaraa slept beside him, although he hadn't heard her come in last night. He headed to the hall and, picking up the phone, heard the familiar click of the long-distance connection, although it was too early to be his father calling.

"Batbold, is that you?" asked the voice on the other end.

"Err...yes."

"Saran-Toya here."

Bat's muscles tensed as he thought of the postmistress, Saran-Toya, a world away in the Erdene Mandal post office.

"Your father's sick. You must come now."

"Sick?"

"Doctor says he won't last. You must come," she repeated.

"Okay," he muttered, even though the line was already dead. Holding the receiver, Bat sank to his knees. His father couldn't be dying.

"Bat!"

Amaraa stood above him in her silk dressing gown and fluffy pink slippers. "Who's calling before six?"

"My father's sick. The doctor said he won't last."

"Are you sure?" she asked, smoothing away imaginary creases from her dressing gown. "Countryside doctors' diagnoses aren't always reliable."

"I know, but Saran-Toya said I must return."

"It's a bit inconvenient," she added softly.

Bat gritted his teeth. "I don't think Saran-Toya would ring at dawn if it wasn't urgent."

Amaraa inspected her nails and polished them against her dressing gown. "In that case, my parents will need to care for the children because I have my students' end-of-term papers to mark."

Amaraa walked to the kitchen and turned the ring on to heat water for tea. Her actions brought Bat sharply to his senses. He needed to get moving. Should he take the children with him? The question flashed into his mind, but by the time he reached Garna's room he'd dismissed it. It was better they go to Amaraa's parents.

Hearing that they were going to stay with their grandparents, the children were up and dressed in minutes. A stay with their grandparents was an unexpected treat. Jargal always returned with stories of the dinosaurs and stuffed animals he'd seen in the museums. Although Bat did wonder whether Jargal's love for his grandmother was because she kept a store of his favourite ice cream in her freezer.

They packed quickly. The children had probably forgotten something essential, but Bat wasn't worried as it was only a short walk back to get what they needed.

At seven o'clock, Bat phoned his parents-in-law. His father-in-law answered and, on hearing of Bat's father's sickness, told Bat that they'd happily take charge of the children. Bat was to drop them off on his way to the bus station.

He was just saying goodbye when the older man coughed. "I am very sorry to hear about your father. He seemed like a decent man. Be sure to pass our regards to your family."

Bat swallowed hard. It was generous of his father-in-law to make such a comment, especially since Bat knew that they'd hardly warmed to his family at Bat and Amaraa's wedding.

He returned the phone to its cradle. "We're ready, Aav-aa," Jargal said, holding a toy car in his hand. Bat quickly pulled on a jacket and collected his bag.

"Be good for your grandparents," said Amaraa, coming into the hall holding a piece of bread and jam. "When will you be back?" she asked Bat.

"I've no idea."

She offered him her cheek, and he kissed her lightly. She smelt as sweet as honey, and he had a crazy desire to carry her away. But he didn't. Instead he opened the door and marshalled the children out. "Will you explain to the principal what's happened?"

"I will," she said, "but why they couldn't bring your father to a city hospital, I don't know."

They walked down the stairs into the freshly washed morning.

"Is Countryside Granddad very sick?" asked Jargal.

"Yes, I think he is," Bat replied.

"If he saw some of my new cars, he might feel better."

Bat ruffled his son's hair.

"Can't we come with you?" asked Garna.

"Not this time, but I will take you one day soon."

They walked, dodging the puddles and muddy stream that gushed down the edge of the road. Bat dropped Garna and Jargal at their grandparents' house and hugged them hard.

"Something for the road," said his mother-in-law, handing him a small parcel of food.

Outside again, he waved a car down and asked the driver to take him to the bus station. The bus to Tsetserleg, the capital of Arhangai, the province his parents lived in, was due to leave at eight, and it was seven forty-five. The driver pushed the pedal to the floor, and the car screamed forward. Bat quietly held the door handle as the driver swung past every other vehicle on the road, leaving behind him a wake of puddled rain. They came to a screeching halt in the bus station car park, and Bat let out a long, slow breath. "How much do I owe you?"

"Save it for your family," the driver replied. Bat thanked him and ran to the waiting Tsetserleg bus.

"Any seats?" he shouted to the bus driver, who was already revving the engine.

"One, maybe two," the driver replied. "Do you have a ticket?"

Bat shook his head—he'd forgotten he needed a ticket. "There wasn't time. I've just heard that my father is very sick, and I need to go home."

"Where are you from?"

"About eighteen kilometres north west of Erdene Mandal."

"My parents herd sheep just outside Erdene Mandal."

"Really? What are their names?"

"Ariubold and Bat-Tsetseg."

"I know them. My grandfather was Namdorj."

The driver scratched his head. "So, you're Altanbaatar's son who made good in the city."

"I am."

"Sorry to hear about your dad." He motioned to the back of the bus. "There's an empty seat next to a drunk, but he'll probably sleep once we're on the road."

Thanking the driver, Bat made his way to the vacant seat, pushed his bag beneath the chair, and sat down as the bus pulled out of the crowded station into the congested Ulaanbaatar traffic.

His companion, a skinny man with blood-shot eyes, offered him a swig of vodka. Bat politely declined, and the man began chuntering. Embarrassed, Bat shifted in his seat, although no one else seemed concerned by the drunk's moans. As they climbed out of the city and headed west towards the open steppe his companion's head began to rock, and it wasn't long before he was snoring. Bat sat back. The bus was warm, and his own eyelids fluttered open and shut. He rested his face on his hand and let sleep carry him away.

With stark clarity, the lens focused. Lush and green with summer brightness, their valley was immediately familiar. Pulling hard on the bit, Bat's bay mare slowed. His legs, hanging loosely around her belly, felt her twitch as she curtailed her speed. They walked, listening to the quiet wind blow through the heat, stirring trees and bending grasses. Abruptly, Bat dug his heels into the animal's side and released her. She responded instantly. Throwing her head back and neighing with delight, she galloped hard across the flat. "Come on, girl," he whispered, "we can fly."

In the eyes of those accustomed to the steppe,
The very edge of heaven appears,
By the actions of horses galloping
Our homeland stretches before us.

Familiar words, although he couldn't recall exactly whose words they were—some poet who died in the late 1970s, Bat thought. Nevertheless, they drew him. He mare was slowing, and he turned her towards home. His grandmother would be there making buuz while his grandfather sat on the thin bench outside, letting his beads slip through his fingers.

Thud! Bat hit something bony. The dream gone, his eyes flew open. He was lying on top of the drunk. "What?" said Bat as the bus pitched and squealed.

"Blow out," his companion replied with cool soberness.

Steering into the skid, the driver braked hard until the bus came to a standstill at the edge of the embankment. No one moved. The driver stood rubbing his head. With trembling fingers, he lit a cigarette and took a long drag. "Gonna need help changing that tyre." He laughed, removing something from the tip of his tongue.

Two men stood, closely followed by another three. Together the five of them made their way to the door. A few minutes later, one returned. "Left tyre's in shreds. It'll take a while to change, so settle yourselves. I think the spirits were with us," he concluded, leaving the bus.

Deciding to stretch his legs, Bat walked past two older ladies.

"Tuesday's always been an unlucky travel day."

"Yes," replied the other. "Although my daughter tells me such beliefs are mere superstition."

"Which just goes to show how little young people know about our world."

The warm breeze touched Bat's face. Summer was here. Other passengers who disembarked before him were examining the smouldering rubber ribbons scattered across the road. Keeping his head down, Bat walked past them all, down the rocky embankment, and out towards the open steppe.

The big blue sky stretched all the way to the horizon. In the distance, the plains rose like crumpled paper to gentle slopes topped with rocky outcrops, shimmering with haze. Horses, tiny against the backdrop of this wildness, roamed free. This was an indomitable landscape, bleak and yet absurdly beautiful. It filled him with intense longing, calling to the depths of his heart.

Squinting, he spotted a lone herder on his horse driving his sheep and goats. That could have been me, he thought with a stab of painful absence.

Pencil-line dirt tracks snaked across the steppe to groups of gers. He imagined families sitting inside, drinking milk tea and talking about the day ahead. The muscles in his stomach tightened.

Why had he returned so infrequently? It had been almost two years since his last visit, and even that had been a fleeting attendance of Altai's wedding to a local herder called Dorj. His family had been kind to him, but they'd wanted him to stay longer. Why couldn't he? Why wouldn't he? As the banished memories surfaced, a single word hammered in his brain. Pride!

At eighteen, he'd been full of it. Bat winced. Oh, the arrogance of his strident judgements that left him believing he knew better than his family, that he knew better than his father! And his father had not reprimanded him; none of them had. Instead they'd let him go, and Bat had gladly gone, escaping to school and then to university, convincing himself that the distance between them existed because Bat was now a professional. Tugging and pulling at this lie, Bat had stretched it over the truth.

But not today. The lie had snapped, and the truth was exposed. He had been proud and conceited. The breath caught in his throat. It wasn't just the pride of seven, almost eight years ago that was the problem. No, there was the stubbornness and arrogance of today, he thought, remembering his inability to remove the wall that stood between himself and Amaraa. He held his hand to his mouth, suddenly aware of his weakness and aware that he had no power to fix it.

"Ooyoo! Ooyoo!"

Bat turned; the driver was waving his arms. Pocketing his thoughts, Bat ran back.

"Thought you'd decided to walk to Arhangai," said the driver, patting his back as they boarded the bus.

The rest of the journey passed uneventfully. His companion, who seemed more lucid after helping to change the wheel, informed him that these days the journey to Tsetserleg was faster as there was more paved road.

By early evening, they were nearing their destination. Weary from the day's travel, the passengers were quiet. The bus passed through the small village of Tsinker, and with his eye Bat followed the rows of brightly coloured roofs of the houses hugging the banks of the River Tamir. Crossing the river's concrete bridge, they snaked through the lush plains and beyond to the Hangai Mountains that cradled Tsetserleg in the crook of their arm. The bus bumped painfully along while passengers gripped the headrests in front of them, straining to catch their first glimpse of the town.

Bat strained forward too, conscious that a voice inside him longed to shout. "This is my province." He was surprised— the city had not severed him from his roots. As dye colours cloth, so this place was indistinguishably part of him.

"You all right?" his companion asked.

He nodded. "It's a long time since I've been home."

"You need to roll in the dirt of the land and cover yourself with the water of the Tamir to be at one with the place of your birth."

"Yes," Bat replied, remembering the feelings of oneness he'd experienced on the mountain tops or on the ledge where he and Altai had sat for hours as children, watching the hawks and kites honk and flick below him.

Tonight, Bat would stay in the town. Tomorrow, he'd find a jeep heading to Erdene Mandal. From there he hoped to get a ride the last eighteen kilometres to his parents' ger. He wanted to be there now, but countryside journeys went at their own pace.

The bus climbed, crunching through the gears as it slowed. Once through the concrete arch that marked the entrance to the town, the driver pushed the gearstick into neutral and freewheeled downhill. They passed gers and wooden homes. After the order of the city, the town looked chaotic and shabby. Passing the disused airfield, they drove through the tree-lined avenue. Cows and sheep grazed on the grass beside two new petrol stations by the edge of the road. The driver swerved to avoid a large pothole as the bus swung onto a patch of dirt that was the official bus stop.

The moment they stopped, everyone grabbed his or her luggage and made for the aisle. His companion was already pressing his way forward towards the door. Bat waited for the rush to subside before retrieving his bag and leaving. The driver was unloading boxes and bags from the belly of the bus. Bat moved through the crowd of hugging relatives and started walking towards a nearby guesthouse where he hoped to get a hot shower and a good meal. Despite the dustiness of the road dirtying his city-clean shoes, it felt good to be stretching his legs.

In less than ten minutes, he'd booked into a room, although the young receptionist dashed his hopes of a shower by telling him that the town's water supply was off.

"The water company is doing repairs, and we don't know when they'll be finished," she said with a smile.

She also informed him that he was too late to get a meal in the restaurant. Bat took his key, grateful for the snacks his mother-in-law had pressed on him that morning.

Chapter 22

Bat had succumbed to sleep the moment his head touched the pillow. Barking dogs woke him, and he lay staring at the whitewashed ceiling, aware of the absence of traffic yet fully aware of the ache in his stomach.

He headed to reception to see whether the guesthouse's water supply had returned. The same receptionist who had been on duty last night greeted him, only to tell him that the water was still off. She did offer him a flask of hot water with which to wash. Bat accepted it and returned to his room. Feeling a little fresher, he decided to head to the market. It was far too early for it to be open, but some drivers might have already gathered.

Cutting across to town, Bat shivered, wishing he'd worn his jacket. He walked briskly down the hushed streets, exchanging greetings with a man stacking trays of eggs into the back of a battered car. As expected, the market's metal doors were closed, although two Russian jeeps stood on a square of land opposite. Two men crouched on their haunches in front of jeeps.

"Sain batsgann uu—Are you well?" Bat said.

"Sain—Good," the two drivers replied.

"Where are you going?"

"Bulgan," replied the stouter of the two. "Muren," said the younger.

Bulgan was a small village forty kilometres south and not in the direction Bat wanted to go. But the town of Muren was beyond Erdene Mandal and even better, the track to Muren passed very close to the track that led straight to Bat's family ger.

Bat knelt beside them and looked the younger in the eye. "My father is very sick, and I need to get home quickly." The driver didn't blink. Bat added, "Our ger is about twelve kilometres off the track to Muren. Would you take me home?"

"I already have one passenger with two sheep," he replied.

"I'll pay extra."

The driver took a long drag on his cigarette and, crinkling his eyes against the smoke, nodded.

"What time will you leave?"

"Eleven," said the driver, offering Bat his hand. "I'm Enkay."

"Bat," said Bat, returning the handshake and stumbling to his feet. He needed to find something to eat and drink.

By eleven o'clock, the market was buzzing. The patch where the two jeeps stood had become a gathering of motorbikes, jeeps, and cars swarming with people searching for rides to the towns and villages around Tsetserleg. Between the vehicles, piles of bloody sheepskins covered the ground as crafty buyers haggled rock-bottom prices from trusting herders.

Bat found his ride. The jeep was locked, and there was no sign of the driver or his passengers. Leaning against the jeep's bonnet, Bat waited until a trader slapped his back and told him to go and sample the season's airag. Bat shook his head. He didn't want to miss his ride.

"You won't," replied the man with a broad smile. "I'll tell Enkay you were here and that you'll be back soon."

Bat threaded his way past the dented vehicles to the market's metal doors. He stopped for a moment to let his eyes adjust to the dim light, and the familiar smell of rancid dairy reached his nostrils, reminding him of the trips he and his grandfather had made to this market. At the end of each summer, they'd come to sell meat and skins in exchange for flour, oil, and cash for Bat's schooling. Those trips were an adventure, partly because Bat never knew what treasures he'd discover hiding beneath the underwear and spare tyres on the sellers' tables.

Today the tables were gone, replaced instead by a collection of metal booths, each housing a seller or two. The booths lined the outer walls, selling vegetables and meat on one side and bread and buns on the other.

Straight down the middle of the hall stood a further double row of booths, from which ladies in pink nylon overalls sold the early summer's creamy dairy that Bat loved. Each counter boasted pots brimming with fresh milk, cream, and yoghurt. Cloth bags spilled yellow curds and hard cheese onto the counter's surfaces, while in the centre of each stall stood a large pot of airag—fermented mare's milk.

Word had it that Arhangai's airag was the best. The grass's lush greenness enriched the milk, making the airag, so people said, more delicious than that of any other province. Bat didn't know whether that was true or not, but he did know that he hadn't tasted any in a long time.

He approached a group of gossiping ladies. "A bowl of airag," he said, watching one of them ladle out a bowlful. Handing it to him, she demanded two hundred turgriks.

Bat blew the grass and the specks of dirt off the surface and drank the contents down in gulps. His tongue fizzed with a sharpness that was mildly alcoholic. His grandmother had always milked the mares early in the morning. Sitting on a wooden stool, she filled her metal pail just after the foals had taken their first drink of the day.

"Two hundred turgriks," the seller repeated.

"Delicious," he said, pulling the notes from his wallet.

He looked at his watch. It was already half past eleven. Shielding his eyes, he stepped into the sun and retraced his steps to Enkay's jeep.

"Leaving shortly, 45-62 HO going to Muren," the muffled loudspeaker announced.

Bat couldn't remember the jeep's licence plate, but he quickened his pace. The driver was leaning out of his jeep, shouting for Bat to come. Bat ran. Breathless, he opened the passenger door and greeted the three sitting on the back seat. "Just tasted my first airag of the year."

"The grass is tender now, so the milk will be energising," said the old man, smiling.

Bat guessed the older man seated next to a woman of similar age were husband and wife. Dressed in thick deels, they were going to get very warm. As for the other passenger, a yellow-faced man of indistinguishable age, he remained silent.

"Are there others to come?"

"No! You're the last," said Enkay.

Bat asked the old man whether he wanted to sit in the front. He shook his head. "No. It's easier to sleep in the back."

Enkay cranked up the engine as the smell of fresh dung hit Bat's nose. Beyond the backseat, two animals bleated.

"Shut up," shouted Enkay. The sheep obeyed. The yellow-faced man snorted. "Don't mind him," added Enkay. "He's been drowning his sorrows."

It turned out that the elderly couple had been in the province capital for three weeks. Rinchin, the husband, had been ill with pneumonia, and the family had sold cattle so that he and his wife Duya could come to the hospital for treatment.

"The hospital here is better than the small one in our village," said Duya.

"I'm not sure about that," replied Rinchin. "Since the Russians left, healthcare has deteriorated."

"The departure of the Russians has brought hardships," conceded Duya.

Enkay honked his horn at a group of stationary cows. "In my opinion, we detached ourselves too quickly from communism," he said, manoeuvring past the obstinate bystanders.

"Perhaps." Bat gave Enkay a brief smile. "But surely it was better to make a clean break than to let the regime linger."

Enkay shrugged his shoulders. "I don't know. Severing links with Russia so dramatically left us all floundering. And as you observed, Rinchin-ax, without Russian funding, our healthcare has declined, leaving hospitals ill-equipped and unable to provide good medical services. And don't get me started on the escalating cost of treatments and the need to pay bribes to doctors." Enkay pushed the screeching engine into second gear.

"You're right," said Rinchin. "The transition towards democracy has been harsh. Education has suffered, and for the first time in living memory, college education is no longer free."

"There are food shortages too," admitted Duya.

"There are," said Enkay. "And the unforeseen struggles have weakened us and increased sickness."

Duya shook her head. "I'm not sure about that. There was plenty of sickness under Russian rule."

Bat nodded. "I seem to remember Orchirbat encouraged us all to tighten our belts."

"He did," said Rinchin. "He is an honourable man and a good first president."

"He is a good man," said Enkay. "But I sometimes wonder whether life under communism was better than it is today."

An uneasy silence fell on the jeep's occupants.

"Communism had its strengths, but it could not continue," said Rinchin, gently pushing a wisp of hair from his whitened cheekbones. "In the early days of his presidency, Orchirbat used to quote that old proverb. Do you remember, dear?"

"There are thousands of proverbs! Which one were you thinking of?"

"'It is better to suffer at your own hand than to live plentifully under someone else's power.'"

"He did," replied Duya with a wry smile.

Enkay sighed and relaxed his grip on the steering wheel so that the jeep nudged its own way to the top of the White Pass. "One day I guess the hardships will end."

"They will," said Rinchin. "And we will prosper again, but the road to true democracy is a long one."

Duya touched her hand to her forehead. "It is, but we have a lot to be thankful for too. Our children and grandchildren are good to us. They organised Rinchin's hospital stay and treatment."

The old man winked. "They did. And my wife stayed with me, cooked my meals, and took care of all my needs, although I was desperate to escape that building."

Duya laughed. "You're a stubborn old fool."

"Probably. But the cold plaster chained my soul to barrenness. I yearned for the closeness of my ger, to see the sky and hear my animals talk."

"You do go on."

"No," said Bat, countering Duya's remark. "I felt the same when I first went to school. The glossed walls and high ceilings made me long for the ease of felt and canvas."

"See. He understands," said Rinchin, pointing to Bat.

"How long have you been married?" Bat asked tactfully changing the subject.

"Nearly forty years." Duya smiled.

"And she's as lovely as ever."

Duya playfully hit her husband with the back of her hand.

Cresting the summit, Enkay paused. Below, the toy-sized town glistened as the noon-day sun dappled across the red, blue, and green roofs. Enkay released the brakes and, finding a rut, let the jeep steer itself down the gravelled road. Descending through twists and turns, they passed venerated trees decked in blue scarves and colourful flags. On the valley floor, the open plain of the Hangai Mountains stretched before them. Hard by, herders pushed their flocks forward to lusher pastures. The gravel road petered out, and they bumped onto the washboard track.

"What brings you to the countryside?" Duya asked Bat.

"My father's sick."

"Sorry to hear that. Has he been sick long?"

"I'm not too sure." Bat rubbed his forehead. "I just got a call from the postmistress of Erdene Mandal yesterday morning."

"That's difficult, son," said Rinchin.

Bat nodded. "It is."

"So how many children do you have?" asked Duya, moving to a happier subject.

"Two."

"Just two?" The old woman pursed her lips. "In my

day, everyone had eight or ten. Young people are leaving our ways..."

Rinchin coughed. "What are your children's names?"

"Gantsetseg and Batjargal, but we call them Garna and Jargal," said Bat.

"How old are they?" Duya asked.

"Garna is six, and Jargal is four."

"Do they like the countryside?"

In his mind's eye, Bat saw the two of them running freely across the plain. "They haven't really visited, but I'm sure they'd love it."

"Haven't visited the countryside?"

"There hasn't really been time. They have only been to the holiday camps around Ulaanbaatar with their grandparents."

"Hasn't been time," Duya repeated. "That's the problem with city people; they're always too busy to be a part of their own country."

"Tell us a little more about them." Rinchin said, holding onto the back of Bat's seat as they jolted towards the village of Ik-Tamir.

"Garna is beautiful like her mother," he said. "She loves poetry and singing and has a mouth full of questions."

"She must like school then," said Duya.

"She thinks it's okay, but she doesn't take study seriously."

"As long as she enjoys life, that's all that matters."

Bat nodded, aware that Amaraa wouldn't have shared the old woman's opinion.

"And your son?"

"Oh, Jargal, he's chubby, round-faced, and loves to eat, even though his mother would rather he ate less. He doesn't like change. But he is fascinated with trains and planes and running fast and free...He wants to fly."

The old man's eyes gleamed. "Don't all boys?"

"They do," said Bat.

"Something in us wants to soar, to be free and live beyond the limits of gravity."

Bat agreed. As they neared the village of Ik-Tamir on the banks of the Great River Tamir the impressive Taikhar Chuluu came into view.

Duya gasped. "And to think a giant hurled that great rock to earth to crush a serpent. That giant must have had enormous strength."

Enkay winked at Bat. "Do people believe in giants?"

Bat shook his head. "I don't think so."

"You can't say that," said Duya. "People believe in many things. In giants and spirits, and in the myriad of beings that live beyond our sight and affect our lives." Touching the palm of her hand to her forehead, she added, "I always pray, asking them to protect me and my family."

A pair of swifts danced before them, turning sharply and smoothly, making visible the invisible path of the wind.

Ik-Tamir appeared deserted. "What's the population of the town these days?" asked Rinchin.

"About two thousand in the town itself, but there are many more out on the steppe," replied Enkay.

"'Course, since the felt factory closed down, there's been little work for people," said Duya.

Driving into the open country, Enkay pushed an ancient cassette into its player. The chrome crackled with haunting melodies. Slumped on the back seat, the three slept.

But Bat could not. His mind, tangled with emotions, followed the changing light across the rugged contours. It was as if part of him were reawakening and becoming visible again. He was a teacher, husband, and father, but he was also a herder and a countryside boy.

The singers sang of mighty wrestlers and sacred mountains, of the sanctity of mother and the holiness of this land. The sky, an endless ribbon of blue, pervaded every area of this world. He thought of his family, living simply under its canopy, inhabiting this place through its story and song.

Once Bat had dismissed this land's stories and music as mere sentiment. He'd pursued knowledge systematically, believing that it would be the key to understanding life. It had been a simple formula. But as he began teaching history himself, he came to understand that legend and song were not so easily dismissible from logic and science. On the contrary, they inextricably intertwined people with their homes and cultures, and as his father had once said, why couldn't story and culture comfortably exist alongside science?

A string of horses galloped across the steppe. Strong and reliable, they were man's best companion, his true shadow. And as all herders knew, a man without a horse was like a bird without wings. Bat watched the horses disappear.

They crawled uphill, and once at the top, Enkay killed the engine. Using nothing more than the footbrake, he let the jeep coast to the bottom. Bat held onto the door handle as Enkay held the jeep tight to the track. They crossed small streams and sped along tree-lined valleys carpeted with vivid alpine flowers.

"It's beautiful," said Bat.

"It is," Enkay smiled.

Almost three hours after leaving Tsetserleg, Enkay stopped beside a forest of silver birch. "There's a brook close by," he said.

Rubbing their eyes, Rinchin and Duya yawned while the drunk huddled tighter into his corner. Bat helped Rinchin down from the jeep, and Duya followed, carrying a large bag over her shoulder. The trees, a cool haven from the sun, introduced them to the grasshoppers' relentless chatter. They passed tree stumps and anthills crawling with workers until they reached a narrow brook tumbling over rocks.

"This brook is fed by an underground spring," Enkay shouted. "The water is always pure."

Smooth stones stood nearby. Duya took Rinchin's arm from Bat and led her husband to a stone seat. Pungent wild garlic filled the soft, moist air. Bat and Enkay sank to their knees and scooped handfuls of water into their mouths. Bat gasped. It was icy and sweet. His grandfather had said that spring water was the purest on earth. It not only quenched a man's thirst, but it also restored a man's soul.

Duya pulled an empty bottle from her bag. Submerging it beneath the surface, she filled it and passed it to Rinchin who slowly drank the contents. "Delicious," he said. "Refreshing to my soul."

Bat laughed. "My grandfather used to say the same."

"Your grandfather was a wise man."

Bat let his hand trail along the water's silky surface. Sunlight cast pockets of golden lustre onto the brook. "He was wise. He was also at ease with this country."

Rinchin squinted and looked at Bat. "To be at ease in one's place is to have a peace of mind that sustains us through the poverty and riches of this world and takes us safely into the next."

Bat raised his shoulders and held his palms open.

"Son," Rinchin answered, "the deepest things in life are beyond reason."

Bat threw a dried twig into the brook and watched it bob gently downstream. "Perhaps they are," he said.

Twenty minutes later, they were back on the road, driving along the track and onto the open plain that would take them to Erdene Mandal. Bat's heart beat hard against his chest. *Would his father still be alive?*

Rinchin patted his shoulder. "You'll be fine, son," he said speaking to Bat's unspoken fear.

The dusty track ran on. Each time they crested an incline, Bat held his breath, imagining he'd see Erdene Mandal in the distance. But he didn't.

Enkay's ready smile had disappeared, and his fixed gaze surveyed the skyline. "There it is," he said, pointing.

Bat let out a sigh. "Okay."

Enkay turned to Bat. "Do you want me to stop in the village?"

Bat shook his head, and Enkay drove straight through. A few kilometres later, Bat indicated that Enkay should take the left-hand track off the Muren road. Enkay turned, allowing the jeep to wind across the valley floor for about half an hour.

"Head for the foot of those mountains." Bat pointed, coughing to clear his throat.

Enkay obeyed, and they rattled along the hardened track. In the distance Bat saw a group of five gers.

"Stop here," said Bat.

"Here?"

"Yes! I want to walk."

Duya leant over and kissed both of Bat's cheeks, while Rinchin shook his hand firmly. The drunk grunted. Bat thanked the driver, slung his bag over his shoulder, and jumped down.

Kicking up clouds of dust, Enkay accelerated away. Bat rubbed the dust from his face and waited. But no one left their gers. The sweetness of dung hung in the late afternoon. All the animals were still at pasture, and the family was probably sleeping. Bat drank in the quietness, letting it soothe his soul and soak up his anxieties.

The snoozing dogs didn't even raise an ear. However, two magpies loudly squawked at his arrival. He wondered whether his mother had heard them and was preparing for the arrival of a visitor.

He passed the Russian motorbike parked outside their gers and guessed it belonged to Zorigo, or to his brother-in-law Lhxaa. Bat stepped onto the shallow wooden step of his parents' ger.

"Help me," he muttered beneath his breath.

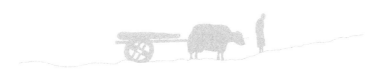

Chapter 23

Bat grasped the plastic handle and entered the ger. Like an old friend, the musty smell of burnt wood welcomed him. Apart from his parents, the ger was empty. His father lay on their metal-framed bed at the head while his mother sat beside him. Their heads were close, and a rush of warmth enveloped Bat's body; it was good to be home.

He coughed, and his mother turned with a start. For a long second, she stared at him and then, calling his name, pulled herself to her feet and rushed towards him. Bat stepped back to steady himself into her embrace as she flung her arms around his middle. Her kisses covered his face, dissolving the distance he'd put between them in an instant.

"I'm here," he whispered.

She pulled away from him. Her eyes were dim and edged with grey. "Thank you," she said, dragging him to his father's side. "Look who's arrived." Bat bowed to kiss his father's papery cheeks which, despite the warmth of the ger, were cold.

"Help me up," his father whispered, opening his eyes as he tried to turn his body towards Bat. Gently, Bat rolled his father onto his side and sat where his mother had sat. Despite his father's sunken eyes and buzz of white hair, there was, Bat noted, the brightest of smiles on his father's face. Bat took his father's trembling hand in his own; it was rough and scarred with the imprint of a herder's life. Again, Bat swallowed. He'd thought this man indomitable.

"I've been waiting for you," his father muttered.

Bat's face buckled, and the tears flowed unchecked. "I'm sorry," he said simply, laying his head on his father's chest.

"Tsuts, tsuts," his father soothed, comforting Bat with the words that he spoke to his beloved camels. "You're here now." Eventually the tears subsided, and Bat felt a tap on his shoulder.

"Come and sit with me," his mother beckoned.

Bat wiped his face with the back of his hand and let his mother lead him to a stool. She carried her bulk less easily, and he noticed her grey hair was starting to thin. With her mouth she smiled, but her eyes betrayed another emotion.

"Your father's illness came on suddenly," she said. "He'd been complaining for days, saying he felt ill, and then three days ago he had an attack. The boys were away so Altai had to ride into town to get the doctor. By the time they got back, all the fuss was over, and your father was lying quietly on his bed. The doctor said it was a stroke."

She released his hands and started smoothing the patches on her old red deel. "We thought we were going to lose him right then. But he rallied, although the doctor said that he won't recover." She removed a piece of fluff from her deel. "I'm glad you got here before the end. Your father is ready to meet his Maker. But he wanted to see you, to talk to you before he leaves us."

The tears threatened to return, but Bat pursed his lips tightly. His mother moved to the tiny kitchen cupboard where she kept all her bowls and spoons. "You must be hungry," she said, handing him a bowl of tea and placing a plate of fried dough ears before him. The tea's milky saltiness revived him. He took a dough ear, dunked it and began chewing.

"Was your journey long?" she asked.

"Yes."

"When did you leave?"

"Early yesterday morning."

"How was the road?"

"Good," he answered between mouthfuls.

His mother groaned as she picked up a large bowl of flour. Jumping to his feet, Bat took it from her and placed it on the table. She sighed. "My old body is worn out. But don't worry, my spirit is still young." She laughed then put her finger to her mouth. "We're trying to keep the ger quiet."

"I haven't been very quiet."

"That's different. It's the constant comings and goings that are wearing." She poured water into the flour, added a generous handful of salt, and began mixing the dough as she'd done a thousand times before. "I thought we'd have buuz this evening."

"Did you know I'd arrive today?"

She winked. "Magpies aside, I had a strong feeling you'd be here before evening." Under her skilful hands, the dough quickly became silky smooth. She shaped it into a ball and covered it with a cloth. "And how are of those grandchildren of mine?"

"They are good."

"And when am I going to meet them? I have photos of their lovely faces but that is not enough for a grandmother."

Bat twisted the button on his shirt cuff. "You are right, photos are not enough. I will bring them this summer," he said with resolve.

"Oh, Bat, that would be wonderful."

"They will love it."

"And how is Amaraa...?"

"She is well—very successful, very beautiful," he said, imagining his wife teaching her classes with a serenity and coolness that made her the envy of her fellow teachers.

The ger door opened, and Zorigo entered. His black hair shone, cropped as close to his head as it had always been. Removing his cigarette from the toothless gap between his front teeth, Zorigo broke into a grin. "Well! Who's this stranger?"

Bat leapt to his feet and gave his older brother a giant hug. "You haven't changed," Bat said with delight. "In fact, I think you're still wearing the same clothes."

Zorigo punched him in the stomach. "Whereas you, my brother, look like a city gent in those clean trousers and open shirt. When did you arrive?"

"About an hour ago."

"We didn't hear a vehicle."

"I got the driver to stop at the bald patch so I could walk the rest of the way."

"Just like you to come by stealth."

Bat laughed. "How are the rest of the family?"

"The lads have gone to Tsetserleg to sell skins and meat. They should be back late tonight. Solyomaa is in our ger. I'll go and get her." And with that, Zorigo was gone.

His mother pulled a slab of meat from under one of the beds. "I saved this beef for a special occasion," she said, dusting the flies off the greening cow's leg. Meals had always been a big part of their lives, thought Bat, rubbing his aching shoulders. The fire's warmth was beginning to make him feel drowsy. He focused on his parents' simple one-roomed home.

Nothing had moved since he'd left. Admittedly, he'd never lived in this ger, but for as long as he could remember, the furniture had never moved or changed.

With just five walls, the ger was small, although everything was in its rightful place. Beside the door lived the same washstand his father had bought when Bat's parents first set up their home. Next to the washstand was the old kitchen dresser that had long since lost its orange paint. The same three beds occupied the same places, one on the left, one on the right, and one at the head. Not that the number of beds mattered, because no matter how many visitors arrived, there was always space for another person.

The once brightly painted chests full of clothes, books, and other treasures had passed their glory days. Zorigo's ornate picture frame, one of the lasting achievements from his school days, sat on top of one such chest next to an ancient frame that his mother's father had gifted her on her wedding day. Both were cramped with family photos. They were his mother's most treasured possessions. He smiled to see Garna's and Jargal's pictures amongst her collection. He really should get his mother some more up-to-date photos.

Above his parents' bed, his father's collection of bullets and knives laid untidily on the shelf. Beside them was his grandfather's single binocular lens, the other lens having been shared with another herder. Balanced at the end of the shelf was *The Red Book* wrapped in its threadbare cloth.

No, this home was neither smart nor sophisticated. But the fire in the hearth kept it warm and comfortable. And there was, thought Bat, a tranquillity in the shabbiness. Even his critical-tongued grandmother had conceded that his mother kept a good ger.

Outside, Bat heard scuffling and giggles. His mother winked as Altai came through the door, balancing a hunk of a baby on her right hip. Grinning from ear to ear, her face was still full of mischief and fun, although, of course, she was a grown woman. Bat enveloped her and the budding wrestler in his arms. Ger smells of smoke and meat clung to her. "So, this is Togs-bilig," he said, pulling away and pinching the bewildered child's cheek.

"It is. Togs-bilig, meet your uncle," she said, encouraging her son to wave his plump hand.

Bat gave the boy a smile, which made him cling to his mother more fiercely.

"He's just learning to walk, so he keeps me busy," said Altai.

"So I've heard."

Altai squeezed his hand. "It is so good to see you." The lump in Bat's throat felt huge. Four years really was too long to have stayed away. Behind Altai stood her husband, Dorj. Bat had only met him once before, and that was at their wedding two years earlier. He hardly knew the man, but he gave him a warm smile and sure handshake anyway. "Nice to meet you again," said Bat a little too formally.

Dorj smiled, returned the greeting, and stood aside to allow Bat's sister Naraa to come forward. She was as willowy and elegant as ever. She held him close. "We've missed you," she whispered in his ear.

He nodded. He'd missed them too. His brother-in-law, Lhxaa grabbed his neck and pulled him close. "Long time no see."

"Yeah," said Bat.

"And you remember Dash, our eldest son," said Lhxaa.

"Of course." Bat hugged Lhxaa's stepson. "And I hear from our father that you've been herding with Lhxaa and my brother for the last couple of years."

"I have," said Dash quietly, pushing the mop of hair away from his eyes. "It took a while, but once I got to know my mother and Lhxaa, I knew I belonged here. And my adopted parents have kindly allowed me to make this my home. Plus, I've got myself a girl from the next valley, and we're soon to be married."

Naraa beamed. "And she's a lovely young lady too."

The ger was starting to get full and noisy. Bat looked at his mother, who'd returned to her seat. "We're fine," she said, waving a hand in his direction.

A woman with a radiant face stood before him. Bat scratched his head. "Solyomaa?"

"Yes. It's me." Gone was her furrowed brow and eyes that jumped like frightened rabbits. Instead she held his gaze with serenity.

"You look beautiful."

"She is," said Zorigo with pride. "Her growing faith in God is really changing her from the inside out."

Zorigo sat next to Dash on the bed on the east side, while Solyomaa uncovered the dough. "I see we are celebrating Bat's return."

"Yes, Solyomaa, we are," said Monkho.

Zorigo straightened. "Before we make food, I think it would be good to give thanks for Bat's safe arrival."

Bat looked from one to the other.

"Good idea," came his father's hushed voice.

They sat, and Bat pulled a stool from the table and sat with them. His hands felt strangely sweaty as he watched his family close their eyes and bow their heads.

"Thank you, God, our Creator and our Keeper," said Zorigo, "for bringing Bat safely home. Give us a good evening, and may our father stay with us until we have all said a proper goodbye. Thank you for this food and our time together. Amen."

"Amen," they replied in unison.

Bat shook his head. Unlike the loud and long prayers of the lamas, Zorigo's prayer was simplicity itself. Bat marvelled; it was almost like his brother was talking to a friend.

Solyomaa, Naraa, and Altai were already dividing the dough. Lhxaa and Dash were off to bring in more firewood, and Zorigo went to make sure all the animals were safely returning for the night.

"What shall I do?" asked Bat.

"Talk," said Naraa.

"Haven't you got any other clothes?" his mother asked.

"What's wrong with my clothes?"

"You look like you've come from the city.

"I have."

"You can't wear those clothes here."

"Why not?"

"They'll get dirty. Haven't you got a deel?" his mother asked.

"No, few people wear deels in the city."

"Don't wear deels?"

"Oh, I'm sure that's just a phase, Mother. Wait till some of those new young designers start making stylish deels. Everyone will want to be wearing them then," Naraa said.

Bat smiled. "You're probably right. How are your girls?" he asked.

"They're doing well." A small pile of dough circles sat on the board in front of her. Holding her tongue between her teeth, she started filling them with meat and skilfully crimping the dumplings closed. Her teeth gleamed white, and she still wore a coat of colour on her lips.

"Father told me that both girls are in the province capital."

"They are. Zyaa enjoyed her first year at the teachers' college. And as you know, Zola has just graduated. She may get a job in the town, but she'd really like to study further and go into banking."

"She'll need to go to the city to study accounting."

"Yes, she will," said Naraa, placing a tray of buuz in the steamer.

"What about Erdene-huu and Gamba?"

Solyomaa laughed. "Oh, they're just like their father. School was an anathema to them. I don't know whether you heard or not, but they've both got young ladies." Solyomaa added more logs to the fire to bring the heat up ready for steaming.

"I thought they were more than just friends."

"Well, yes, you're right. We've already met the parents and spoken of weddings."

"Father told me that Erdene-huu's young lady is pregnant."

"I see our father keeps you up-to-date with all the important news," said Altai referring to their father's monthly phone call to Bat.

"He does."

"We're expecting an announcement from Gamba's young lady soon too."

"So, you are going to be grandparents?"

Solyomaa grinned, clasping her hands "Exciting, isn't it?"

"It is," Bat replied.

"And I'll get to see the next generation before I die," said his mother, placing the steamer above the fire. "God is good."

Bat coughed. "I hear Erdene-huu and Gamba are herding close to our grandparents' old ger."

"They are, and they're doing well. Although their father thinks they've let their herds get too big, which is a worry with the coming winter."

"Ah," said his mother, prodding the buuz to check whether they were ready. "Inexperience imagines it can defy nature. But the young have to learn by their mistakes too."

Solyomaa took a pile of bowls from the cupboard. "Is there any other way to learn?"

"No," said Bat, aware that his own mistakes were becoming his teacher.

Bat's eye moved to the steam escaping from the wok's ill-fitting lid. He grasped his grumbling stomach. The dumplings were calling him, which was hardly surprising since he hadn't eaten a proper meal in two days. Altai filled bowls with buuz and placed them on the table. Bat picked one up and popped it into his mouth.

"Fffffff," he spluttered, dropping the dumpling into his hand. "It's hot!"

They laughed. And after gulping draughts of water, Bat laughed too.

His father tapped the metal frame of his bed. "Lift me up."

Bat and Zorigo propped their father up with pillows, and he smiled a weak smile, although his eyes gleamed. Monkho fed him a few mouthfuls of watery soup.

Sitting on stools and beds, they ate and talked. The evening passed easily, reminding Bat of what it meant to be absorbed in the rhythms of his family, of this landscape. They laughed, reminiscing over funny and painful stories, of happy times and sad, of wealth and poverty. Each story formed a memory woven into these people, woven into this land. Memories of the living and the dead and memories that, Bat realised, joined him to his family and formed the touchstone of his identity.

"I'm so full." Bat groaned, yawning.

"I think we should call it a night," said Zorigo, standing to leave.

"Yes," added Naraa, pushing the rest of the family towards the door.

His mother pointed to the bed to the left of hers. "You can sleep here," she told Bat.

Bat sat on the metal frame, feeling the thin, matted horsehair mattress between his fingers. His head throbbed with tiredness. Bending to untie his shoelaces, he tried to understand the unexplainable. His father was dying, he was sad, and yet there was a calmness in his soul that defied logic. All he could say was that the peace had come when he'd entered his parents' ger.

This is where I belong, he thought letting sleep overtake him.

Do you?

His eyes flew open, and he shivered with cold.

Chapter 24

"Monkho, Monkho," Altanbaatar croaked, feeling as limp as a washed-out piece of muslin.

"I'm here." Monkho was at his side with a bowl of tea. "Have something to drink," she said, pushing the spoon to his mouth. Altanbaatar parted his lips to let the liquid run down his throat. His heart felt like it was leaping again, which wasn't good. The doctor had told him that his body would not recover. Altanbaatar was not afraid of death, but one thing pressed hard; he wanted to speak to Bat. He reminded God of the prayer he'd often prayed: "Just one chance. Just give me one chance to talk to Bat."

The tea finished, Monkho rubbed his face with a warm cloth and helped him get comfortable.

"You...are...a good wife."

"And you are a good husband."

"I am sorry to leave you."

Tears formed in her eyes. "I am sorry to let you go." He hated causing her such pain. "But," she continued, "I do not want to see you suffer. And I will not be alone; the Lord is with me, and the family will care for me."

He nodded. She was right, although her reassurances did nothing to remove the knot in his stomach. They'd been together for more than forty years. It had been a good marriage, especially since the living God had found them and become a part of their lives.

Altanbaatar wanted to lift his hand to stroke Monkho's forehead, but his hand refused to move. As if reading his thoughts, Monkho caressed his brow. "At least I know you are going to be safe with God."

"Bat," he said.

"I understand." She closed her eyes and lifted her hands. "Lord, free my beloved's tongue so that he can talk with Bat."

Altanbaatar marvelled; his wife truly had learned the secret of placing everything in God's hands.

"Did I hear my name?" Bat asked, coming back into the ger.

"You did," said his mother. "Come and sit with your father." Monkho winked at him.

Unless God loosened his tongue and opened his mouth, Altanbaatar knew he wouldn't be able to speak. Bat kissed his cheek, and Altanbaatar caught the freshness of the morning on his son's clothes. Oh, how he longed to be outside with the animals.

"Did you...did you have a good sleep?"

"The best sleep I've had in a long time," answered Bat.

"Help me sit up."

Bat lifted his body while Monkho packed pillows behind him so that he was upright.

"That's better. Talk to me, Bat."

"Of course."

"You have done very well, son."

"I have, Father. At the end of this term, I've been promised a promotion to head of the history department."

"Congratulations. Do you enjoy teaching?"

"I do, particularly the interaction with the students."

"I can understand that. There was a time when I wanted to become a teacher too."

"Grandfather told me about that."

Altanbaatar shuddered. "My feet are cold."

"The blood's not reaching them," said Monkho, placing another blanket over his legs. "'Keep your feet warm and the rest of your body will take care of itself,' your mother used to say."

He nodded, remembering the force of his mother's words. "So, in your success as a teacher, what have you learned?"

Bat pressed his hands together and held them to his lips. In the stillness, Altanbaatar heard the call of the cuckoo. She'd be out of sight, hidden in the foliage of the trees beside the river, singing her summer song.

Bat cleared his throat. "I am learning that education and knowledge have little to do with a person becoming a wise, mature individual."

Altanbaatar coughed. "That is an interesting observation. What drew you to that conclusion?"

Bat smiled. "Remember how I used to extol the virtues of education, believing that knowledge, alongside man's logic, was the key to a correct understanding of life?"

"I remember."

"Well, I was wrong!"

Altanbaatar's heart took a jump. Monkho handed Bat a bowl of buuz, and his son carefully placed a dumpling into his mouth.

"Of course," Bat continued, "I do not deny that education is useful. We all need to be educated, but so often it's impersonal."

"Impersonal?"

"Yes, education concentrates on facts and figures, explanations and definitions. It explains how things work, but by itself it adds nothing to the character of a man."

Altanbaatar's fingers tingled with anticipation. "I would agree with your conclusions."

"Education, knowledge, logic, all those things that I prized, have not made me a better person. I had thought knowledge and therefore education was to be prized as the ultimate truth but teaching history has shown me that things that were regarded as truth in one period can be discarded by the next generation as new truths are discovered."

Altanbaatar tried to focus on Bat's face but couldn't. "You are right, son. History testifies to the progress of knowledge as man's understanding grows. But to place our hope in education, or even in man's reasoning, will, eventually disappoint because education by itself leaves the real questions of life untouched."

"Untouched is an apt word."

"Mmm! Education is useful, Bat. It has its place in our lives, but it cannot assuage the restlessness of our souls."

Bat took another dumpling, bit off one side, and sucked out the hot fat. "Restlessness," he repeated. "Yes, it's there beneath the surface, isn't it?"

"It is, touching all that we seek to do and all that we are. Our beliefs constantly urge us to be better people, to do good to remove the restlessness that covers the endemic sense of shame we carry with us on the inside."

Monkho refilled Bat's empty bowl with hot tea. The sun streamed through the toono, touching the old woodburning stove and making it shine.

Altanbaatar's head ached. "Even after examining our religion, our worship of the earth with its mountains and rivers, our wise words and traditions, I found nothing to satisfy my soul's longing for wholeness."

"I think Grandfather felt the same," said Bat.

"I believe he did. Do you remember his desire to find a Being beyond the gods and spirits of this world?"

"I do, although at the time, I didn't fully understand."

"Neither did I. Only after his death did I recognise that I too was asking the same question—was there a Being beyond our world?"

Bat laughed. "Study and my thirst for success caused me to disregard such ethereal ideas. Plus...Bat fixed his eyes on his bowl. "Buyeraa bagsh convinced me that any form of mysticism was obsolete in modern Mongolia."

"Buyeraa bagsh is a good teacher."

"He is," Bat agreed.

"But he was a broken man. He's better these days, but those early years after the devastating loss of his wife and son were brutal. Hopelessness overwhelmed him, and he rejected all religion and his heritage. 'Religion defies logic,' he used to say."

"I remember. And there's one incident in particular that's stayed with me. Some of Grandfather's words about religion must have stuck with me. Because after his death, I returned to school and told Buyeraa of my young desire to know truth and find God. On hearing my thoughts, Buyeraa reacted with such fiery rage that the memory still makes me shake."

"He spoke from his grief."

"I see that now. And Buyeraa bagsh's care did propel me forward, and for that I am thankful."

"Yes, it did."

Bat looked his father in the eye. "So, you've never told me how you found freedom from shame."

Altanbaatar took a breath. "It was a journey. I was living for my family, for their future, but there was a growing disquiet inside me."

"I can understand that. We all live for something."

"We do, and we think that *something* will give us a good life, but if that *something* isn't rooted in eternity, then we find it's as empty as a wasp nest in winter."

Bat laughed. "Like chasing the wind," he said, staring into his empty bowl.

"Like chasing the wind," Altanbaatar repeated.

"When I used to ride my bay mare across the steppe it seemed possible not just to chase the wind, but to outrun it. If my bay could gallop just a little faster, if she could stretch herself full length, then the wind would gather us up and we'd be flying with it, galloping on the thermals until, we were beyond it and in the place of true freedom. It sounds childish to speak of it now, but it was real to me then."

"It is not childish. Every boy and every man longs to soar above the earth. Something in us hungers for that freedom."

"Jargal has the same longing."

"It is in all of us, but the reality is, if we could fly, our euphoria would be short-lived."

"For a start, we'd return to earth with a bump."

A smile touched Altanbaatar's lips. "We would, and the despair we'd experience after would be greater than before," he said, trying to point to the shelf where *The Red Book* lay. "But reading *The Red Book* started to answer some of the questions in me. It told me that my heart's longing for freedom, for cleanness, was right, but that I wouldn't find it through endless good acts or through worship of this place with its rivers, hills, and incredible blue sky."

Bat's eyes narrowed, as he weighed his father's words. "On the journey here, I felt overwhelmed by the wonders of this land. It was good to have my feet on the grass that my ancestors touched and be under the covering of the blue sky. I felt like I belonged here and that my despair was because I'd abandoned it, and my family."

"Knowing we belong to the land and to our family is very important for us Mongolians, but it is not the focus of our worship; rather the land and our family reveal the wonders of their Creator." Altanbaatar held the blanket close. "As I desired to see beyond my physical eyes and to know the creator God, it was as if He drew back an imaginary curtain over the world and let me see behind the scenes and for the first time, I realised that *He* was the Master of the world."

His heart was pumping hard against his chest, and the pain in his head was sharp. Monkho squeezed his leg; she was with him. But did Bat understand? Altanbaatar twisted the blanket tighter. "Why is it that when you want to speak clearly about the wonder and greatness of God, you end up reducing Him to the size of your own words? If only I could open my chest and show you the inside of me."

Bat placed his hand in his father's. "Don't fret, I understand. I can see it. The bird songs, the running brook, the thunder of horses' hooves, everything points to the presence of a creator God."

"It does." Altanbaatar gasped, "My mouth's as dry as a camel's."

"And that's pretty dry." Bat smiled.

"I'm not surprised; you've been talking non-stop," said Monkho with a wink. She left his side to put another log on the fire and returned with a fresh bowl of milk tea.

"I hope that fire banishes the chill covering my body," he

said, grateful for the warming tea. "Now, where were we?"

"Acknowledging the presence of a Creator," said Bat.

"Yes," replied Altanbaatar, eager to tell Bat the most important thing. "Do you remember Tseren-ax, the old storyteller, sharing with us a story from *The Red Book*?"

Bat grinned. "Of the shepherd boy Dav-it who defeated the evil giant?"

"Yes."

"I do, and I've been thinking of that story recently."

"Mmm!" Altanbaatar said, aware that God was already at work in his youngest son's heart. "*The Red Book* is full of stories that eventually lead to God overcoming man's inherent badness by sending His own perfect Son, Jesus Christ, into the world to pay the price for man's badness. Because Jesus was a pure, holy Man and His sacrifice was perfect, death could not hold Him."

Bat's eyebrows rose a notch or two. "Rose from the dead?"

"He did, and His perfect sacrifice stands not only for me, but for every person. Believing in the creator God and His Son enables me to surrender my efforts to be good. To have the shame of my constant failures removed by God's complete forgiveness and to be honoured with His perfect gift of freedom."

Bat ran his hand through his short hair. "So, you are no longer chasing the wind."

"No, Bat, I am no longer chasing the wind. And I am no longer trying to make myself a better person."

"One thing I have learned," said Bat, pursing his lips. "It's impossible to make myself a better person on the inside."

"It is. Because no one other than God can truly change

a man's heart. But God's love touched my heart, it cleansed me, and it is changing me."

"And you know God?" asked Bat.

"I have a friendship with him that I believe man cannot destroy, that even death cannot steal. After death I will be with Him." His limbs were heavy, and his breath wouldn't come easily. He wanted to rub his chest to ease the pain, but his hand refused to move. *Just a little more strength, please give me a little more.*

"*The Red Book* speaks truth. I've experienced it. Bat, believe; it will change everything." The pain in his head was piercing his temple, making him sick to his stomach. Down his arm the pain ran, gripping his chest in an iron fist and coursing into his legs until they burned. He closed his eyes. *Thank you, Lord.*

Bat saw his father's face contort, heard his faltering speech. "Aav-aa, Aav-aa," Bat cried.

Altanbaatar said with the utmost calm, "God will never disappoint you, son."

Altanbaatar heard the ger door open and close. He'd miss them, he thought, but suddenly all that had been so important to him a moment ago dropped away. There was a small light above him.

"Please don't go." Bat gripped his hands. But Altanbaatar was already moving away. The clouds were so white. He breathed softly and let go of Bat's hands. Bat picked up his hand again— it was cold and clammy. "I know it's true," Bat said.

The clouds were beginning to thin. The sky...Altanbaatar was just catching his first glimpses of it. Blue beyond blue:

rich and velvety, pure and transparent. He'd never seen such a sky.

Zorigo, Nara, Altai, Dash, they were all there, standing by the bed. Bat moved, and Monkho drew closer to her husband. She took his hand in hers. "My love, my love?" she spoke softly in his ear.

"Beautiful," he replied.

"Then go," she said.

Bat's hand flew to his mouth.

Zorigo's arm was on his shoulder. "It's time to let him go."

Bat pushed his brother away. "You don't understand. You never left. You've never been away."

"You were never lost to him," Zorigo said. "He was just waiting for your return."

Bat sat down hard on the bed. The old deel that he'd used as a blanket lay crumpled where he'd left it. Solyomaa came in, stood beside Altanbaatar's bed, and beckoned to Bat. Bat stood with his brothers and sisters. His father's face was white, and his glazed eyes were more deeply sunken in their sockets. Altanbaatar's shallow breaths scraped like a file against wood.

Zorigo laid his hand on his father's head and asked that the Lord take him swiftly and without further pain.

"He's gone," said Monkho, holding two fingers to her husband's throat. She closed his eyes and wiped a tear from her face.

Ah, so this is what it's like to fly, thought Altanbaatar, emerging fully from the clouds into the true presence of the dazzling sun.

Chapter 25

Monkho pulled her deel around her shoulders and left the ger. If anyone were to ask where she was going that early in the morning, she would say that said she was checking the animals. But no one stirred. The grey night was already dropping below the horizon as she opened the small four-walled ger where her husband's body lay. Like her worn hips, the door creaked on the threshold.

"Why did I let you talk me into burying you on the hillside," she said, rubbing her side. "I'm definitely going to need help getting up that slope."

Needles of light filtered through the gaps in the ger walls. Piercing the gloom, they flickered along the side of the coffin. Monkho's hand traced the light along the silky wood. Zorigo and Lhxaa had crafted a box of simple beauty.

Altanbaatar lay undisturbed. In death, his haggard look had disappeared and he was again her handsome herder. Longing to kiss him awake, she touched his cold forehead.

"More than forty years we were together. It was a lifetime, but still, you left me too early."

She straightened the collar of his best deel and tried to fasten his top button, but her knobbly fingers refused to perform the task. She sniffed.

"You'll go to your grave with your button undone," she said, pulling his sleeves straight. "Although your boots are shining. I wish you could see them. Bat made the polishing of them his project. It was something he could do while we made buuz. He cleaned off the dirt, applied layers of polish, and rubbed until they glowed."

His hand was clay in hers. "Oh, my love," she said, biting her lip. "You have been my best earthly companion. Death may have separated us, but I know that nothing can separate us from God's love." She'd read that in *The Red Book* somewhere, not that she knew where. It was a confusing book, with so many parts written by so many authors. "Your funeral will be the celebration we discussed."

The door squeaked. "Eej-ee." It was Naraa.

She smoothed the sides of her deel. "I was just making sure that everything is in order."

"We are about to start making the salads," said Naraa.

"Is it that time already?"

Naraa's hand was on her arm. "He's handsome, isn't he?"

"He is," Monkho agreed. Turning to the door, she wiped a tear from her cheek. Naraa linked her arm through her mother's. The sun was soft with early summer warmth. Already on their feet, the sheep and goats were lazily heading towards the pasture.

Monkho entered her ger, surprised to see it a hive of activity inside. Absorbed with saying goodbye to Altanbaatar, she'd heard no opening and closing of ger doors or footfall on the hardened ground, and yet here they all were.

Solyomaa and Altai were making potato salad, Bat and Lhxaa were filling buuz, and Zorigo was trying to manhandle the roasted sheep onto Monkho's large serving platter. Monkho quickly steadied the platter while Zorigo centred the sheep's long carcass. "It's going to be a feast," she said.

"Indeed," answered Zorigo. "Although some of our neighbours may not understand."

"Since we embraced the God of *The Red Book*," said Monkho, "many think we've lost our way."

"We don't need to worry, though," said Solyomaa, piling sliced apples into a bowl and covering them with a cloth.

"You're right," said Naraa. "Whatever they think, I'm guessing they'll all enjoy the food."

"They will," said Bat squeezing the dough of his dumpling together in a most professional way. "But it is a sad day."

"It is, Bat," said Monkho. "Although I trust there will be joy in it too." She sighed, knowing there'd be plenty of sorrow and tears in the days ahead. The watch on her wrist read after ten. "Lads, it's time you went up the hill." Her fingers ran over the scratched face of Altanbaatar's watch. After his stroke, he'd insisted that she wear it. "The young ones can finish those. You need to get up the mountain and dig your father's grave."

Monkho shooed them towards the door, but Bat hesitated. "Yes, that includes you too, Bat. There are three shovels in the store."

Bat followed them a little reluctantly. Picking up a knife, Monkho shook her head. There was no time for comforting conversations today; people would be arriving at midday and they needed to be ready. She sliced pickled cucumbers, laying them on a plate between slices of salami and spoonfuls of bottled carrot salad.

It would take the boys ten to fifteen minutes to walk to the burial spot. That mountain was a special place. Even before Altanbaatar became a follower of Jesus, he'd worshipped what he'd thought was the spirit of that place. After he got to know the true, living God who created not only his beloved mountain but the whole earth, the mountain had become his sanctuary: a place where he worshipped his Creator. In the warmer months, he'd trekked the ridges daily, although recently he'd stuck to the lower grassy banks. Occasionally, she walked with him, but her aching hips had stopped her. Today, however, she would walk with him one last time.

"Eej-ee, we're going to get washed and changed," said Naraa.

"Is everything ready?"

"It is," answered Naraa, following Solyomaa out the door.

All the preparations seemed to have been completed very quickly, thought Monkho, taking her best deel from the avdar. She held it in her hand for a moment; the purple brocade was rich. Solyomaa had bought the fabric and made the deel for her this past New Year. It was beautiful, but had Monkho chosen the fabric herself, she'd have bought something less colourful and less expensive.

Removing her old working deel, she pulled her new one on. Its silver edging, crisp with newness, made the buttons harder to fasten. She unwound her grey hair and started brushing. I hope people appreciate the day, she thought. It was strange to long for gladness on a dark burial day. But she wanted people to see that there was hope beyond the grave. She coiled her hair, piling it on top of her head, and slipped the gold drop earrings Altanbaatar had gifted her on their wedding day into her lobes.

Her eyes were hot again. "My love," she whispered. "You're gone, but I feel like you're still near."

She tried to remember when Altanbaatar's family had first arrived in the valley. "It was March, wasn't it," she said. Monkho's mother was the first to hear news of a new family trying to find the right spot for their ger. Word had it that they'd moved from Hovd to start a new life in Uvs. But why? This tasty morsel fed the imaginations of the gossips until they started spreading the tale that Namdorj's family had fled the surveillance of local officials.

Eventually, Namdorj and Yanjaa settled a little over a kilometre away from Monkho's ger, and the two families became acquainted and learned the true reason for their move. Three years of losing animals to the spring famines and summer floods of the great Hovd River convinced Namdorj that it was time to move his family to a kinder climate.

Monkho had immediately noticed Namdorj's handsome youngest son, Altanbaatar. A year above her at school, he excelled in his studies and was one of the few students offered a place at university in Ulaanbaatar or some other exotic foreign city. However, Altanbaatar's mother was adamant that he was a herder, not a scholar, so he never left his ger.

She poured warmed water into the bowl and washed her face and hands. The first summer that Namdorj's family were in their valley, Monkho had spied Altanbaatar herding horses. Concealed behind a rock on the slopes, she'd become fixated on his lean figure and his long hair bound in a tail. He stood effortlessly in his saddle, tilting to the left and the right as horse and rider gently nudged the strays back to the herd. Morning and evening Monkho had watched, knowing that her heart was quietly slipping into his pocket.

The cream Naraa had given her for New Year smelt of roses and was one of Monkho's luxuries. She smoothed it over her wrinkled face, remembering the days when she'd had no wrinkles.

"Oh, how I schemed, trying to manipulate a meeting with my parents and yours, but I needn't have worried," she said, remembering that thundery summer afternoon when the sky, black with fury and providence, had opened its door.

Her father had been trying to gather his restless horses into the safety of the corral. Panicked by cracks of lightning, one colt had dashed headlong towards the valley's edge. Before Monkho's father could mount his own stallion, Altanbaatar, who was tending his father's herds, had flicked his reins and turned his horse to chase after the runaway. Once, twice, three times, Altanbaatar had swung his lasso pole above his head. Casting it forward, he threw so that the lasso hovered just beyond the reach of the colt, waiting for the young horse to bolt straight into the noose.

Altanbaatar saved that colt from certain death. Indebted to the young man, Monkho's father had bought him into their ger where the tale was told and retold.

It had been better than any introduction she could have imagined. Within a few short weeks, the two of them were firm friends. Captivated by Altanbaatar's hard work and gentle spirit, Monkho's parents readily agreed to their marriage. Altanbaatar's family embraced Monkho. In the time-honoured fashioned, the marriage was sealed with Altanbaatar carrying her away to his own ger, where she'd lived ever since.

She pulled the sash tight around her waist. "Where are those boys?" Her watch said twelve. They should be back by now. Ah, there were voices outside and feet on the step. The next moment they were through the door. "Quickly, we need to leave in five minutes," she said.

Zorigo smiled. "There's no rush."

"We'll be washed and changed in a moment," said Lhxaa.

Five minutes later, Lhxaa and Zorigo were wearing their smart deels and Bat, looking a little out of place, was in his city shirt and trousers.

"Right, Eej-ee, are you ready?" asked Zorigo.

"I've been ready for the past ten minutes."

Zorigo took her arm, and they stepped out together. A few neighbours had gathered. Solemnly, they watched Bat, Lhxaa, Gamba, and Erdene-Huu bring the coffin out of the small, darkened ger.

"We will bury my husband's body on the hillside. You're welcome to join us," said Monkho, extending her hands to encourage people to walk with them. Their eyebrows rising, her neighbours stepped back. Monkho repeated the invitation, knowing that some were probably offended that her invitation included both men and women. Women, after all, were supposedly more susceptible to influences from the evil spirits that lurked beside graves than men were. Monkho smiled. "Or you can wait for our return, when we will celebrate Altanbaatar's life together."

Her old friend Sara, the postmistress, wore a pained expression. Sara touched her forehead with her beads and bowed slightly. Monkho guessed she'd scared Sara by speaking Altanbaatar's name. No doubt Sara was praying that such a declaration would not interrupt Altanbaatar's journey to his final resting place. Poor Sara, thought Monkho, her beliefs still hold her in the grip of fear.

The four boys hoisted the coffin onto their shoulders, and the people parted to allow them through. Her husband led the procession. Hanging onto Zorigo's arm, Monkho followed with Solyomaa, Naraa, Naraa's two daughters Zaya and Zola, and Dash behind. Dressed in matching deels, Naraa's daughters were as pretty and willowy as their mother.

The procession moved slowly, and Monkho prayed that Lhxaa's ill-set leg, broken years earlier, would hold up. Not that Lhxaa ever complained, but there had been times when his leg had buckled beneath him. But, loving Altanbaatar as his own father, Lhxaa had considered it an honour to bear his father-in-law to his grave.

Starting the slow climb, Monkho turned back; their neighbours were following. Admittedly, their faces were downcast and they walked in silence, but still, they were following. Monkho squared her shoulders and inhaled.

"Heavenly, powerful Lord." Her voice was shaky, but she carried the tune. Solyomaa and Naraa joined her, and Zorigo's voice, smooth, clear, and soothing made the hymn swell with power. They sang, and the singing strengthened her steps, carrying her to the grassy knoll they'd chosen for Altanbaatar's burial.

"I'd forgotten how lovely this place is," said Monkho observing the bright faces of the flowers with their heads tilted sunwards. The family gathered as the boys laid the coffin next to the hole they'd dug.

"Stand with us," said Monkho, inviting their neighbours nearer. They shuffled but moved no closer.

Zorigo pulled *The Red Book* from his deel pouch, turned the pages, and cleared his throat. "I tell you the truth, unless someone is born again, he cannot see the Kingdom of God. Do not marvel that I say, 'You must be born again.' The wind blows where it wills, you hear the sound, but you do not know where it comes from or where it goes. So it is with everyone who is born of the Spirit."

Blank, emotionless expressions held their neighbours' faces. They didn't understand! And why should they? thought Monkho. There'd been a time when she hadn't understood. But those words they'd first read in that tiny, inconsequential scrap of a volume they'd found after her father-in-law's death had been the beginning of opening their understanding to the true and living God.

"Father God." Lhxaa spoke with clarity. "Thank you for showing us Yourself and leading us in the true way. For cleansing our black hearts and for giving us the strength to live right each day. Thank you that our father found this strength, that he found Your hope, which changed his life and gave him joy. We are grateful. Father God, give us strength when we are weak. Amen!"

They sang another song and without further ado lowered the coffin into the grave. Dash, Gamba, and Erdene-Huu, retrieved the three spades hidden behind a tree and piled earth on top of the coffin.

"Walk with me," Monkho said motioning to Naraa and Solyomaa. Each woman took one of her arms, their strength lightening her steps. The pale afternoon sun dappled the trees with light. Stroking her face, the breeze carried the sharp scent of pine. God was refreshing her, reminding her that He alone was the source of her confidence.

"I love these long summer days," said Solyomaa.

"Me too," said Naraa.

"My body loves the warmth," said Monkho.

Her daughter and daughter-in-law laughed. The three of them were the first to arrive home. "I'll just change my deel," said Monkho. The girls nodded and headed to their own gers.

"Fires are lit," said Solyomaa, returning to Monkho's ger. "Let's get the buuz steaming."

Bat and Lhxaa followed. Pouring bowls of steaming tea, they handed one to each person who came through the door. Monkho hadn't expected so many people all at once. Tying her own door open, she invited their guests to sit in any of the family's four other gers or on the grass. No one moved until the food was uncovered, and they started filling their bowls with salad, slices of mutton, and buuz. Only then did the sombre mood disappear, their tongues loosen, and they began to seek more comfortable places to sit.

Even Bat appeared comfortable and relaxed. Catching his eye, Monkho winked, and he winked back.

Zorigo took the bowl of steaming buuz from her hands. "Go and chat," he said.

Monkho moved amongst the mourners, thanking them for coming and giving each a word of encouragement. In return, most had a touching remembrance of Altanbaatar.

As the day wore on and the afternoon slipped towards evening, an atmosphere of relaxed ease descended. Some guests left, but many stayed, content to talk, play cards, or just snooze. Ladies helped clear up, and a few herders brought the family's cattle home from the hillside.

With darkness approaching, their guests announced that they should return to their own homes and animals. The family stood at Monkho's door waving them off. Bat towered above Monkho, holding her close in the crook of his arm. "It's been a good day," she said, thankful for the answers to her prayers. "Of course, there was sadness, but there was also a quiet joy."

"Thank you, Lord, that you care for all our needs," Solyomaa prayed.

Monkho felt Bat's grip tighten. Standing tall, he pulled her closer, and she turned her face to his. Bat was smiling.

Chapter 26

For the last hour, the family had been sitting by the fire chatting. Bat longed for sleep, but he also relished this time of drinking tea and nibbling leftovers from the funeral party. He sighed, wishing he visited more often, aware that it was his foolish, stubborn pride that had kept him away. How he longed to be different.

Eventually the family retired to their own gers, and Bat, pulling his father's old deel over his body, slept. The next thing he knew, the dogs were barking. The silver sky was turning softly blue through the toono. He rubbed his head, squeezed his eyes shut, and turned over.

"God will not disappoint you," his father had said. Bat wanted to believe this, but something stopped him.

Shafts of light touched the wood-burning stove. Sore from the boards and the horsehair mattress, Bat pulled himself up. City life had made him soft. Although, he recognised, he'd had it easy in the countryside too. As he grew up with his grandparents, his grandmother had constantly indulged him. "'Her little king,'" she used to call him, granting him his every wish and helping him to become the petulant, headstrong young man he was today.

His grandfather had tried to stand up to her, tried to give Bat guidelines, but Bat never listened. When his grandmother died, it felt like comfort and ease had been ripped from his life. What a spoilt brat he was.

His grandfather had crumbled without her. At the time, Bat hadn't the eyes to see the old man's brokenness. Yet that brokenness had quickly carried him to his own death. Bat pressed his hand hard against his mouth, afraid that the anguish rising in his throat would escape. His grandfather was a faithful, good man who cared for his sheep and goats, shod his horses, and took his cows to the best pasture.

His grandmother had been a small woman. He remembered that, at least, but the details of her face were gone. His grandfather's face, on the other hand, was etched in his mind. The wiry old man's brown face, weather-beaten and deeply lined, seemed close. And with every remembrance, he saw the worn beads dangling from his grandfather's hands, pointing to the unseen world.

"Listen to other people's words," his grandfather had said. "Don't let yourself be wounded or offended by every strong word that comes your way, but humbly accept it, weighing its value."

Bat clenched his teeth. He'd never been a good listener. Even when people advised him with their so-called wisdom, he'd simply smiled, letting their words fall from his memory, certain that he knew what was best for him.

Realising he would not sleep again, he got up and quietly moved to the kitchen dresser. The funeral wasn't what I'd expected, he thought, picking up a hunk of bread and filling a flask with yoghurt. Before they'd taken the coffin up the hill yesterday, he, Lhxaa, and Zorigo had climbed to the burial spot and dug his father's grave. The morning light had coloured the valley amber, which prompted Zorigo to speak of God's closeness with a devotion that surprised Bat.

He put the yoghurt and bread in his rucksack and crept to the door. Beneath his foot a board creaked, and his mother opened her eyes. Bat motioned that he was going out. She smiled. There was something different about her. Yes, despite his father's death, there was a calm steadiness in her manner and he noticed that she'd stopped quoting old proverbs.

He walked towards the mountains, watching the waking sky tint the clouds pale pink. Sheep and goats dozed close by. Only the lambs and kids stirred and, rushed to his side with unusual friendliness. Six or seven darted in between his legs. He stumbled, imagining they'd follow him all the way up the hill, but he needn't have worried as they quickly abandoned him in favour of other entertainment.

The morning light cast ghostly shadows across the valley.

"Ulaan-aa, Ulaan-aa." Altai was calling him by his childhood name. "City life has made you deaf," she puffed, drawing alongside him. Her tussled hair swung loose as she pulled her orange belt tight around her deel.

"What are you doing up so early?"

She linked her arm through his. "I heard our mother's ger door open and guessed it was you. I'm coming with you."

Bat half-laughed. "What about Togs-bilig?"

"There are plenty of people to look after him."

He nodded, remembering the ease with which the family cared for one another's children. "Just one son...? I thought you'd have a tribe?"

"Yes, just one." Her grip loosened. "I lost two from my stomach. The doctor said I couldn't keep them inside for nine months. We prayed, and I felt that God promised me a son." She looked up into his eyes. "God kept His promise and we have a lovely boy. And Togs-bilig is enough."

Bat's face glowed red; he knew so little of Altai's and Dorj's struggles.

They climbed easily, passing their father's burial spot before heading into the trees. Bat led and Altai followed. The air was cool and the ground a carpet of flowers beneath their feet. Close by, he spotted the tiny white flowers that would soon form alpine strawberries. Bending, he held one between his fingers. "I used to love picking strawberries."

"Yes, but it was always a race to get the ripe ones before the red ants gobbled them up."

"I used to eat them when they were green." Bat groaned, patting his stomach.

Altai giggled. "I remember our grandmother sending you over with pails full of berries."

"Yeah...and all those extra pails of yoghurt and milk that we couldn't drink. I'd carry them in my saddlebags with Emee's warning ringing in my ears. 'Don't spill our precious bounty.'"

"Of course, that was before plastic bottles with screw lids."

"Life is easy now," he said.

"If you live in the city!"

"Perhaps." He stopped, listening to the merry twitter of the wagtails and swallows. Somewhere in the lattice of trees, a woodpecker was tap, tap, tapping a trunk for tasty grubs.

Altai slipped her arm around his waist. "Wherever we live, there are challenges."

Bat took her rough hand in his. "That's true," he said, thinking of Amaraa. "When we used to walk this path, you always used to beg me to take you to the top of the world."

"I did."

"Shall we go there now?"

"Sure, if you know the way."

He playfully punched her arm. "Of course, I bet I can even find the ledge we used to sit on."

"Let's see." She winked.

"You doubt me?"

"Entirely! You've forgotten your countryside roots."

He hit the side of his leg. "I could never forget my roots."

She narrowed her eyes.

"Honestly!"

"We used to sit on our ledge, thinking we were the king and queen of all we surveyed."

"We were." He grabbed a branch to steady himself as he freed his leg from tangled roots.

"Careful," said Altai, falling in behind him again. They climbed the steep path, zig-zagging their way to the ridge. Bat reached the top first and stopped to let the sweet air fill his lungs.

The mountain dropped to the valley floor. "We are on... top of the world," Altai said between gulps.

"We are not there yet," he laughed.

They headed north along the narrowing ridge. The grass was sparser, and the path was punctuated with rocky outcrops and stone kerns decked in blue cloths and abandoned walking sticks.

Far above the tree line, Altai stood still. "It's a long time since I climbed any mountain."

"Me too...the landscape is huge," he said, letting his eyes follow the folds of the valleys. "I used to think I could step off the peaks and fly."

"I'm sure we all thought we could fly."

"Probably...my son bombs around our apartment pretending he's an aeroplane."

Altai smiled. "We'd love to meet your children."

"Yeah, they'd love it here."

"You must bring them."

"I will." A black kite soared on the thermals. Turning with ease, the bird circled, spied an innocent hare and, faster than a stone, dropped to snag his prey. How many times had he watched these birds, envying their freedom? Too many times to number. "This place hasn't changed."

"No, Bat, the rhythms of the seasons, the rhythms of our lives remain the same."

"You sound like our father or grandfather."

They walked on quietly, navigating the unprotected ridge. "I think the ledge is just ahead," Altai said, biting her lip as she placed one foot in front of the other on the thin stony path.

"Look straight ahead and you'll be fine." Bat's own legs felt shaky as they approached the gap that separated the ledge from the path. Bat held his breath and jumped. Altai gingerly extended her hands, and Bat grabbed them and pulled her over the gap. She let out a sigh. Cautiously, he cleared the gravel from the flat red slab, and they sat.

Resting their backs against the bare rock of the mountain, they dangled their legs over the ledge.

"It must be more than nine years since we were here."

"It seems smaller," said Altai, shifting as far back as she could.

"Perhaps we were smaller." He opened his rucksack, handed her the yoghurt, and broke off a piece of bread for himself. It was stale. "The sky is brighter here."

"It is. I don't know how you can live in the city, with all the cars and the smog."

"You get used to it," he said, aware of the ache in the pit of his stomach.

"I love the way the mist hovers ghost-like above the ground in our valley, mysteriously disappearing as the sun climbs." She grinned. "I will never leave this place."

"You're a poet, a dreamer."

"True! I never want to stop seeing the beauty around me."

"You shouldn't." He picked up a stone. Red and flinty, it crumbled between his fingers, scattering specks across his palm that glistened like gold. He used to dream of digging up precious veins of metal and making his fortune. "But life does change."

Altai knit her brow. "Of course, it changes. We grow up, we marry, take on responsibilities, and have children."

"We do. I'd imagined those responsibilities would bring fulfilment to my life. But they haven't really."

Altai passed him the yoghurt pot. He took a swig, holding the sharp creamy liquid in his mouth before swallowing it. Altai trailed her fingers in the sand beside the rock. She seemed distracted, he thought. Sharp stones stuck to his trouser legs and bottom, and he wriggled, pushing them aside. Why didn't she say something?

He coughed. "Oh, Altai. My wild younger sister, all grown, beautiful, sensible, and compassionate, you possess a satisfaction, a kind of simplicity and dignity that I neither understand nor can explain. And yet, like the warmth of the fire on a cold day, it beckons me."

She drew patterns in the sand. "That tranquillity is not mine. It comes from God. It's the result of my faith in Him."

"What is this faith in God? Before our father died, he told me the land and our family were signposts to the Creator. That I can see. That I can understand. But to have faith in God—I can't work it out. How do I do that?"

"You don't need to do *anything*," she said, looking him in the eye.

"I must need to do *something*." Bat picked up a stone, hurled it over the edge, and listened to it ricochet against the rocks.

She put her hand on his shoulder. "Bat. The key is to stop doing. To stop trying to save yourself, to stop trying to make yourself a good person."

"I know I can't save myself," he said quickly, letting his gaze fall to the tiny figures below. Zorigo and Lhxaa were pushing the sheep and goats towards the steppe while a small child bounced after them. Monkho, seated on a stool with the horses, was milking the mares. Wiry bushes lined the banks of the river that shone as it snaked its path along the valley floor. "But how do you let another save you?"

"By admitting that you cannot save yourself."

"I cannot," he said.

"Then let God rescue you from yourself."

"But surely, letting myself be rescued would be like walking off this ledge. I'd plunge to my death."

"Exactly, Bat."

He scrunched his eyebrows. "You want me to walk off this ledge?"

"Not literally." She giggled. "But placing our faith in God *is* like walking off this ledge. We let go and step into the unknown. However," she raised a finger, serious again, "that step doesn't kill us physically; it allows us to know God."

Bat slapped the rock. "It is hard to take that step. Hard to give myself up to another."

"It is. Such submission does not come easily. But putting our trust in God plunges us into the vast landscape of His love."

"I thought I belonged to this landscape, to this place and its people." His neck felt stiff and painful.

"You belong to God."

"Belong to God?"

"Yes. Yearning to know we belong is a natural human desire. But only knowing that we belong to God brings true meaning to our lives. God's Son, Jesus, came to establish a way for us to have a relationship with the Father by making us all God's sons."

"I need to know that I am His son." Bat held his chest; it ached with an agony he'd never known before. "I want to be free," he said, not sure what he was grasping after. Tears splashed down his face, and a howl, like a wolf bereft of her cubs, wracked his body. Altai put her arm around his neck and drew him closer, rocking his shaking body as she might rock and comfort Togs-bilig. The loss, the emptiness, his own blackness: it was all exposed.

"I've been trapped—enslaved to the god of success. Consumed with jealousy and anger." It felt like the lid was being prized off his despair. "I've hated Amaraa, hated the ambition in her. Resentful of her success, I responded to her with anger and a coldness that froze the love between us." He turned to Altai. "Why do I do this?"

Altai brushed the crumbs from her lap and pulled her hair into a bunch in much the same way she'd done as a child. "We are like mirrors," she said quietly.

"Mirrors!"

"We only clearly see the faults in others because they are in us."

Had she hit him in the stomach? Winded, he spoke, "That is true. Ambition has driven me. But all my efforts, all my achievements..." He sighed. "They are nothing before God, are they?"

"No, Bat. *The Red Book* calls all our so-called achievements and good deeds 'filthy rags.'"

"It's all so chaotic, like life is beyond my control."

"Life is beyond our control. Even when we think we have it in our grip, its unruly nature refuses to fit neatly into logic's narrative. But if our eyes are open, the chaos can move us towards the presence of God."

"I need to find this new way."

"Coming to know the living God is not about finding a new way. It is not about adding power to your horse. Nor is it exchanging one set of beliefs for another or adding something more to your life. It is about entering a new relationship that changes life's perspective completely—like giving your horse wings.

"I need those wings."

"Then stop living in denial," she said abruptly.

Bat laughed. "Uvoo said the same thing to me once."

"Our grandfather was a wise man."

"He was." Bat, his face bright with smiles, continued, "To become a wise man, he told me to listen and allow other men's words to influence my life. I've never done that before."

"Then it is time to do that now. Listen to God. Follow His living Word, Jesus Christ, and let that Word change you."

Twists of dust rose from the track below; a motorbike approached their family's ger. "I will," he said, staring at their gers standing in a row like buttons on a shirt. His legs hung loose over the ledge's edge. His grandfather's old bench was gone, replaced by another that stood outside his parents' home. He imagined his mother and father sitting there talking; talking about God and the world and, perhaps, remembering him too. He was firmly seated on the rock. He was not flying, but the lightness, the unalloyed joy bubbling inside him told him that he had stepped forward.

"Love like this," he said, "that can rescue me from despair and hopelessness, that can change me and make me clean, calls for love in return."

Chapter 27

Altai scrambled to her feet. Stumbling forward, she lurched towards the edge. Bat was up in a moment, grabbing her wrist and yanking her to safety. "There's no need for you to step off the ledge," he said, holding her close for a moment. He pulled his rucksack onto his back, took Altai's hand, and drew her back over the gap that separated the ledge from the path.

"I made it," she shouted in triumph.

At the fork, they took the narrow path that descended gently into the woods. Tightly knit trees formed a canopy that muted the sun's heat, reminding Bat of the soothing coolness of summer milk against his hot skin.

"Why did you run away?" Altai suddenly asked.

Surprised by her question, his hand flew to his throat. A week ago, he'd have given her a list of excuses, but he no longer needed those excuses. "I was afraid," he said.

"I can understand that. It was a confusing time after our grandparents' deaths."

"It was," Bat agreed. "And somehow my grief became full of anger and ambition."

"Why?"

"I'm not altogether sure. I was angry with our parents. I thought our father's questioning of our traditions was a challenge to my desire to gain further education."

"Oh, Bat! You were silly."

"It's easy to say that now, but at the time my feelings were hot and real."

"You always were obstinate."

"I know. But I thought they were trying to change me."

"Did our parents ever try to change us?"

Bat shrugged his shoulders.

"Never, Bat!"

He winced; she was right. "I am sorry."

"I am sure there have been times when they've wanted us to follow a certain path, but they never tried to make us anything other than the people we were and are today."

Bat nodded.

"When our father was seeking to find the creator God, all he ever wanted was for us to enter into the discussion with him."

"I said I'm sorry."

She marched on ahead. "We made the journey towards discovering God's saving power together. But belief in the living God was never foisted on any of us."

"Altai," he shouted.

She stopped and stared. "What?"

"I said I was sorry. Isn't that enough?"

A flush crept across her face. "Of course, it is enough. I am sorry too. I just couldn't bear the thought of you misunderstanding our parents."

Bat leant on a tree trunk and started rubbing his back against the bark. "I don't misunderstand them anymore," he said, letting the crude massage relieve his aching muscles.

She touched his arm. "I'm glad."

The sun danced on the flowers and their leaves. "Although," he added, remembering the way her chatter used to irritate him, "I see that following God has not quieted your passionate soul."

Altai squatted to examine the yellow celandine and ground-hugging irises. Picking a posy of blue butterfly flowers, she held them beneath Bat's nose. "People say these flowers represent our harmonious life with nature, but I simply see them as evidence of God's care for each one of us. Their scent is faint, but these delicate lavender petals are another miracle of creation."

"They are." Bat smiled and, linking his arm in hers, led her out of the woods and onto the plain. Close to the river a group of horses, ankle deep in the cool water, swished their tails back and forth.

"How did you and Dorj discover God for yourselves?"

Altai sighed. "Through the misery of childlessness. I'd accepted our parents' new beliefs but they weren't real in me or in Dorj until we experienced God's peace personally."

She twisted the long-stemmed flowers between her fingers. "When it became clear that I couldn't carry a baby full-term, a new god entered our lives, dominating our every waking hour and driving us both to near-madness. In despair, we asked God to release us from the desire to have a child. Instantly an unexplainable peace settled, allowing us to relax our grip on our longing to be parents and assuring us that with or without children, we were already complete."

"But you have a son?"

"Remember, I told you that God spoke a promise into our lives, telling us that He would give us a child."

"I remember."

"One year after that promise was given, Togs-bilig was born."

"That explains his name."

"'Perfect-Gift.' Yes, he is God's perfect gift to us."

They turned away from the river and passed the sheep and goats as they made their way towards their gers. Two horses stood alongside Zorigo's stallion, hitched to the hitching post. Zorigo's big brown stallion was neighing and scraping his front hooves in the dirt. Bat's own mare had been the same.

Zorigo's horse jerked his head this way and that. Bat ran to the post and retied the reins more tightly. Flaring his nostrils, the horse screamed for freedom. Bat pulled the reins close, but the animal rolled his eyes backwards and stamped the ground. Still Bat pulled, drawing the horse's head closer and whispering, "Chu, chu. You're okay. You're okay."

"The city hasn't taken all of the countryside out of you then." Altai grinned.

"It hasn't," he said, scratching the stallion's withers as the agitated horse became calm.

As they reached their gers, Altai ran on to her own while Bat walked to his mother's open door. His mother was there, singing: "Holy Spirit, fill us with Your power that we might shine for Your glory."

Bat didn't understand the words, but it didn't matter. That unspeakable peace, telling him that he was bound to God, now filled his being. He ducked through the door into the warm ger. His mother was wearing her old red deel, and a matching scarf held her hair in place. She sat beside the fire, stirring a wok of soup. Her gold earrings hanging in her stretched lobes glistened as the sunlight caught them.

Bat gathered her to him. "I'm here."

Her arms tightened around his waist, and her body convulsed against his. "You've come home."

He stroked her head. "I have. Not only to my family's home, but to my heart's real home."

She sniffed and pulled away from him.

Bat sat down on a bed. "I'm just sad it has taken me so long to find the way."

"Don't be. Each of our journeys is different. We cannot dictate its length, or even the direction it will take. All we can do is walk, praying that we will find the truth, and in finding the truth, have the ability to embrace the reality of God and His desire for us to know Him through His Son, Jesus Christ."

"I want that."

"I know you do. So, you should return to the city and talk to Amaraa."

Bat dropped his gaze to the shabby carpet that laid beneath the low table. "I have treated her very badly."

"Yes, son. And now it's time to fix it."

"Can a relationship be fixed?"

"It can. But you must be willing to humble yourself and confess your wrongdoing. Are you willing to do that, Bat?"

"I am," he said, rubbing the carpet with the toe of his shoe, just as he used to do.

"Then there is hope."

"More than anything," he said, raising his head as the confidence grew inside him. "I want to cherish and support Amaraa in a way that I've never done before."

His mother rubbed her hands together. "You must leave tomorrow. You must speak to her."

"I will. But how do I rebuild trust when trust has been shattered?"

She took a rag, wiped the sweat from her brow, and came closer. "It will not be easy. You will need patience." She mopped her brow again. "No, it will not be easy. But God will help you. He will give you the strength to walk this untrodden path. And let's pray that the change in you touches Amaraa, giving her a desire to walk this way with you as God creates a new landscape in your marriage."

Bat would go. He would leave early tomorrow morning and head back to Ulaanbaatar. He would talk to Amaraa, ask for her forgiveness, and ask her to allow him to nurture her. He knew that with God's help, he could be a different husband.

His mother pulled herself to her feet and moved to the avdar.

"What do you want? Let me get it for you."

"I'm fine," she said, stretching her arm to his father's shelf to pull down the tattered brown package. "Your father wanted you to have this."

"I can't take it," he said, pushing the book back into her hands.

"No, Bat! It's your turn to discover its secrets. It will guide you as you seek to walk in the way of truth. It will help you discover the wonders of your relationship with God and will teach you that His Spirit's power, just like the wind, surrounds you."

He held the book. Through the threadbare silk, he could see the faint imprint of the once-gold letters. It didn't feel valuable. But the old storyteller had pushed it onto his father in much the same way his mother had just pushed it on to him. "You'll find the answers to your questions," the storyteller had said. And evidently his father had.

Bat held it to his chest. "I will read it."

She drew back the sleeve of her deel and squinted at his father's old watch. "All this talking," she said, moving to the door to call the family to lunch. "It's time we ate."

Zorigo, Lhxaa, Naraa, Solyomaa, Altai, his nephews, and nieces crowded into his mother's ger. Sitting on beds and stools around the low table, they ate and chatted as they'd always done. The air hung heavy with the warmth of the fire. His grandmother used to say that the seat of the fire was the centre of their home, banishing the cold, cooking the food that sustained their lives, and holding their family together.

He looked at their warm faces, the familiar squared brows, the blunt ended noses that he shared with Zorigo and his sisters. They were his family, bound by more than the hearth, more than flesh and blood even. For the same invisible, unbreakable cords that secured them to the living God bound them to one another. And this, Bat knew, was where he truly belonged.

Acknowledgements

A book is never written by one person alone, for without realising it, many contribute to the telling of a story. In sharing their lives with us, the Mongolians have stretched our understanding, deepened and enriched our lives, so that lines from their stories have woven themselves into this story. We are thankful that God has given us the privilege of living in Mongolia, where we have many friends. However, one in particular deserves a mention. When we first moved to the Mongolian countryside, possessing little language and even less cultural understanding, Davaajav, a lady in her mid-forties, readily welcomed us into her home, her family and her life. Hospitable, always ready to forgive our ignorance and, most of all, loving us, Davaajav's friendship is a continued blessing.

I long to write well, but don't always manage it, so I am thankful to friends who constantly help me unravel my mistakes. Thank you, Peter Inchley, who for more than twenty-five years has sagely corrected my newsletters, articles and blog posts; I couldn't have got this far without you. Mike Burnett, thank you for the fresh perspectives you challenge me to consider. Dave Stewart, thank you for believing in me, and Nick Horgan, for pressing me to keep on going. Doreen Sharp painstakingly read through this manuscript several times. Thank you, Doreen, and Tony Roe too, who saw this manuscript when it was just a rough collection of ideas. Stephanie Ricker, your excellent manuscript critique and great editing skills have helped me immensely. And finally, thank you to Mark, my amazing husband, who encourages me to write even when I think I have nothing to say. You're a star.

Any cultural anomalies or mistakes are, of course, wholly mine.

Printed in Great Britain
by Amazon